Murder, Served Simply

AN AMISH QUILT SHOP MYSTERY

Isabella Alan

AN OBSIDIAN MYSTERY

OBSIDIAN
Published by the Penguin Group
Penguin Group (USA) LLC, 375 Hudson Street,
New York, New York 10014

USA | Canada | UK | Ireland | Australia | New Zealand | India | South Africa | China
penguin.com
A Penguin Random House Company

First published by Obsidian, an imprint of New American Library,
a division of Penguin Group (USA) LLC

First Printing, December 2014

ISBN 978-0-451-41365-9

Printed in the United States of America
10 9 8 7 6 5 4 3 2 1

continued . . .

"This series starter set in Amish country will delight readers with its details of the community's culture and lifestyle. The contrast between the simple life and a grisly murder plays out nicely in this well-done cozy.... [The] author does a good job of introducing several key players in the community, which develops a strong sense of place and provides plenty of material for future mysteries."
—*Romantic Times* (4 stars)

"This is a community you'd like to visit, a shop where you'd find welcome . . . and people you'd want for friends. . . . There's a lot of interesting information about Amish life, but it's interwoven into the story line so the reader learns details as Angie does."
—Kings River Life Magazine

"Alan's take on the Amish is not necessarily what the reader might expect, and there is plenty of action to keep those pages turning. Cozy readers and Amish enthusiasts alike will be raving about this debut. It proves to be a great start for Isabella Alan."
—Debbie's Book Bag

"A new series that I look forward to reading. . . . It is well-plotted and has an intriguing cast of characters. . . . . If you like your mystery with an Amish flair, then you should be reading *Murder, Plain and Simple*."
—MyShelf.com

Also by Isabella Alan

For my sister-in-law
Nicole Flower
with love

ACKNOWLEDGMENTS

To my readers, who follow me as I switch from writing as Amanda Flower to Isabella Alan and back again, *En frehlicher Grischtdaag!* Merry Christmas!

When I started writing the Amish Quilt Shop Mysteries, my mother, Rev. Pamela Flower, and I went on many research trips to Holmes County. Because Amish Country is so close to where I live, it was always a day trip. However, one weekend we decided to stay overnight to attend the Amish-themed play showing in the hotel's theater. It wasn't until the first scene began that we realized the play was a musical. In surprise, we laughed so hard, tears streamed down our faces. Knowing how some Amish would react to an Amish-themed musical, I realized I had the setting for the third mystery. It was as if it had been wrapped up with a Christmas bow and set at my feet. Thank you, Mom. You remain my partner in crime, who can never be replaced.

Thanks to my dear agent, Nicole Resciniti. Your friendship is one of the best parts of my career. And thanks to my editor, Laura Fazio, for pushing me. Sheriff Mitchell thanks you too.

Love to my family: Andy, Nicole, Isabella, and Andrew; and to my dear friends Delia, Mariellyn, Meredith, and Suzy, for your unfailing support.

Finally, gratitude to my Heavenly Father. You teach me something new about faith with every book.

Chapter One

Water fell from the faucet into the old porcelain sink in Running Stitch's tiny bathroom. Through the closed door, I heard the cheerful Pennsylvania Dutch chatter of the ladies from my quilting circle. Normally, the sound would have made me smile. Today, any noise was certain to cause an instant migraine.

I dabbed my face with a damp paper towel, careful not to mar my eye makeup. When Ryan Dickinson showed up at my door, I wanted to look my best. Not for him but for me. Didn't every girl feel like that when confronted with her ex-fiancé? Of course, most girls don't have their parents to blame for the reunion. I rested my forehead on the mirror and willed myself to get a grip.

A tap came at the door. "Angie, are you okay in there?" asked Anna, who had been my aunt Eleanor's closest friend.

I opened the door. My kitten, Dodger, and French bulldog, Oliver, sat on either side of her. Concern was plastered on all three of their faces.

"I'm fine," I said, forcing some Christmas cheer into my voice.

None of them bought my act.

"*Ya*, you sound like it."

If you had asked me before my move from Dallas to Ohio's Amish Country whether Amish women were sarcastic, I would have said no. Boy, did Anna prove me wrong.

"I *am* fine."

She stepped back to give me enough space to exit the bathroom.

"You didn't seem that way earlier today. When your parents and Ryan arrived, you practically threw them onto the progressive-dinner sleigh. You barely gave Mattie and me enough time to introduce ourselves."

I crossed the shop to the long table lined with tureens of soup, each made by a lady from my quilting circle, and chili made by me. I had to bring a little of Texas to this Christmas in Ohio. "The sleigh was leaving," I said as I stirred my chili. "I didn't want them to miss this important event in Rolling Brook. It's not like they will have another chance to have an Amish progressive dinner."

"They will if they come next Christmas," Anna said.

I shivered. "Mom and Dad are welcome back, but this will be the *last* Christmas Ryan Dickinson spends in Rolling Brook if I can help it."

Mattie Miller, my young assistant in the shop, said, "Ryan is very handsome."

I scowled at the chili. *Maybe I should add some more hot sauce and show them how we really do chili in Texas.*

"He's no more handsome than the sheriff. The sheriff is distinguished," Anna said.

I flinched. There lay the heart of the problem. Ryan Dickinson, my ex-fiancé, and Sheriff James Mitchell, my kind-of boyfriend, were together in the same county for Christmas. I never thought I would see the day, not even in my worst nightmares. And it was all thanks to my mother, the mastermind behind the drama.

Suddenly, the chili didn't seem all that appetizing. I debated going back to the bathroom in case I needed to toss the half dozen Christmas cookies I had pilfered from the tray Mattie had brought across the street from her family's bakery. I placed the glass lid back on the Crock-Pot.

Mattie's thin eyebrows wrinkled. "Angie, you don't look so good. Are you ill?"

"I'll be fine. The holidays are always stressful, right?"

Anna sniffed. "The *Englisch* make it stressful. It's not that way in the Amish world. We know Christmas is a time of reflection on our faith, and to be with family."

"I think most English folks know that too," I said. "But there are also credit cards involved."

Anna shook her head as if I'd hit her with yet another mysterious English riddle.

Mattie unwrapped a third stack of plastic bowls from their packaging and set them on the edge of the table. "The progressive dinner is across the street at the bakery."

"Already?" I swallowed hard. The next stop would be Running Stitch. I hurried to the front window. Sure enough, the progressive-dinner sleigh was off-loading customers, most of whom were local English folks, with the exception of Ryan and my parents.

Before the cold could seep through their heavy winter coats and parkas, they dashed into the bakery. My best friend and Mattie's sister-in-law, Rachel Miller, would warm them up with hot coffee and some of her prizewinning friendship bread.

Maybe if Mom and Ryan overeat, they will be too ill to talk to me about whatever brought them to Ohio this Christmas, I thought, feeling more cheerful. Then I could spend the rest of the week avoiding talking to them about it. I wouldn't mind talking with my dad though. I suspected he was on my side. Plus, Dad had the ability to pack away a couple of pies single-handedly. The progressive dinner wouldn't even be a challenge for him.

Mattie patted my arm as she carried a tray of crackers to the second long table along the quilt shop's front window. "Angie, don't worry so much. It will all be fine."

When had Mattie become the calm, reassuring one? When she'd started working for me four months ago, she'd been a quiet, unassuming Amish girl. I liked the new Mattie, but I wasn't sure how her conservative brother felt about her new confidence.

I peered out through Running Stitch's display window. One of my favorite quilts, a double wedding ring pattern done in Christmas red and green, hung over the quilt stand next to a five-foot Christmas tree decorated with white lights and pincushions as ornaments. The Amish don't have Christmas trees in their homes.

Like everything else, their Christmas decorations are modest—some greenery and maybe a string of popcorn at most. I shuddered at what my Amish friends would think of the nine-foot glitzed-and-glittered tree that sat in the front hall of my parents' home back in Dallas. There were enough electric bulbs on it to light up an aircraft carrier. Dad always said it wasn't worth putting up a Christmas tree unless you could see it from space. Thinking of the tree made me nostalgic and happy that both of my parents were in Rolling Brook for Christmas.

The sleigh shifted forward a foot as the two draft horses shuffled in place. Steam escaped from their nostrils as they stamped the snow-covered road. Jonah, Anna's son and my childhood friend, sat on the driver's seat of the sleigh. He spied me in the window and waved. He arched his sandy-colored eyebrows as if to ask a question. *Great,* I thought, *even Jonah wonders how I'm going to handle Ryan. Does the entire town know my ex-fiancé is here for Christmas?* I already knew the answer to that one.

Behind me, Anna and Mattie spoke in hushed tones. I walked across the room in time to hear Mattie say, "Aaron said it's wrong for the *Englischers* to portray the Amish that way."

Ahh, I thought, *the play. An Amish Christmas* was the second hot topic in town, and I was happy to have it. At least it took some of the heat off me.

"Did you hear what it's about?" Mattie asked.

"Judging from the title," Anna said, "something about the Amish and Christmas."

"Nee." Mattie put her hands on her hips. "I mean yes, but it's mostly about an Amish girl who falls in love with an *Englischer* and leaves the community. My brother says that it belittles our way of life."

Anna snorted. "Let the *Englisch* have their fun."

"If it were just *Englischers*." Mattie lowered her voice until I could barely hear her. "Eve Shetler is in the play."

Anna clicked her tongue. *"Ya,* I heard that. Eve is an *Englischer* now. It's not our concern what she does now that she has left the community."

"Many don't feel that way. It's fine she left the community, but why would she come back and mock it?"

"I don't think the play is meant to mock anything," I said, jumping in for the first time.

"Have you seen it?" Mattie asked.

"No, I heard bits and pieces when I was at the inn setting up for the Christmas quilt show. Tonight will be the first time I'll see it run all the way through." The progressive dinner would end at the Swiss Valley Hotel on Rolling Brook's border with Berlin. The grand finale of the evening would be the opening of *An Amish Christmas.* Perhaps now was not the best time to mention the musical numbers in the production.

Mattie smoothed the pile of napkins on the table. "Then you can't say for sure."

I opened my mouth to protest, but the bell over the front door rang. Progressive diners poured into the quilt shop. Cheerful chatter quickly filled the small shop. The women raved over the quilts, and the men made a beeline for the tureens of soup. Anna and Mattie took up their posts behind the soup table and began dishing hot soup and chili into bowls.

Mom, Dad, and Ryan were in the back of the pack. My father gave me a huge grin, and it took all my will-power not to run over to him and give him a big bear hug like I had when I was a little girl. The man behind him, Ryan, stopped me. Ryan had a pained expression on his face as he rubbed his arms, as if to get blood circulating. Clearly, spending the night freezing in an Amish sleigh as it moved from business to business in Rolling Brook and eating heavy Amish food were not what he expected when he arrived in Ohio. I knew Ryan, the fitness fanatic, was already calculating the number of calories he'd consumed since his plane landed and how many hours it would take in the gym to burn them off.

His gaze zeroed in on me. Could I be wrong, but did his expression soften? My stomach did a little flip. I wouldn't let Ryan's chocolate puppy-dog eyes work their magic on me. I wasn't going to be fooled this time. Never again.

I broke eye contact, and I took a deep breath. It was just a week. What could possibly happen to ruin Christmas in a week?

I glanced down at my beloved Frenchie, Oliver. He covered his nose with his white paw. Oliver knew better. He knew all the players on and off the stage.

Chapter Two

I reeked of chili. And as delicious as it was, it was not a scent I wanted to be breathing the rest of the night, especially through *An Amish Christmas*, which promised to be a three-hour affair. So while the progressive diners were at their next stop, the Amish mercantile, for pickled Amish delicacies like eggs, onions, and peppers, I locked up Running Stitch and made a quick stop at home to change my outfit and drop off Dodger. Oliver was welcome at the Swiss Valley Hotel. Dodger was not. He was my problem child.

I was in and out of my rented house in Millersburg inside fifteen minutes. I turned my little SUV into the parking lot of the Swiss Valley Hotel.

I patted myself on the back. While Ryan and my parents had been in Running Stitch, eating soup and chili with the rest of the progressive diners, I had done an excellent job of looking *really* busy and unable to talk to them. In truth, that hadn't all been for show. Having thirty-some shoppers suddenly descend on my shop was more than I was used to. Both Mattie and I had made quite a number of sales, which would please my accountant. Unfortunately, at the main-dish portion of the meal at the hotel, I would no longer be able to ignore my family and their stowaway.

Oliver placed his paws on the dashboard, and his stubby tail wagged with excitement. He loved the hotel, and the staff loved him. I would have to keep an eye out to make sure they didn't slip him too many treats. Both Oliver and I had gained weight since moving to Ohio. We planned to get back on the wagon in the New Year.

We had visited the hotel often in the last few days as Mattie and I set up the Amish quilt show in the front sitting room. I had been honored to be asked to sponsor and manage the show, especially since I was still new to the community, until I was told I would be doing it with a rival quilt shop. Martha Yoder was my sullen partner for the event and the owner of Authentic Amish Quilts, which unfortunately was right next door to Running Stitch. When I first moved to Holmes County, Martha had been my employee, but when she didn't like the direction I was taking my shop, she decided to open her own right next door. The location was intentional.

Now we were working together. I hoped this would lead to some type of truce, but so far, all that had come of it were scowls and thinly veiled insults. All coming from Martha, of course. I knew when to keep my insults to myself.

I'd been gritting my teeth and taking Martha's jabs

because the show was excellent exposure for my shop, and I needed that to compete against her. If she'd thought about it for just a moment, she would have realized that we could work together to help both of our shops, but she was too busy being angry.

"Well, Oliver," I said, "let's be civil with her. The quilt show is only up for a few more days."

He woofed sympathy. I can always count on him.

My little SUV shifted into four-wheel drive as it made the climb up the steep hill to the hotel. As the tires ground through the snow, I felt bad for the horses that would be pulling the sleigh loaded with tourists for the entire progressive dinner. Beyond a double row of pine trees iced with fresh snow, the Swiss Valley Hotel came into view. The hotel was a grand white building four stories high. It reminded me of an overgrown gingerbread house with electric candles flickering in every window and a garland of pines over every doorway. More greenery with clear twinkle lights wrapped over the whitewashed fence surrounding the property, and the pines trees closest to the entrance sparkled with blue, red, and green lights draped over their limbs.

Even though the hotel was "Amish themed," it very much was owned and operated by its English proprietress, Mimi Ford. She inherited a sizable fortune at her father's death and used that money to purchase the hotel, or so Sarah Leham, my quilting circle's good-natured gossip, had told me. Amish women worked as maids and cooks in the hotel. Amish men served as its carpenters and handymen. I wondered what the Amish employees thought about the controversial play going on in the barn.

With that in mind, I was curious to know what Martha thought about it. She wasn't a fan of English impacting Amish culture. Wasn't that the greatest complaint about the play?

The parking lot was half full, and I circled the lot to find the space easiest to get out of when the play ended. It would fill up closer to showtime, and I didn't want to be trapped in parking-lot gridlock when it was time to leave.

There had been some speculation at the last trustees' meeting whether or not tourists and locals would be willing and able to come out on a cold night this close to Christmas for the play, but Mimi reported at the meeting last week that the first five shows had sold out. Since a portion of the proceeds would go toward building a new playground for the township, this was excellent news.

I shifted the car into park and was relieved to see I had beaten Jonah and the sleigh there. Good. It would give me enough time to settle myself before Ryan showed up on the scene. I still didn't know what he came all the way to Ohio to say that he couldn't have told me over the phone, assuming I would have answered the call. I had my suspicions, but I did not want them confirmed.

I reached into the backseat of the SUV and grabbed Oliver's travel bag. Yes, my dog has his own accessories, and I refuse to believe that is strange. I rooted around in the bag until I came up with Oliver's Christmas sweater and boots. The sweater was red and had Rudolph's face knitted into the pattern on the back.

Fannie Springer, an Amish friend of my aunt and owner of a yarn shop just up the road from Running Stitch, made him the sweater. It would keep him warm in the drafty barn during the play, and the red boots would protect his paws from the snow and ice. Bonus: He looked darn cute in the getup. At least I thought so. Oliver seemed to disagree.

My Frenchie whimpered as I slipped the reindeer sweater over his head. "Count your blessings," I said. "I'm not asking you to wear your antlers."

He stopped fussing when I said that. He *hated* the antlers.

With Oliver appropriately dressed for the arctic, I climbed out of the car and grabbed my ever-present hobo bag.

Oliver hopped out behind me and snuffled as he shook his four paws one at a time, trying his best to fling the boots off his feet. I knew all of his tricks and reinforced the closure with extra-strong Velcro. I snapped a leash on his collar.

The whimpers became stronger.

I patted his head. "Sorry, buddy. There are a lot of cars around here, and I don't want you getting hurt."

Oliver and I shuffled across the icy parking lot. The surface was a sheet of ice. I may have had Oliver outfitted for the weather, but I hadn't thought of my own footwear. I should have left my cowboy boots back at the shop and traded them for my ugly black snow boots, but I was convinced those had been commissioned by a prison guard in Siberia. I really needed to go into the city, the closest being Canton, and buy some more-attractive snow boots. I may have never wanted to be the pageant girl my mother hoped I'd become, but I still had some fashion standards, and it was time my snow boots got the heave-ho.

I shuffled forward on the ice bit by bit, so focused on not falling that I didn't hear anyone approaching. Oliver froze, which told me something was amiss.

A voice broke through the swirling snow and wind. "Hey, you! You!"

I scooped up Oliver and held my huge purse at the ready to strike.

"You!" the voice called again. A figure stumbled forward in the snow-filled air. I made out the outline of an Amish felt hat before I saw his face. Snow swirled around him, and his grizzled beard whipped back and forth, peppered with ice crystals, and he looked like Rip Van Winkle just awakened from his long nap.

I took a big step back and had to steady myself as the smooth soles of my cowboy boots slid on the icy pavement. "Who are you?"

The elderly Amish man shook his fist. "The curse of *Gott* is upon you for this abomination!"

"Um, sorry?" I wrapped the long strap of my purse more tightly around my hand, better to whack him with. "What abomination would that be?"

He pointed at the large white barn adjacent to the hotel. "That," he hissed. "There will be the wrath of *Gott* for it."

Warm yellow light glowed out of the barn's four-pane windows as final preparations were made for the opening performance of *An Amish Christmas*.

"The play?" I asked.

"*Ya!* It is a disgrace to our people, a disgrace!" Rip Van Winkle's doppelganger shook his fist.

An abomination and a disgrace? I guessed I shouldn't ask him if a complimentary ticket to the show would make him happier. "I think you should go," I said, expecting him to argue.

"I will," he spat. "But mark my words. You will rue the day you chose to put on this atrocity. You will rue the day."

Some spittle landed on my face. Gag. I wiped it away. Was there a five-second rule for spit like there was for a dropped cookie on the kitchen floor as far as germs were concerned? I needed Purell stat.

He stepped backward into the snow flurry. "You tell those heathens what I have said."

"Sure. Consider your message already delivered," I said, thinking I'd tell the sheriff about this nutcase first and clutching Oliver closer to my chest.

The man melted into the snow. I took a few deep breaths, because there was nothing like a close encounter with an Amish abominable snowman to give a girl a shock. Oliver's solid body pressed up against my leg. I scratched him between the ears, his favorite spot, before setting him back on the ground. He'd been shaken by the incident too.

My Amish aunt Eleanor had been like a second mother to me, and I've always had many Amish friends. I knew the Amish disapproved of much in the

English world, but they usually did so quietly and without confrontation. It was not the Amish way to threaten or be so outspoken. There was only one other Amish man I'd known who had behaved like that, Joseph Walker, and he had ended up dead. I had been the one who made the gruesome discovery. I shivered. I wasn't interested in reliving that memory, especially standing alone in the dark in the middle of a frozen parking lot.

I would have to ask Anna about this man. I wished I had thought to ask his name. The spit threw me off my game.

A hand rested on my shoulder. Rip Van Winkle was back! I swung around and smacked my assailant with my enormous purse.

"Oomph!" the attacker cried, and I found James Mitchell, the sheriff of Holmes County, standing two feet from me. He was holding his stomach.

I rushed toward him. "Ohmigosh, Mitchell, are you okay?"

He straightened up. "I think so. What do you have in that thing? If you swung any higher, you would have cracked one of my ribs."

I winced. That was a good question. There could be anything in there from a stapler to a brick. My purse was the catchall for everything in my life. If I pick something up, into the purse it goes. As I do this, I always think I'll remember to put whatever it is back where it belongs, but items rarely make it to their final destination. My purse is sort of like a purgatory for the lost, encased in fine-grain leather.

"I'm so sorry!" I rubbed his arm. "I didn't mean to do that. I thought I was being attacked by Rip Van Winkle."

He narrowed his startling blue-green eyes and placed his hand over mine on his arm. "Say that again."

"Oh! It wasn't the *real* Rip Van Winkle."

"Well, that's a relief."

"You can cut the sarcasm."

He grinned. "Okay, I will try to refrain from comment. Please tell me what happened."

I frowned. "Oliver and I were heading into the hotel, and we were stopped by an angry Amish dude, who looked a lot like . . . Rip."

"Hence the name."

"Yes, hence the name. Anyway. He called the play an abomination and said that we would all rue the day that the play was put on."

"I wouldn't expect anything else from old Rip."

"Are you laughing at me? I never should have told you the nickname I gave him," I grumbled.

"I'm not laughing at you," he insisted. But the glint in his aquamarine eyes told me otherwise. "That must have been Nahum Shetler you came across. We have gotten complaints from the hotel that he's been stalking around the place during play practice. I'm not at all surprised he showed up on opening night. I'm sorry if he scared you."

Shetler? Where had I heard that name before? Then it hit me. That was the last name of the Amish girl in the production.

"Shetler? Is he related to Eve, who has the lead in the play?" I bounced on the balls of my feet to fight the cold. Cowboy boots weren't made for this weather. Not only could I trip and fall, but frostbite was totally possible.

"He's her uncle. Let's go inside, and I will tell you more about him. You're shaking like a leaf."

"No, I'm not," I said through chattering teeth. "But Oliver is cold, so let's go."

Mitchell scooped up my stocky dog as if he weighed no more than a pillow. Oliver licked his cheek. It seemed we were both smitten with the handsome sheriff.

As we navigated the icy parking lot, I asked, "What has Nahum been doing? I mean other than accosting innocent bystanders in the parking lot?"

"I think that's the most of it. One of the deputies had to escort him off the property twice for trying to scare off the actors from rehearsal."

I slid on a patch of ice, and Mitchell protectively stuck a hand under my elbow. "You're not wearing the best footwear for the weather."

"I know. I should have been more practical, but I had a strong feeling this morning that I would need the boots today." As slippery as my footing was, my cowboy boots gave me confidence. They were good at stomping things.

"That wouldn't have anything to do with the arrival today of your parents and Ryan?" he asked, trying to sound casual and failing miserably.

"What do you think?"

Mitchell opened the front door to the inn for me. "When will I get to meet them?"

"You'll see them tonight."

"See and meet are not the same thing."

I squatted next to Oliver and removed his boots, but I left on his sweater.

The Frenchie whimpered.

"You look adorable, trust me."

Mitchell tapped his foot. "You are avoiding the question."

"You will get to meet them, I promise, but not on the first night, okay?" I placed my hand on his chest. "I haven't told Mom and Dad about you, and I don't want to in front of Ryan."

"Is it wrong that I want to meet your parents? You've met my family."

"No, of course not." I folded my coat over my arm. "But I know Mom and Dad won't be the main attraction for you."

"So he did come." He covered my hand with his and squeezed it. "I was hoping the little weasel would back out."

"Please don't call him a weasel to his face. That would be awkward." I slipped my hand from his chest.

Mitchell chuckled. "I can't promise you that."

I rolled my eyes. "I've barely said two words to him since he got here, so I still have no idea why Ryan came all the way to Ohio for Christmas."

The sheriff's expression turned serious. "I know why, Angie, and so do you."

I looked up at him. "Why?"

"You. He wants you back. I have to say it's a pretty romantic gesture to come all this way to win you." His right eye twitched. I would have missed it if I hadn't been standing so close to him.

I rocked backward onto my heels. "And is that what you want?"

He reached out and grabbed both of my hands. "No. But I can't blame the guy for realizing he made a huge mistake. But it's too late for him, and I will do everything in my power to make sure he fails."

"You don't have to worry about it," I said.

"I know."

Mitchell squeezed my hands one last time. "Don't wait too long in introducing me to them, okay? Or I might just have to introduce myself."

Knowing the sheriff, that was not an idle threat.

Chapter Three

I stood up. "Can we get back to the conversation about Nahum Shetler?"

Mitchell took my coat, and I followed him into the small coatroom next to the hotel's registration desk. The wooden hangers clanked together as he hung up my coat and then his own.

"You're in uniform," I said. Outside, his long wool coat had almost completely covered up his navy sheriff's department uniform. "I thought you were here tonight as a guest, not on official business."

For the inaugural progressive dinner and play, the hotel invited all the Rolling Brook dignitaries, or at least, the closest thing we had to them. Mitchell was invited as the county sheriff, and I was invited as a township trustee, a title I still wasn't completely comfortable with. I had agreed to the appointment with the hope that I would be able to better represent the wishes of the Amish, but it was hard to think of myself as a politician.

Mitchell put his stocking cap and Oliver's boots on the shelf above the coats. "It's turning into a little bit of both. Farley was concerned about the problem the hotel had been having with Nahum, so he asked me to come as the sheriff."

Farley Jung was the immediate past head trustee of Rolling Brook. Because of governmental term limits, he had to step down in November and was just your average trustee like me. After six years at the top, he retained his control over the trustees through the mouthpiece of his replacement, Caroline Cramer.

"Nahum did seem to be very outspoken for an Amish man." I adjusted my huge bag on my shoulder. "But why are you involved? There's nothing to investigate, right? Does Farley think something criminal will happen?"

"I'm just here to put the play's cast and crew more at ease. Some of them have been shaken by Nahum's appearance at practice."

"I could see how Eve would be shaken," I said. "Her own uncle called the play an abomination. What about his bishop? Could he talk to him?"

"From what I gather from the Shetler family, Nahum doesn't attend church services or pay much attention to anything their district or any Amish bishop has to say. He lives outside of any particular Amish community."

"He's a rogue Amish?" I asked as I followed Mitchell out of the coatroom.

The sheriff stopped beside the eleven-foot-tall Christmas tree to the left of the main entrance. I inhaled the heavy scent of pine. Oliver wriggled under the tree, and I heard him taking a drink from the tree's water bowl. White twinkle lights and handmade blue and white ornaments covered the tree. The white pine was halfway between the registration desk and the doorway to the sitting room where the quilt show was taking place. Just beyond the sitting room's archway, the grand staircase began. It curved in a great C shape. I made a mental note to check on the quilts in the sitting room before I left the hotel that night.

The heavenly aroma of the progressive dinner's main course wafted across the lobby from the dining room. A line of open French doors separated the dining room from the lobby. The hotel didn't have a full Amish restaurant, but it provided an Amish breakfast for the guests each morning and Amish baked goods in the afternoon. Tonight the hotel dining room was where the main course of the progressive dinner would be served. Actors in costume from the play wandered around the lobby in character as they waited for the progressive diners to arrive.

Mitchell turned to face me in front of the tree. The white lights reflected off the silver in his hair, making his unusual aquamarine eyes sparkle—or that sparkle could have been from his amusement at my comments. "I suppose you could call him that." He nodded to Oliver. "Are you sure he's allowed in here?"

"Mimi doesn't mind. He's been with me all week while Mattie and I have been preparing for the quilt show."

He arched an eyebrow. "And Martha?"

"Martha too, but we are working independently, for a lack of a better description. I have yet to get a smile out of her, much less a direct conversation. She will speak to Mattie though, so I'm trying just to ignore it."

"Will she be here tonight?"

"I don't think so. She's participating in the quilt show, but I can't see her having anything to do with a play called *An Amish Christmas*. That would go against every protest she has ever made about English and Amish relations."

The front door of the hotel opened again. A gust of arctic air buffeted the tree and blew my wild blond curls into my face. I pushed them away to see the first of the progressive diners step inside the hotel. The noise volume inside the lobby rose as their happy chatter filled the room.

Mitchell squeezed my elbow. "Remember what I said about introducing me to your parents *and* Ryan," he called as he melted into the crowd.

I couldn't be more grateful that Mitchell was giving me the time to tell my parents about us my way, but I also knew that time was limited.

As my father stepped through the door, he waved at me. With a new full beard on his face and belly to match, he looked like a stand-in for Santa, a role he'd played before. I couldn't help but smile, and a pang of homesickness swept through me. Holmes County was home now, but I would always be Daddy's little girl.

Ryan's face brightened as if I had been waving to him. I dropped my hand. Mom scrutinized the chandelier above. Her sleek blond hair fell perfectly to the shoulders of her cranberry red wool coat. Her scarf and gloves matched the coat.

I was happy to see that many of the progressive diners had wandered into the large sitting room where the quilt show was happening. Maybe I would drum up some business from this dinner and play after all. It certainly couldn't hurt business.

My parents and Ryan wove through the other progressive diners to reach me.

"Angie Bear! There you are." Dad wrapped his arms around me. "I didn't get a chance to give you a proper hug back at Running Stitch. You were so busy, but I could see you were in your element."

It felt so good to be squeezed against his soft tummy. Clearly, my mother had not been successful in making him stick to his diet. Maybe I could give him a talking-to about it. My father had always been big, which wasn't a problem. I couldn't imagine him as thin, but he could lose a few pounds. I worried about his health.

He let me go.

"Thanks, Dad." I hugged my mother. "You too, Mom."

She was in head-to-toe Chanel and smelled like No. 5. She kissed both of my cheeks. "Angie, couldn't you have put on a dress for tonight? You are a township trustee, after all."

I glanced down at my cords and pink snowflake-patterned sweater I thought I was dressed pretty fancy for my life in Rolling Brook. My typical outfit consisted of jeans. It was a far cry from the suits and dresses I had worn to my advertising job in Dallas.

I nodded to Ryan. "Hello, Ryan."

His face broke into a boyish grin. "Hi, Angie. I was afraid that you were going to pretend I wasn't here."

"The thought did cross my mind."

"Angie," my mother reprimanded.

"I don't deserve anything more," he said with the lopsided grin still intact. "I hope we—"

"So, how do y'all like the progressive dinner?" I interrupted him, and noticed that my Texas twang re-emerged as I spoke to them.

My father beamed. "It's been wonderful. I forgot how much I missed good old Amish cooking. I had three helpings of Amish noodles at the yarn shop up the street from your store. The noodles were just like the ones Eleanor used to make."

My mother folded her thin arms, and a wave of perfume filled the air. "Kent, I don't know what I am going to do with you. You aren't even pretending to stick to your diet."

"Aww, it's the holidays. Everyone gains weight this time of year. I would hate to be losing weight and making everyone around me feel inferior. I'll just have to wait until after New Year's to start my diet. I can't insult Angie's Amish friends by turning my nose up at the food that they have to offer me, now can I? That would be rude." He winked at me.

"What a lovely hotel," my mother said, changing the subject. "It wouldn't be fair to compare it to the finer hotels in Dallas, but it's quite a step up from those I remember when your father and I lived here."

"How kind of you, Mom," I said.

The hotel appealed to those looking for Amish sensibilities with its sturdily built and impossibly shiny Amish wood furniture. However, it clearly was not an

Amish business. Twenty feet above me in the main lobby was an electric crystal chandelier that shimmered and sparkled. Of course, the Amish wouldn't use electric lighting, but more than that, they would never have something so extravagant in their homes. It provided so much light that even standing beside the large Christmas tree at the very front of the hotel, I could see the sparkling indoor pool on the other side of the dining room.

The long registration desk was made of polished dark wood. Two receptionists stood behind it, ready to answer questions. The guests stopped there and then moved through the lobby into the dining room. Many of them were chatting with the actors as they went.

I stood there, taking it all in.

Oliver, on the other hand, reached up and put his paws on Ryan's legs.

Ryan squatted in front of the Frenchie and scratched him between the ears just how Oliver liked it. A pang of memory hit me. Ryan had been with me when I adopted Oliver as a puppy. He'd helped me housetrain him. If nothing else, he had always been kind to my dog. To me, that goes a long way.

"Hey, you old rascal," Ryan said. "Did you miss me?"

Oliver licked his face in reply.

Ryan looked up at me with those chocolate brown eyes, which were as familiar to me as my own. "Did *you* miss me?" he whispered.

I pretended not to hear the question.

"Angie, who was that man you were talking to when

we came in?" my mother asked with a raised eyebrow. "He seemed very interested in what you had to say."

"Oh, that was the sheriff. He's attending the dinner tonight too."

"They must have had some township business to discuss with all the trustees, Daphne. Don't read so much into everything."

"Trustees?" Ryan asked.

"Didn't we tell you, Ryan?" my father asked. "Angie Bear is a township trustee for Rolling Brook. I'd say that was mighty impressive for a gal living here only a few months. I always knew you were destined for politics."

Yep, the next stop is the White House.

My mother jabbed him with her elbow. "How can you say that you *always* knew that? You never said that about Angie a day in her life."

"I thought it."

I smiled at my parents' good-natured squabbling. As much as it drove me crazy when I was a teenager, I missed it now. It remained to be seen if I would still miss it by the end of the week.

"Being a township trustee is impressive," Ryan said with awe in his voice. "You look like you fit in here." He frowned. "That came out wrong."

I gave him a genuine smile. "No, it didn't. That's probably the best compliment you've ever given me."

Ryan frowned as he thought about that.

A round woman in Amish dress rang a bell. "Dinner is served in the breakfast room. Please find your place cards as you go in."

We followed the actors and other diners through the French doors. A long table with a navy cloth over it dominated the room. It was elegantly decorated with pine and holly, white dishes, and polished silverware.

In addition to the actors and progressive diners, there were the sheriff, the other township trustees, and Mimi Ford, the hotel owner. I found myself seated between a young, striking girl in Amish dress and a tall, thin man in a charcoal suit and shiny black shoes. I couldn't see her place card, but his said WADE BROOKLYN.

I picked up my water glass and asked the girl, "Are you an actress or Amish?"

She rolled a baby carrot across her plate with the back of her fork. "I'm both."

I started coughing and almost spat water across the table onto Ryan's plate. Fortunately, I was able to regain control of myself. Remembering my encounter with Nahum, I thought there had already been enough spitting for one night. I felt Mitchell watching me from the farthest end of the table.

"I'm Angie Braddock," I said. "I'm one of the township trustees."

She blinked at me. "You don't look like a trustee."

"What does a trustee look like?"

"Older. Irritable."

I laughed and lowered my voice. "We have some of those, but we have some cheerful people on the board too," I said, thinking of my friend Willow Moon. If the girl thought I didn't look like a Rolling Brook trustee, then she would never believe Willow was one. Willow was at the end of the table near the sheriff in an animated conversation with a brunette girl in English dress. Her lavender hair was cropped close to her head, and she fingered the purple crystal pendant resting on the front of her signature gauzy blouse.

The girl next to me nodded her head. "I'm happy to hear that. Not everyone would agree with me, but change is good for Rolling Brook. When I came back, I thought everything was exactly as I left it. I'm glad to see I'm wrong."

I shook her hand. "And you are?" I asked, although I had already guessed.

"I'm Eve Shetler," she said, confirming my suspicions. "I'm sure you have heard about me."

I didn't deny it. I wanted to ask her about her uncle Nahum, but it didn't seem right to ask the girl about her crazy uncle just before she went onstage for her big opening night. She must know that Nahum was causing problems for the play.

The roast turkey, baked ham, roast beef, boiled potatoes, carrots, and Amish casserole were served, which saved me from making a choice about asking her about her uncle.

"Gracious," said my mother, who sat on the other side of Eve and typically had water and salad for three meals a day. "How are we ever to eat all of this food?"

"You just have to take it on as a challenge, my dear," Dad said, with knife and fork at the ready.

I picked up my own knife and fork, ready to dive in. I thought I would follow my father's lead and worry about my diet after the New Year. Besides, that's when it's trendy to worry about your weight anyway.

Eve stared at her plate.

"You aren't hungry?" I asked.

"Opening-night jitters, I guess." She smiled. "Usually, I can push my nerves away, but there's something completely different about acting here, so close to my old community."

"You have the lead." I cleared my throat. "I—I saw it in the program."

She chuckled. "I know the entire county is talking about me. You don't have to pretend that you didn't hear the gossip."

"Okay." I cut a roasted carrot in half with my knife. "I won't."

The man to my left leaned into our conversation. "Eve is the star of our little production." He held out his hand to me. "I'm Wade Brooklyn, the director. She is magnificent in the play. I'm taking all the credit for discovering her when she becomes a star on Broadway."

"From your lips to the casting directors' ear," Eve said with a smile, and then turned her head to reply to a question that my mother asked her.

Farley, who was also representing the township trustees at the dinner, patted his perpetually greasy hair. "I appreciate you wearing your uniform tonight, Sheriff. We don't want any trouble from Nahum."

Beside me, I felt Eve tense, and across the table from me, Ryan's head snapped in the direction of that conversation.

Mimi pursed her lips. "Farley, I don't believe there is any reason for concern."

"Who's Nahum?" one of the progressive diners asked.

"Just a crazed Amish man," a handsome man in English dress and a surprising British accent said from across the table.

My mother leaned forward. "What crazed Amish man?"

I'd forgotten that my mother's love of gossip was rivaled only by that of Sarah Leham, a member of my quilting circle. Sarah knew more about the lives of the Amish in Holmes County than anyone—just as my mother had the same level of information on the socialites in Dallas.

"The man is a menace." Wade gripped his water glass so tightly, I was afraid it would crack in his hand. "He shouldn't be allowed anywhere near the property. Mimi, you should take out a restraining order."

Mimi forced a laugh. "Nahum is all bluster. There will be no need for that."

I watched Eve out of the corner of my eye. She shifted in her seat.

Behind me there was a crash. Everyone turned to look. An Amish girl—I believed this one really was practicing Amish—put a hand to her mouth. "I'm so sorry." She stood over the remains of a glass coffee carafe.

"Junie, please clean up." Mimi's brow furrowed. "And then go back to the kitchen for a fresh pot of coffee."

The girl dropped to her knees and started to gather up the pieces.

Eve stood up. "I can help her."

Wade reached across me and stopped her with his

hand. "No, Eve, I don't want my star taking any chances, like getting cut by glass before her big debut."

Eve rolled her eyes. "Don't be ridiculous."

"I don't need anyone's help," Junie said barely above a whisper. I wouldn't have heard her if she hadn't been directly behind me.

I jumped out of my seat. "I don't have any reason to fear broken glass."

As I knelt beside her and put pieces of glass on a plastic tray, she whispered, *"Danki."*

"Wilkumm," I whispered back and smiled as her eyes widened.

Eve turned in her seat and peered down at us. "Junie," she whispered.

Junie wouldn't look at the other girl and fled with her tray.

I gave Eve a questioning look, but she faced forward without a word.

Chapter Four

Shortly thereafter, the actors excused themselves to prepare for the performance, and the guests bundled themselves back into their winter coats and scarves to make the short but chilly walk from the hotel to the barn where the play would be held.

I followed the crowd with my parents and Ryan, preoccupied by the encounter I had witnessed between Eve and the Amish waitress. I was thankful the wind was too brisk for much conversation, so Ryan could not attempt to ask me whatever he had wanted to say in the hotel lobby.

Inside the barn, padded folding chairs twenty rows deep were set up for the audience. The hand-built stage was at the far end of the barn. Blue velvet curtains had been installed and the stage floor polished. It seemed Mimi had spared no expense on the new business venture.

High above, three ceiling fans turned lazily, pushing the warm air from the central heating back down onto the onlookers. The place was packed. Attendees who weren't part of the dinner were already seated, but there were two rows in the middle and front that remained open. I knew those were reserved for the progressive diners.

Just inside the barn door, my mother brushed snow off her coat with her gloves. "I forgot how cold it is here. Maybe my blood has thinned since I've lived in a warmer climate. I saw a special on one of those science programs on television about that. People who live in extreme heat often can't stand polar temperatures."

My father chuckled as he removed his own gloves. "Daphne, you don't live in extreme heat. Ninety-nine percent of your time is spent in air-conditioning."

"You never take my ideas seriously."

My father smiled. "I take all of your ideas seriously."

Willow pushed her way through the crowd toward me. She was hard to miss because she had styled her supershort hair into tiny spikes for opening night. Despite her looks, everyone in Holmes County accepted Willow, even the Amish. I suspected that they just found her to be eccentric. She was one of the longest-standing township trustees. I partially had her to blame for my post on the board.

Willow's gauzy blouse ballooned around her as her blouses always did. "Angie, thank goodness you're here. One of the ushers called in sick, and I need someone to pass out programs." She shoved a stack of glossy programs into my hands. "If you run out, there are more of those behind the hay bale there in a cardboard box." She pointed at the hay bale.

"Sure," I said. "I'm happy to help."

My mother gave a tense smile. "My daughter is a township trustee. Isn't there someone else who can pass out the programs?"

Willow held out her hand to shake my mother's. "Of course, I know she is. That's exactly why I asked her. Willow Moon. I'm a trustee too. It's all hands on deck for such a little township when it comes to events."

Reluctantly, Mom took it.

"You must be Angie's parents. I can't tell you what a ray of sunshine your daughter is to this township. She's smart too. Without Angie, a few mur—ouch!"

I stepped on Willow's foot because I knew she was about to talk about the recent deaths in Holmes County and my part in their investigations. My parents didn't need to know more than what I had told them about that.

Willow stepped away from me and twirled her crystal.

"Really, I don't mind. The house is almost full," I said. "It won't take long to hand out these last few programs."

Willow's smile widened. "You must be Ryan. I've heard *all* about you."

The corners of Ryan's full lips turned up. "All good things, I hope."

"None at all," Willow said.

My father covered his laugh with a cough. I winced.

"You had better get to your seats." I handed them each a program.

Ryan's fingers brushed my wrist as he took the paper. I blushed and felt my face heat up even more as I was angry at my body for betraying me. Ryan shouldn't make me blush. I prayed Sheriff Mitchell had been called away and wasn't within the viewing area.

Ryan smiled at me, and I scowled back. Any sympathy I had for him evaporated.

I pointed down the aisle. "Your seats are in the middle section, down in front. They are the best seats in the house."

My parents and Ryan had been standing there too long. Those waiting to get from out of the cold and into the barn slid past them impatiently. I shoved programs at them as they went. "Go on. I got this," I said. "The show starts in five minutes."

"Where will you be sitting?" my mother asked.

"I'll grab a seat as soon as everyone else is seated."

"Can't you sit with us?"

I shook my head. "That place is reserved for the progressive diners. I wasn't going to be sitting there anyway."

Mom pursed her lips. "I feel like we have hardly seen you since we arrived. I hope the entire visit won't be like this."

A pang of guilt hit me. "It won't, I promise. Today was exceptionally busy. Tomorrow will be calmer, you'll see."

"Yes, of course it will be," my father said as he led Ryan and my mother to their seats.

Willow knelt down and scratched Oliver under the chin. "I'm glad you brought Oliver too. We need him for the play."

"Wh-what?" I asked.

Oliver gave me a pleading look.

"There is a dog in act two. He sits with Eve's character as she sings to him about leaving the Amish. Any dog will do. Plus imagine how dashing he will look onstage!"

Oliver bumped his head against her leg as if to say, "Well, that is true, but please don't embarrass me."

"What happened to the other dog?"

"He belonged to an animal trainer in Canton. The snow is really bad in Stark County, and she couldn't get him here."

"I don't know. Oliver has never been on a stage before. The bright lights might bother him, or he might become afraid and run off. What if a bird gets into the barn? Then we'll really have some trouble."

"Don't be silly. We don't have to worry about Oliver's fear of birds. There aren't any in the barn. We would have seen them by now in all this commotion. He will do great. He has that star quality."

Oliver shuffled behind my legs.

Before I could argue, Willow took Oliver's leash from my hand and led my Frenchie away. I watched them go with a knot of dread growing in my stomach. As Oliver went, he looked back at me forlornly. I trusted Willow with my dog, but Oliver, although a ham, simply wasn't an actor.

I continued to hand out programs and point out open seats to guests. The sheriff came up to me.

"Program?"

He patted the back pocket of his uniform. "I got one.

What's wrong with you? You look like you lost your best friend. Did Ryan say or do something?"

"Ryan is a problem, yes, but I'm frowning because I did lose my best friend. Willow took Oliver backstage."

"Why?"

I interrupted our conversation to pass out three more programs.

"It seems the dog actor in the play is snowbound, and she needed Oliver as the stand-in. He knows Willow, but you know how scatterbrained she can be. Oliver could get scared back there by himself with no one he knows."

"I'll send Anderson backstage to keep an eye on him. I need to put someone near the back anyway to keep an eye on the south entrance to the barn."

"Would you?" I sighed with relief. "Thanks." I considered his last statement. "Do you suspect trouble tonight?"

"I always suspect trouble. I'm a cop."

I frowned.

"But nothing out of the ordinary. My deputies have canvased the property. Nahum isn't around."

"Good."

The houselights flashed, warning the audience the play was about to begin.

"You'd better get to your seat," I said.

He winked. "You too."

I snapped up an empty hay bale near the barn door. It was a chilly post, but I would be able to see any latecomers and hand them a program.

As I settled onto my hay bale seat, I wondered how

Oliver was getting on. I was just about to get up and check on him when the curtain went up. The opening scene was an Amish farm. I thought the life-sized wooden cow was a nice touch. Eve Shetler glided across the stage with her arms held wide as she breathed in the farm air. Since the theater was an old barn, that was very close to the true scent in the air. Her twirling movement was very Julie Andrews, and I wondered if she had seen *The Sound of Music* recently.

Eve was beautiful, thin, and lithe; she seemed to float across the stage. When she sang, her voice came out as a perfect soprano.

The scene changed to the inside of an Amish kitchen. Eve was cleaning and suddenly broke into song and dance. I had to cover my mouth to stifle a giggle. I think it was more the thought of an Amish woman tap-dancing in her kitchen that tickled my funny bone than anything else.

"What am I to do? Do I stay with my family, or do I follow my heart?" she sang.

Okay, the cheese-o-meter was officially off the charts. I watched the members of the audience. They were wrapped up in Eve's performance. I didn't know much about acting, but even I could tell that Eve was a special talent and one that was wasted here in Holmes County. I hoped that this play would catapult her career. Wade had been right. She was a star.

At the beginning of the second act, Eve's young English beau, played by the handsome actor with a British accent, was alone onstage, singing about his love for the pretty Amish girl. One of his lines was "Could I give up my cell phone for her?" His native accent was gone onstage, replaced by a flat and spot-on midwestern twang.

I nearly choked. Although Eve had owned the stage, this young actor struggled and would pause as he tried to remember his lines. For the first time, I wished I had sat beside my mother during the play just so I could see her reaction to his performance. I was sure I would hear about it later.

Eve was lowered on a swing made to look like a tree limb while her beloved looked on. The ropes and pulleys groaned as they lowered her. All the while, Eve sang about the choice she must make. She sang with such passion that I couldn't help but think she poured some of her own anguish about leaving her community into the song.

As the number ended, Eve climbed back onto the swing and was lifted up into the air. We could just see her feet below the top curtain. She was nearly at the very top when a scream reverberated through the barn, and Eve's tiny body smacked onto the stage with such force that a table overturned on the set. The unlit lantern sitting on top of it also fell and shattered into a thousand pieces across the stage.

That was when I realized I'd lied to my mother. There was no way tomorrow would be calmer.

Chapter Five

Screams filled the barn. Some of them might have been my own. The members of the audience were out of their seats as they all seemed to want a better look at the stage.

"Everyone stay where you are!" Mitchell's commanding voice broke into the sound of screams and gasps.

Without thinking, I dropped the stack of programs I had been holding onto the ground in front of the hay bale and rushed toward the fallen actress. I ran up the side aisle and stopped just short of the stage.

I prayed Eve was all right. She fell at least twenty feet to the hard stage floor, but there was a chance she could be fine. Through the crowd, I couldn't see if she was moving.

My Frenchie bolted from backstage and ran straight to me. He catapulted his black-and-white body into my arms. I caught him with an "Oof!"

"It's okay, Ollie," I murmured to the little dog and

rested my cheek on top of his solid head. I tucked Oliver under my left arm and approached the side of the stage where Eve lay. My steps were tentative. A part of me didn't want to confirm whether she was okay, because I felt like I already knew the answer from the murmurs and whimpers coming from the audience. But I had to see for myself. I propelled myself forward.

Deputy Anderson, Mitchell's young, gawky officer, stood over Eve. I gripped the edge of the stage with my free hand and watched as the sheriff knelt beside the motionless body in Amish dress.

I looked down at Eve, and then up at the sheriff. Mitchell's gaze met mine, and he shook his head ever so slightly just once. There was no doubt about it. This rising star, this former Amish girl, was dead. I sucked in air as my body began to shake. I had just spoken to her at the dinner an hour ago. How could a bright, vibrant light be so quickly extinguished?

The sheriff waved over another deputy I hadn't even known was there. The two men spoke into their radios in hushed voices, which were impossible to hear over the noise from the crowd.

The actors and stagehands poured onto the stage. The heavy stage makeup on the actors' faces amplified their horror. The British man, who played the male lead and had been onstage when Eve fell, clenched his fists. "The structure wasn't reliable. How dare you let us perform under these conditions? Poor Eve." He choked on her name and bit his fist.

Something about his reaction seemed off. The fist biting was a little much, as if he were still playing a part.

Director Wade Brooklyn ran onto the stage. He dropped to his knees next to the lifeless girl. "My star! My star!"

Mitchell grabbed Wade's hand before he could touch Eve. "Sir, do not touch her."

"She was so talented, so beautiful. She was destined for a long career on the stage. She could have made it on Broadway, in Hollywood, anywhere. She just had that *it* factor. I will never again work with such raw talent."

There was a sharp intake of breath on the other side of the stage at the director's comments. A second girl, whom I recognized as the one in English dress during the progressive dinner, was now dressed as an Amish girl. She twisted her onstage prayer cap in her hands. A tear slid down her cheek. "That could have been me."

The British actor galloped across the stage and put his arm around the girl.

I frowned. "That could have been me" seemed like an odd statement to make on seeing a fellow actress die onstage. Yes, there were tears streaming down her face, but were those tears for Eve or for this girl's supposed close call? Had I even heard her correctly? It was difficult to hear anything over the shouts and cries of the audience. I spun around and searched the crowd for my parents. They stood in the middle of their row. Ryan appeared stricken, and my mother had her face buried in my father's broad shoulder. The same combination of disbelief and horror was registered on the faces of everyone sitting and standing around them.

Deputy Anderson stepped onto the stage and peered

at the swing Eve fell from. He picked up the heavy rope that had been used to raise and lower the swing. "Sheriff, look."

Mitchell slapped his forehead. "Anderson, drop that right now."

As if he had been shot, Deputy Anderson dropped the piece of rope onto the stage. It landed with a thud. The severed end pointed at me. It had a clean cut halfway through it. The remainder was torn.

"The rope was cut," Willow said loudly in a rare moment of silence, so that her voice projected across the barn.

I turned. I hadn't even realized that she'd been standing there next to me.

"Close the curtain!" Mitchell ordered.

No one moved.

He pointed at Anderson. "Close the curtain."

The deputy sprinted to the ropes. Slowly the curtain came together, and with one final pull, Anderson, the actors, Mitchell, and Eve's body disappeared behind a blue velvet sheet.

Pandemonium erupted as the playgoers pushed out of their rows in their haste to escape the barn. There was a mad rush for the one exit through the front of the barn. Someone was going to get trampled. Again, I looked for my parents and Ryan. They were seated. Ryan was talking to Mom and Dad, probably telling them in his logical-lawyer way that it was safer and smarter to remain where they were until the barn emptied. I had never been so grateful for Ryan as I was in that moment.

"The ropes have been cut," Willow whispered, bringing my attention back to her.

"This can only mean one thing," I whispered.

Willow gripped my arm. "What? What does it mean?"

"Murder," I murmured, so that only Willow and Oliver could hear me.

Willow's hand went to her crystal.

Mitchell appeared through the curtain and put two fingers in his mouth. He let out a whistle that would have made a shrill harpy fall from the sky.

Everyone in the room froze.

In the silence, the sheriff spoke. "Please, of those of you who are still here, I will have to ask everyone to remain in your seats for the time being. We will dismiss you from the barn after we ask a few questions about what you saw. More deputies and police officers assisting from Millersburg PD are on the way. We will do everything that we can to make this process go as quickly as possible."

More people moved toward the door.

"If you leave, we will be calling or knocking on your door to interview you."

A few reconsidered and took their seats; others kept heading to the exit. I couldn't blame them. The sheriff didn't chase them.

Mitchell held up a hand. "Please, please, I know this is very upsetting, but a young woman is dead. You may have seen something that can give us a clue as to what happened. I'm asking you for your patience. It won't be long—"

The wail of a siren approaching the barn interrupted his speech.

"For pity's sake," Willow whispered. "I can't believe we're dealing with another murder." She smoothed her gauzy sleeve. She sniffed. Her black eye makeup streaked across her cheeks. "And Eve Shetler of all people. It's a terrible, terrible shame."

I touched my own cheeks. They were dry. I was too shocked to cry. I knew the tears would come later. "I sat next to her at dinner. She was so . . ." I searched for the right word. "Alive."

"Eve had an infectious quality about her. That's why everyone thought she was going to be a big star. And now—" Willow covered her mouth.

I didn't want to think about it. "Who was that actor on the stage with the British accent?"

"Ruben Hurst. He's English—I mean *real* English, not just what the Amish call us. Isn't his accent swoony?" she asked, but the usual twinkle was missing from her eyes.

My brow wrinkled. "What's he doing in a production in the middle of Ohio?" I knew a better person would not ask such inane questions at such a time, but my curiosity kept my mind off the image of Eve's body and that was top priority at the moment.

She shrugged and removed crumpled tissue from her pants pocket. "Times are tough. Maybe this is the only place he could find a part."

I frowned. I supposed that she was right, but it was so far off the normal beaten path for an actor, let alone one from England, that it was hard to believe.

"Who's that actress with Ruben?" I whispered to Willow.

She wiped at the mascara on her cheek with the tissue. All this accomplished was pushing the makeup into a set of wrinkles I had never noticed before. "Lena. She plays Eve's sister in the play, but she is also Eve's understudy for the lead." She twisted her crystal in her hand. "I guess that part is all hers now if the play is to continue."

It seemed I had suspect number one, who also had seemed to be concerned more with herself than over the loss of Eve. "Did she and Eve get along?"

Willow twisted the crystal hanging from her neck. "Why do you ask?"

"Just curious," I said, hoping Willow would buy it.

Willow dropped her crystal. "I don't believe you. You want to find out what happened."

The main door into the barn opened and in stormed a half dozen officers, some from the Millersburg police department and some from the Holmes County Sheriff's Department. Mitchell and Anderson went over to meet them. As the audience waited to be interviewed, conversation resumed, and it was becoming more and more difficult to overhear what the police were saying to one another—not that I was trying or anything.

"I didn't know Eve long," I said. "I hardly knew her at all, but I liked her."

Willow forced a smile. "Well, I wouldn't let your sheriff know what you are thinking."

"First, he's not *my* sheriff, and second, I'm not thinking anything that he wouldn't expect from me."

"The last part of that statement I believe."

Mitchell completed his powwow with the other officers, and the men and women in uniform fanned out across the audience. While they began their interviews, the main entrance opened again, and three EMTs and the county coroner entered the barn. Mitchell waved them to the small opening in the curtain.

Willow shook her head. "I hate to even ask this under the circumstances, but do you think the play will go on? We have another progressive dinner and performance the day after Christmas. The hotel can't refund all those tickets. We would lose all that money to build the new playground for the kids. What will the children do if we don't get a new slide and swing set? The one out there is twenty years old. It's a wonder a child hasn't killed him- or herself on it yet." She grimaced. "Poor choice of words. Sorry."

I grimaced too. "That's up to the sheriff as well as the play director. Maybe they won't want to go on without their star."

Willow snorted. "I don't think the play people are going to be the ones stopping the performance."

I was just about to ask Willow what she meant by that when she said, "Maybe you can talk to the sheriff and convince him not to close down the play and the progressive dinner."

"I don't know why he would close the progressive dinner. Most of that took place away from the hotel. I don't know what I can possibly say to convince him to do anything."

"Sweet-talk him."

I gave her a look. "Sweet-talk?"

Oliver cocked his head too. At least he agreed with me that the senior trustee was nuts.

Willow gripped my free hand. "Angie, you have to. Do you know how bad it would look for the hotel and the township if the play was canceled? Rolling Brook is gaining a reputation for this sort of thing. It could hurt tourism. It could hurt business, your business."

"Let's move away from the stage if you really want to discuss this." I led Willow to the side aisle and leaned against the wall. Audience members were being interviewed. Once an interview was completed, the individual was dismissed. The police had broken the crowd up into a grid system, and it was surprisingly organized. It was going more quickly than I expected, but then again, more than half the audience had left before reinforcements arrived. "How many people are in the acting troupe?" I shifted Oliver into my other arm. He didn't seem to mind as long as I didn't put him down. My little Frenchie was still shaken; we both were.

"I don't know right offhand, but I can get you a list." She smiled at me knowingly. "You will talk to Mitchell?"

"I didn't say that. I think it's good to know all the cast and crew names just in case."

"In case of what?"

I ignored her question. "I'm not asking because I am afraid for the township or for my business. I'm asking because a young girl I had just met and liked very much is dead. Let's pray it was a terrible accident."

She dropped her head. "I'm sorry. You're right." She twirled her crystal again. "The police will want to talk to us too, especially you, Angie. You sat next to Eve at dinner. Did you notice anything strange?"

I shook my head, but then I remembered the odd

encounter between Eve and the Amish girl who dropped the tray. The pair knew each other, of that I was certain. How well did they know each other?

Actors, including Ruben and Lena, and the stagehands appeared from the other side of the curtain. A deputy was with them and instructed them to sit in the first two rows of the audience. They would be interviewed too. I noticed Wade, the director, wasn't among them.

I stared at the blue velvet curtain. I had to get back there.

Willow held out her arms. "Here, give me Oliver and go back," she said as if she read my mind.

I handed her my Frenchie and hurried up the three steps to the far side of the stage. Before I disappeared behind the curtain, my eyes fell on my parents' row. They each were being interviewed. However, Ryan was not. He had his attention firmly fixed on me before I slipped behind the curtain.

I stood at the end of the stage in the shadows. A spotlight pointed down from the rafters onto Eve's body, making the stillness of her body more apparent. Overhead, flashes of light went off. I glanced up at two police officers I didn't know. One from the Millersburg police department and one from the sheriff's office were inspecting the rigging. The sheriff's deputy took countless photographs of every inch of it.

"How is that possible?" bellowed Wade, who was being interviewed by another deputy on the opposite side of the stage from me. He voice carried, and I wondered if he had started his theater career not as a director but as an actor.

"Wade, when was the last time the set was checked for safety?" Mitchell asked.

"Any questions you have about our set should be directed to our stage manager, Jasper Clump."

A small wiry fellow dressed all in black stepped forward. His gray hair was slicked back with enough styling gel to make the folks at Deb stand up and cheer. I imagined a last name like Clump would belong to a huge beast of man. The beast Jasper resembled the most was a rat, or if I was feeling charitable, a possum.

"Jasper Clump?" the sheriff asked.

The possum folded his arms. "That's me."

"When was the last time you gave the swing and scaffolding a safety check?"

"Just an hour before curtain."

"Who had access to the scaffolding?" the sheriff asked.

"Anyone on the set. We don't police it, but only the stagehands, Eve, or I needed to climb up there during a production. No one else would have reason to climb up there."

"But they could have climbed up there, if they wanted to," the sheriff said.

Jasper's eyes narrowed. "Yes, they could have, but someone probably would have seen them." He pointed to the top platform. "As you can see, there is nowhere to hide."

"So between the safety check and the time Eve fell, no one could have tampered with the ropes."

"That's what I'm trying to tell you. I can prove it to

you." Jasper turned and snapped his fingers at a skinny boy in his late teens. "Blake, tell them."

The boy, presumably Blake, swallowed, and his pronounced Adam's apple bobbed up and down. "Yes, I did a safety check at seven o'clock. You can look at the log in the back. I signed it with the time I finished my check."

"I'm going to want to see that log," Mitchell said. "Could you have missed something in the check, Blake? Maybe something was faulty you didn't realize."

Jasper's face flamed red. "There was nothing wrong with the setup of that stage. I checked it myself."

"When?" Mitchell's voice was sharp.

"This morning. The pulley was oiled, and the rope was new and solid. I rely on Blake to do final checks but only *after* I do my own daily check."

Blake swallowed. "When I saw it, the rope was fine. I always check the rope. It's the most important part."

The EMTs helped the coroner roll Eve onto a gurney. I had to look away.

Chapter Six

I was one of the last people to be interviewed. By the time Deputy Anderson got to me, he was clearly shaken.

"How did you know Eve?" he asked.

"I just met her a few hours ago at the progressive dinner. She sat next to me during the meal."

"And—" The deputy's eyes flitted over to the sheriff, who was consulting with the coroner at the foot of the stage. Eve's body had been removed from the scene. The curtain was open again.

"Anderson, calm down," I said. "The sheriff isn't going to fire you."

"He's not?"

I shook my head. I didn't add that if Mitchell was going to fire the young deputy, he would have done it a long time ago. "Do you have any more questions?"

"No . . . ," he said uncertainly.

"Then I'm going to take off. My family is here visiting."

The deputy didn't bother to stop me. He was too distracted by his fear of termination.

Mom and Dad had been questioned more than an hour ago, but they were still sitting in the audience when I said good-bye to Officer Anderson.

"You didn't have to wait for me," I said. "Why don't you go into the hotel and settle into your rooms?"

"I canceled our hotel reservation," my mother said. "Your father and I want to see as much as possible of you this week. By the way things are going, I'm afraid that your house will be the only place we will be able to catch you."

"You're welcome to stay with me. I had said that from the beginning. I just thought you would be more comfortable at the hotel." I swallowed and looked around the barn. "What about Ryan? He kept his hotel reservation, didn't he?"

Dad stood up from the folding chair, which served as theater seating in the barn. "Don't you worry about that; Ryan is still staying at the hotel."

I gave a huge sigh of relief.

"Angie," my mother said, "you should really be more hospitable. Ryan came a long way to see you. The least you could do is offer him a bed to sleep on."

"I would," I lied, "if I had a bed for him. The best I could do is my lumpy sofa. As it stands, you and Dad will get my bed, and I will sleep on the futon." I waved my hands to stave off any protests. "Not that I mind. I'm very happy that you two and only you two will be staying at my house. Why don't you head over there now, and I'll be heading home soon. I want to check in on the quilt show before I leave. Judging for best quilts is early tomorrow morning." I handed Dad my keys and Oliver's leash. "Do you mind taking Oliver home? He's a little shaken up by everything."

"Not at all," Dad said.

My parents left shortly after that. I glanced back at the stage. The coroner, Eve's body, and the EMTs were gone. So were the police from Millersburg, but Mitchell and a handful of his deputies were still on the scene. How much did I want to go over there and question the sheriff about what he knew? I knew better than to do that. Instead, I ventured out into the snow.

I pulled open the hotel's heavy wooden doors and brushed off what snow I could from my coat and boots before stepping into the hotel. Irritated theatergoers crowded the lobby, waiting to complain about the night's performance, which had been cut short by Eve's fall. Mimi gave them an option of tickets for another night or a full refund. A refund seemed by far the more popular choice. I wanted to talk to Mimi about the play's future, but that would have to wait, as she was surrounded.

Instead, I stepped into the large sitting room where the quilts were and gave a sigh of satisfaction to find that all of them were undisturbed. The quilts, each one hung from a wooden quilt rack, were made by both English and Amish women in the county. Finding twenty quilt racks for all of the quilts had been the biggest challenge. Mattie had resorted to giving away free pies from her brother's bakery in order to borrow a quilt rack. All the quilts were handmade in the traditional Amish patterns from Double Wedding Ring and Four Patch to Goosefoot and Tumbling Block. The colors were the easiest way to distinguish the Amish from the English quilts. The Amish ones tended to be more sedate and darker. The English ones included every color of the rainbow. But not all Amish quilters kept to the dark-colored tradition, because they knew that brighter colors sold better to the English tourists.

A well-dressed couple admired a queen-sized Rolling Block quilt made by an Old Order woman from Charm. Her color choices of pinks, reds, and whites were unconventional for the Amish.

The woman, wearing chiffon, brushed her fingers across the quilt's fold on the wooden rack, then turned to her husband, and said, "It's so lovely. Don't you think our granddaughter would love it?"

I stepped forward. "Interested in purchasing a quilt?" I held out my hand. "I'm Angela Braddock, owner of Running Stitch, a quilt shop in town. I'm managing the quilt show along with Martha Yoder, another local quilt shop owner."

The woman's face brightened. "Oh yes, I think my granddaughter would love this. Pink is her favorite color."

I nodded. "It's a beautiful piece. The woman who made it is over ninety, half blind, and does most of her quilting by feel."

"Amazing."

"All the quilts will be for sale through the end of the show on New Year's Eve, but if you really like that one, I can reserve it for you."

She clasped her hands together. "Would you? It's just perfect for our granddaughter. Don't you think, dear?" she asked her husband.

"Whatever you think, my sweet."

The woman smiled as she wrote the check. "It is so nice to come into this room and see all of these beautiful quilts after such a terrible night." She met my gaze. "Were you at the play? Did you see what happened? It was such a horrific scene. That poor girl. She had her whole life ahead of her. I heard that she actually was Amish."

"She grew up Amish," I said as I wrote her a receipt.

The woman's husband peered at a goosefoot-patterned quilt on the next rack and said, "If she was in that play, she's not Amish anymore and her family won't even miss her."

My jaw twitched. "My aunt was Amish."

"Oh," the man said. "But you are not."

"No," I said, refusing to explain any further. "But I can assure you that she loved me like a daughter, even though I am English." I glared at him.

"I didn't mean any offense."

I clamped my mouth shut to hold back a smart remark. "You can pick up the quilt at my shop." I handed the woman my card. "Or call the telephone number, and we can make arrangements to get it to you."

"Thank you," she said, and her husband put his hand under his wife's elbow and led her from the room.

"You almost lost a sale there," a voice said to my right.

I jumped and found Ryan sitting in the corner with a novel on his lap. "I'm frustrated by the assumptions people make about the Amish. They think that they are all the same, but that's not true. It's like saying everyone from Texas is a cowboy."

He pointed to my cowboy boots. "Like you?"

I frowned in return.

"I know how much you miss your aunt, Angie." He closed his book and stood up. "I know how important she was to you."

I blinked away tears. Does grief ever truly go away? I was beginning to doubt it. I refused to think of Eve's family. If I even started to, I would never stop crying. Ryan's wasn't my shoulder to cry on any longer, and I didn't want it to be. "What are you doing in here sneaking up on people?"

He held up his book, a thriller. "Just reading and waiting for you. I thought you might want to check on your quilts before you headed home. We need to talk."

My shoulders sagged. "Not tonight, Ryan. I don't have the energy for it."

He stepped toward me. "I came all the way here to see you, and you won't even speak to me."

"We will have plenty of time before you go back to Texas. After what happened to Eve—"

"Who's Eve?"

"The girl who fell during the play." I paused. "I don't have it in me for any more high emotions tonight. Can we talk later?"

He stepped closer to me, and I took two huge steps back, bumping into a quilting rack.

"This isn't about the girl. It's about the sheriff. Is he the reason you don't want to talk to me?"

"What are you talking about?" I asked, my voice alarmingly high.

"I could tell by the way you reacted when your mother asked about him. She thought you two had much more to discuss than official township business."

A young girl came into the room carrying a watering can. "Oh, I'm so sorry," she said. "I didn't know anyone was here. I will come back and water the plants later."

"No!" I said a little too quickly. "Water the plants now. We were just leaving."

She hesitated.

Ryan picked up his book from the chair. "Good night, Angie," he said as he left the room.

"Night," was all I could manage.

After Ryan left, I realized the girl watering the spider plant in the corner of the room was the same girl who dropped the coffeepot during the progressive dinner. "You were at the dinner earlier tonight," I said.

She turned to look at me. There were tears in her blue eyes.

"Are you all right?" I asked.

She swiped at her cheek. "I'm fine."

"Is something wrong?"

She dropped the watering can. Tears flowed down her cheeks. "I'm so clumsy. What else am I going to drop today?"

"I'll go get some paper towels," I said, and ran to the public restroom on the first floor. When I returned with a wad of paper towels, I found the girl sitting on the edge of an armchair, staring into space.

I righted the watering can and sopped up what water I could with the paper towels. They were soaked through in seconds. I tossed them into a discreet wastebasket in the corner of the room.

"I'm sorry," she said. "I can't believe what has happened."

"Do you mean the accident at the play?"

She nodded, and fat tears rolled down her pale cheeks.

"It's been a shock for everyone."

She whispered something I couldn't hear.

I pulled a footstool close to her. "What was that?"

This time it came barely above a whisper. "She was my sister."

I rocked back on my stool. "Your sister?"

She nodded. "And it's all my fault."

I sat across from her on a love seat. "Why's that?"

"Because I'm the reason she came back. She would never have come back without my meddling, and she would still be alive."

"How did you convince her to come back?"

"The play. My mother knew from her letters she was struggling, finding any small part in New York, so *Mamm* asked me to write her about this theater troupe coming to the hotel and urge her to contact them and try out. I never thought she would actually do it or that they would give her the lead part. *Mamm* was overjoyed when I got her letter telling us she was coming home. And now she's gone forever." She buried her face in her hands.

I remembered now at the dinner when Eve offered to help the girl clean up the spilled coffee and Wade stopped her. "I'm so sorry," I said. "I'm Angie Braddock."

"I know who you are," she said. "You are the new trustee. My father says that you will look out for the interests of the Amish in Rolling Brook."

If she was Eve's sister, Nahum was also her uncle.

"Nahum Shetler is your uncle?" I asked.

"*Ya*. He believes he is in charge of the family like he's our bishop, which he is not." She covered her mouth. "I shouldn't have said that. It was unkind. He is my elder. I should respect him."

"Even if he is crazy?" I asked with a smile.

She gave me the tiniest smile in return. "Even if he is crazy." Tears returned to her eyes.

"What's your name?" I asked gently.

She removed a soggy tissue from her apron pocket and balled it in her hand. "Junie Shetler."

"It's nice to meet you, Junie. Is there anything I can do to help you? Ice cream works wonders for me. It doesn't make anything better, but it does take the edge off."

She shook her head. "*Nee, danki.*" She stood and picked up her watering can. "I should return to work."

"Shouldn't you go home? I'm sure Mimi would let you take some time off."

"Mimi has been very kind. She was the one who told me, and she offered to take me home." She swallowed. "I would rather work. I'm sure the police have told my parents by now, and—and I just can't be there."

I stood. "All right."

Her whole body shook as she tried to restrain a sob. "I wanted her to come back, but not like this, I wanted her to rejoin our community. *Mamm* did too. We didn't know what the play would be about or that it would make so many people angry. If we had known, we would never have told her about it."

"Who did it make angry?" I asked.

She started to cry in earnest and left the room without another word.

My heart ached for the girl, but I couldn't help but wonder why she didn't want to go home. Wouldn't she want to be with her family at a time like this? Was whatever kept her from home tonight the reason her sister left the Amish in the first place?

I finished straightening the quilts on their racks and left the hotel, more certain than ever that Eve Shetler was not the victim of a tragic accident but of premeditated murder.

Chapter Seven

My alarm, set to "kill," went off, and I fell with a thunk from the futon in my tiny guest room onto the cold hardwood floor. Everything hurt. When I was in my twenties and slept on my friends' futons, I had been able to hop up like the Easter bunny, bright eyed and bushy tailed. Not anymore. A girl gets over thirty, and everything begins to creak.

I struggled to my feet and rubbed my hip. It was still dark outside, but there was no time to delay. Quilt show judging was that morning at eight thirty sharp. If I was ten seconds later, Martha Yoder would never let me forget it.

Oliver and Dodger were MIA. I heard murmurs coming from the first floor. No doubt they were trying to talk my father out of his substantial breakfast.

When I finally stumbled downstairs, I stepped into my retro kitchen to find my dad at the olive green stove, flipping pieces of French toast. Bacon crackled on a second burner. Oliver and Dodger were at his feet, rotating their begging tactics between "I'm starving to death" and "Aren't I the cutest thing you have ever seen?" Sitting at the tiny kitchen table, which had been left by the previous tenant, Mom sipped coffee and read the local newspaper.

I filled my favorite French bulldog coffee mug and took a long pull before I said good morning.

Dad waved his spatula. "Breakfast, Angie Bear?"

"Sure," I said, feeling more human with caffeine in my veins. "I only have a few minutes. Quilt show judging is this morning."

Mom folded the paper. "You didn't tell us you would be busy today."

"Oh, well, I'm telling you now. Afterward, I will be at the shop until four." I sat across from her at the table, and Dad set a plate of bacon and French toast in front of me. I doused both with Amish maple syrup.

My mother sighed. "And what are we supposed to do all day?"

"You're welcome to stay here, hang out at the shop, or go see the sights or old friends. Whatever you like. My Christmas vacation starts tomorrow. The shop will be closed Christmas Eve and Christmas Day."

Dad dropped two pieces of bacon on the floor. Dodger and Oliver pounced on them. There was a quick flurry of garbled snuffling, and then a hiss. Oliver retreated between my legs under the table, but I saw one piece of bacon sticking out between his teeth.

"Dad," I complained, "that's not good for them."

He pulled out a chair. "Oh, it's just a little treat. It's Christmas."

My sigh sounded frighteningly like my mother's.

Mom didn't touch the French toast or bacon. Instead, she opted for the small serving of plain oatmeal Dad placed in front of her. If that was what I would have to eat to have her figure, being skinny was overrated.

She stirred her breakfast. "I was hoping that you would spend some time with us *and* Ryan today."

I concentrated on my plate. "I wish you hadn't brought him here."

"Angie," my mother reprimanded, "that's not a very nice thing to say."

"I can't even tell my parents how I really feel?" I blamed the whine in my voice on the early morning. Have I mentioned I am *not* a morning person?

"I can understand why you wouldn't want to see him, Angie Bear, after the way he treated you. It took me a long time before I could look the boy in the eye without wanting to pop him in the nose over breaking your heart."

"Kent!" my mother chastised.

I beamed at my father. "Thanks, Dad. That might be one of the nicest things anyone has ever said to me."

Mom shook her head. "What am I going to do with the two of you?" She continued to stir her oatmeal. I wondered if she had any plans to eat it or if just looking at her breakfast was enough. Maybe *that* was her secret to staying so thin.

"What do you think about Ryan now?" I asked my father.

"He's sorry," Dad replied.

I popped my last piece of bacon into my mouth to stop a smart remark. "Got to run. Come, Oliver. It's time to suit up for the elements." I grabbed the Frenchie's sweater off the bench by the laundry room door.

"You are going to take him to the hotel? Won't that upset the staff?" my mother asked.

"Oliver will be on his best behavior."

Oliver sat up straighter as if to prove how good he could be.

I knelt in front of him and slipped the reindeer sweater over his square head. "He was with me when Mattie and I set up the show last week. Mimi should be glad I'm not bringing Dodger. He's the real trouble-maker in the family."

Dodger tilted his fuzzy head up to me and mewed, complaining that I didn't trust him. I knew better than to trust that mischievous little kitten.

It was just after eight when Oliver and I stepped through the front doors of the Swiss Valley Hotel. Guests were slowly coming down the grand staircase on their way to the dining room for breakfast, which smelled heavenly. I would've certainly been tempted to finagle a plate if my father hadn't made breakfast.

The Amish girl behind the registration desk smiled at me, and I snapped off Oliver's leash, shoving it into my bag. He gravitated toward the dining room. Oliver believed in second breakfasts the way a hobbit does.

"Oliver, come." I crossed my arms. "You already had your serving of people food for the day."

He dropped into a downward dog move and did his best to look like a starving orphan.

I shook my finger at him. "Not going to work."

The girl behind the counter started to giggle, and I grinned. "He's a handful."

"You are the lady from the quilt shop, aren't you? I saw you with Mattie Miller last week setting up the quilts."

"Do you know Mattie?" I asked.

"*Ya.*" She folded her hands on the counter. "Mattie and I used to go to school together many years ago."

The girl couldn't have been more than seventeen, but she spoke the truth when she said "many years ago," because the Amish stop schooling at the eighth grade.

"It's always nice to meet one of Mattie's friends. She's a good worker, and I'm lucky to have her with me at Running Stitch. What's your name?" I asked.

"Bethanne Hochstetler."

I decided to press my luck with Bethanne's friendliness. "Do you know if Junie Shetler is here today?"

She shook her head. "Junie works afternoons and evenings, most of the time. She might be in a bit early because we have so many guests here for the play. Ms. Ford wants everything to be perfect, especially after last night." She dropped her gaze to the polished counter in front of her.

"After Eve fell," I said.

"*Ya.* I was at home and didn't learn of it until this morning. It's so sad. I went to school with Eve too, and Junie of course. I feel terrible for Junie."

"She was Junie's sister, right?"

Bethanne frowned slightly. "*Ya.*"

I knew I couldn't push Bethanne too far or she wouldn't tell me anything. Most Amish weren't that forthcoming with English people, especially English people whom they didn't know. "I'm very sorry for Junie. I just met both her and Eve yesterday at the progressive dinner. I was surprised to see Junie working at the hotel after the accident. I would have thought she would have gone home to be with her family."

"I—I just don't think they were that close. Eve lived in the hotel the last two weeks during rehearsals, and I never saw her and Junie speak to each other even when they were in the same room." She tapped her pencil on the desk. "Junie may have just been following her family's rules, but if it were my sister, I would talk to her when I saw her. I wouldn't care what my bishop had to say about it."

"Was Eve shunned for leaving the community?"

"*Nee*, but everyone is so upset over the play that no one wanted to speak to her."

"No one? You mean none of the Amish."

She nodded. "When he heard about the play, I thought my *daed* would ask me to quit my job here at the hotel, but he didn't." She hung her head. "But I didn't speak to Eve either while she was here. I was too afraid to. I was afraid my *daed* would find out and make me quit. I love working for Ms. Ford." She lowered her voice. "I'd like to run my own inn someday. Not as big as the hotel, but I've always dreamed about having a little bed-and-breakfast. I know that must sound silly to you." She squatted to scratch Oliver between the ears.

"Not at all. Before I inherited my aunt's quilt shop, I never thought of having my own business, but now I wouldn't do anything else. Being a small-business owner is hard but rewarding work."

Across the lobby, Martha stood in the doorway of the sitting room with her arms folded across her chest. Of course she beat me to the hotel. Martha was set on beating me at everything.

"I'd better go."

Oliver whimpered.

"He can stay here with me if he wants," Bethanne said. "I'm not going anywhere. I will watch him."

I glanced back at Martha, who was now tapping the toe of her black boot on the carpet. "Maybe that's a good idea."

As I walked across the lobby, I heard Bethanne ask, "Do you like cheese, Oliver?"

"Good morning, Martha," I said.

She nodded. "I have already prepared everything for the judges. They will be here soon."

Her comment put my teeth on edge, but I held my temper. "Thank you." I stepped into the sitting room. Mattie was there, smoothing quilt edges. She shot a glance at Martha.

I wondered what the other woman had said to her before I arrived to make her so nervous.

"Thanks for being here so early, Mattie. I hope Aaron and Rachel didn't mind."

My assistant shook her head. "Rachel dropped me off on the way to the bakery."

"I was chatting with Bethanne at the desk. She says she knows you."

"Everyone knows everyone in Rolling Brook," Martha said.

I frowned.

Mattie watched Martha out of the corner of her eye. "We went to school together."

"Did you two hear about the accident last night?" I asked, including Martha in my question.

Martha perched on the edge of an armchair. "Of course we heard about it. It is the main topic of conversation in the hotel. I am sorry that Eve is dead. She was a bright young woman, but she should have known better than to come back to Rolling Brook." She eyed me. "Some people just don't know when they should stay away."

I was about to open my mouth to rebut when Mattie asked, "Will the play continue?"

"I don't know," I said. "The actors are still here. I saw them eating breakfast in the dining room with the other guests when I arrived."

"It would be best if the theater troupe left," Martha said.

If the theater troupe left, we might never know who cut the rope that caused Eve's fall, and the township might get into some serious financial trouble over the new playground. I didn't share either of these arguments with Martha. Neither would change her opinion. "I thought I would go for a walk around the hotel while we wait for the judges to arrive. Martha, you have everything in order here, don't you?"

"Angie, you are supposed to be here for the quilt show."

"That's exactly why I'm here. See you ladies in a bit."

Martha scowled at me.

In the lobby, I made a beeline for the front door.

"Angie, wait." Mattie came running up behind me. Her cloak was draped over her arm. "Can I go with you? I don't want to be left in the room alone with Martha."

"Why not? Did something happen?"

Mattie frowned. "I'd rather not say."

I planted my feet firmly into the carpet. "Mattie, tell me, or neither of us are going anywhere."

"She offered me a job," she said in a small voice.

I closed my eyes. "And what did you say?"

She squeezed the chestnut bun on the back of her head as if to make sure it was still there. "That I was happy working for you."

I smiled. "Thank you. I would hate to lose you."

"You won't," she said. "As you can guess, Martha's not too happy with me right now. Exploring the hotel seems like a great idea."

"Okay then," I said, zipping up my parka. "Put your cloak on. We aren't going to walk around the hotel. We are going to the barn."

She let the bottom of her cloak hit the carpet. "But the play people will be there."

"They are at breakfast, remember?" I pulled on my own coat and winked at her.

With a dramatic sigh, Mattie picked up her cloak and bonnet, just as I knew she would.

Chapter Eight

The wind picked a layer of snow off the ground. It swirled in our faces as we hurried across the parking lot. The cold walk was much easier for me this morning because I had left my beloved cowboy boots at home and opted for my much more practical black snow boots.

When we reached the barn's huge sliding door, I yanked on it, but it didn't budge.

Mattie held on to her cloak so it wouldn't fly into the air. She was a dead ringer for a flying nun. "See. It's locked." Her teeth chattered. "They don't want anyone going in there, and we shouldn't be there."

"There's a back door." I shuffled to the corner of the barn.

Mattie's sigh was lost in the wind, but I knew it was there.

I jogged around the building. My footsteps crunched in the fresh snow. It'd be obvious that someone had been around the barn today with all the footprints Mattie and I left, but it couldn't be helped.

The back door was a normal hinged door. I turned the knob with my gloved hand, and it opened.

Mattie caught her breath as she stopped beside me.

"Open sesame," I crowed.

"What?" Her forehead wrinkled.

I inwardly groaned. So many pop culture references were lost on my Amish friends. "Never mind. Let's go."

We crept into the barn. This was actually better than my first idea to go in through the main entrance. The single back door led us directly into the backstage area. The area was dimly lit. There was one high window where the barn's hayloft had once been. Mimi had the loft removed when she converted the building into a theater.

"Why are we here? What are we looking for?" Mattie asked.

"That's my girl," I said. "We are just getting an idea for where people would have been during the play. We need to know who might have seen what so we know who to talk to about Eve's tumble."

"Why do *you* need to talk to anyone about Eve? Isn't that the sheriff's job?"

"Officially. But I'm unofficially making it mine too."

She folded her arms. "Is this because you want to avoid Ryan?"

"What? This has nothing to do with Ryan."

"Doesn't it?" she asked. "If you are running all over the county, you won't have time to talk to him."

I narrowed my eyes. "You have a very suspicious nature for an Amish girl."

She grinned. "I have been working for you for four months."

Oh great, she was giving me credit for corrupting her.

"Maybe you are right a little, but Ryan isn't the only reason."

"What's your other reason?"

It was a simple question, but I didn't know how to answer. My shoulders sagged. "I met Eve, and I liked her. Because Eve was too young with too much promise to have this happen to her. Because I think I can help, and if I think I can help, I have to try."

Mattie placed a small hand on my arm. "Angie, you have a big heart, and I shouldn't have questioned your motives. My family knows that better than anyone. You helped my brother last fall when he was accused of murder, but I don't think this was such a great idea. We should go back to the hotel and prepare for the quilt show judging. Let the sheriff take care of this one. Martha must be livid that we left."

"Martha is always mad about something. That can't be helped." I ignored her comment about Mitchell because I knew Mitchell would agree with her one hundred percent. I tilted my head back and peered up at the scaffolding that had held Eve's swing.

Mattie removed her large black bonnet. "Angie, let's go back."

"We're here now. We might as well take a look around." I stepped onto the main stage. The curtains were open, and I looked out onto the empty seats. Would an audience ever sit there again?

I returned to backstage crime-scene tape wrapped around the ladder leading up to the platform. I pursed my lips. That was problematic, but then again it was winter and I was wearing gloves. I wouldn't leave any fingerprints behind. I shook the rung of the wooden ladder, which led up to the platform above. It didn't budge. It was sturdy, Amish made. I was sure the swing had been the same way.

Mattie stood a few feet away from me. "If there is another performance, when will it be?"

I delicately removed the crime-scene tape and let it hang loosely from the ladder. "I thought there was going to be one tonight, but the next combo with the progressive dinner is the day after Christmas." I gave the ladder another yank.

"What are you doing, trying to pull it down?"

I placed my right foot on the bottom rung. "I'm making sure it's stable."

Her eyes narrowed. "Stable for what?"

"For me to climb. What else?"

She gripped her bonnet. "You can't climb up there."

Both feet were off the ground, and I stood on the third rung. "Why not?"

"Because I'm sure you're not allowed. You could get caught."

"Caught by whom? I will be up and down before you know it." I started to climb.

"It's not safe. Look what happened to Eve."

"Someone had cut the rope holding up the swing.

There was nothing wrong with the ladder or platform itself." I climbed to the next rung. "At least I hope not," I muttered under my breath.

The rung creaked under my weight. I froze. The ladder held. My heart skipped a couple of precious beats. "See. Solid, Amish craftsmanship. You can always count on it." I continued the climb much faster, not wanting to have my full weight in one place for too long.

She stared up at me. "You are as foolish as my brother claims."

"I won't argue with that." At the top, I hesitated for a moment before stepping onto the wooden platform. My knees shook. Usually, I'm not afraid of heights, but in my mind's eye I relived Eve's fall. Gripping the railing, I straightened my knees.

From the scaffolding loft, I couldn't see the audience seats because the bottom of the velvet curtain obscured my view. However, I had a clear view of the stage, both the main stage and the backstage area. If Eve had been paying attention, would she have seen the person cut the rope? I shook my head. It was unlikely that the culprit would do it in the middle of the play. There was too great a risk of being caught in the act. If Blake checked the ropes an hour before the curtain went up, the murderer had to have cut the rope during the progressive dinner. I shivered. We had all been sitting in the dining room enjoying the good Amish food while someone plotted murder. I tried to think back to the meal. Had anyone left the table? I just couldn't remember. But someone could have slipped away unnoticed when Junie dropped the tray.

Feeling more comfortable on the platform, I leaned over the railing and examined the backstage from my vantage point. An area was partitioned off for the wardrobe and props behind two Chinese screens. Plain dresses, trousers, and simple leather shoes made up the wardrobe, hanging from a metal rack. The props consisted of pots and pans, rakes, a basket of silk flowers, and bonnets of various sizes. Two makeup tables sat outside of the screened-in area.

"Are you coming down now?" Mattie asked. "I think you should come down now."

"Almost," I called, and carefully walked along the platform. At the end, a person-sized hole was cut into the wood. I looked up and saw a large pulley dangling above that lowered Eve onto the stage. It would have been very simple to stand above this hole and cut the rope. Why hadn't Eve seen the cut rope? Was it because she was too nervous about the show? I bit my lip. Or because she trusted the crew to take care of her?

I imagined Eve, climbing onto the swing and nodding to someone backstage or even on the platform when she was ready to go down. Who would it have been? Stagehand Blake? Or stage manager Jasper Clump? Or a third person I didn't know about?

From the platform, I could see everything backstage. So couldn't anyone backstage see me if they thought to look up? That was another reason that the rope had to have been cut when the backstage was empty.

"Angie, please come down." Mattie's voice jumped an octave in the time I had been above her.

Mattie was on the stage now, rubbing her hands together as she watched me. I really should stop being such a bad influence on the Amish girl, or her brother would tell her to quit working for Running Stitch and work for Martha. Martha would never climb a ladder to get a better view of a murder scene.

I stood. "All right. I'm coming." As I climbed down the ladder, I wasn't sure I had learned anything new other than confirming, at least in my mind, the time of the crime.

On the stage once again, I replaced the tape and dusted my hands off on my jeans. The swing Eve fell from was shoved back in a corner. I walked over to it and examined it, wondering why I hadn't seen it from above. Looking up, I saw that my view would have been obscured by a beam. So it wasn't completely true. Not everyone on the stage could see what was going on on the platform. "I guess they don't plan to use that again," I said.

"What happened to Eve seems like such a waste. Why did they even need to lower her on a swing in the first place?"

My mouth fell open. "Mattie, that is a brilliant question! Why haven't I thought of that?"

She twisted her bonnet ribbon around her fingers. "It is?"

"Sure. The lowering of the swing really didn't add anything to the play. I know it was dramatic, but was it necessary? Maybe I should find out whose idea it was and that will lead us to the killer. If you look at it that way, it could have been completely premeditated." I warmed up to the idea. "The swing may have only been added with the murder plot in mind."

Mattie shivered. "Then who put it in the play?"

Jasper Clump materialized from the shadows and gripped a sledgehammer in his hands. "It was my idea."

Chapter Nine

"Oh, hey, Jasper," I said as if we were old friends. I tried not to stare at the sledgehammer.

Mattie stood behind me.

Jasper's well-endowed eyebrows knit together. "Do I know you?"

"I'm Angie Braddock, and I own Running Stitch, an Amish quilt shop here in Rolling Brook." I grabbed Mattie by the arm and yanked her close to my side. "This is my assistant, Mattie."

"An Amish quilt shop? You're not Amish."

Like I've never heard that before.

"Got me there. We will just be on our way now." I took Mattie's hand and squeezed it hard, hoping that would send the message for her to pay attention.

Jasper stepped into our path. Even though there wouldn't be a performance that day, he wore all black like he would as the stage manager during a play. "Wait! You can't just walk away. What are you doing in here?"

I gave my most dazzling smile. "We're hosting the quilt show in the hotel, and we thought we'd just pop over while we waited for the judging to start to check out the stage. Mattie hadn't been in the barn since it'd been converted to a playhouse, and she wanted to see it. Isn't that right, Mattie?"

Mattie didn't say anything.

I elbowed her.

"*Ya*—I mean, yes, that is what we are doing here." She sidestepped away from me. "It is amazing how the barn has been transformed."

I shared another big smile. "We got a good look, so now we will be on our way. We can't keep those quilt judges waiting." I forced a laugh.

He smacked the sledgehammer in his palm and his opossum-like nose wrinkled. "You aren't going anywhere."

Mattie began to tremble.

"Why not?" I squeaked. I cleared my throat. "Why not?"

"Because I heard the two of you talking just now. You are about to go to the cops and tell them I was the one who cut the rope."

"Nope. That thought never crossed my mind," I lied.

Jasper's lip curled. "I'm not going to be blamed for what happened. Sure, the swing was my idea, but it was safe. I'd stake my life on it."

Sadly, it was Eve who staked her life on it, not Jasper.

"Angie," Mattie hissed.

I ignored her. "Maybe you should go to the police and tell them what you know."

"You aren't going to pin this on me! No way! I do everything I can to keep the actors safe. It's not my fault if they sneak about the stage trying to off one another. I don't condone that kind of behavior."

"What do you mean by saying 'trying to off one another'?"

Jasper turned red. "Everyone knows how actors are. Someone is always trying to beat or better the next person coming up. It's a constant battle to stay on top."

"And was Eve like that?" I asked as I inched Mattie and myself toward the back door.

"Oh no. She was different." Tears sprang into his eyes. "She was a good girl, treated me like a person. Unlike the ungrateful others. What right do they have to be all hoity-toity with me? Newsflash, you are in a stage production in Holmes County, Ohio. It's not exactly Broadway, if you know what I'm saying. But Eve was different. It may have been because she was raised Amish. She was a sweet girl." He reached into his back pocket and removed a handkerchief to wipe his eyes. The sledgehammer fell limply from his left hand.

My shoulders relaxed. "If you think an actor is behind this, is there one actor in particular that you suspect?"

His jaw twitched. "I'd put my money on Lena. She's made it no secret that she wanted and thought she deserved Eve's part in the play. Then again, her boyfriend, the Brit, is just as likely."

"You mean Ruben?"

"Is there another Brit in the play?" he snapped.

None that I knew of. I swallowed. "He and Lena are a couple?"

"Oh yeah, from what I hear, he flew across the pond for her. They were going to be the next Broadway power couple by way of Holmes County." He snorted.

"Angie, we need to get back to the quilt show," Mattie said. "The judging starts in five minutes."

"Be on your way then." Jasper gripped his sledgehammer with both hands again. He marched across the stage to where the swing lay. Before I could even fathom what he was about to do, the sledgehammer came down on the swing with a crack. Wood splintered and flew across the stage.

I dodged a flying wood chip. "What are you doing?"

The sledgehammer came down again. "No one will be hurt by something I created ever again." Tears coursed down his weathered cheeks.

"Okay then. We'll see you later." Pulling Mattie by the wrist, I fled through the back door to the stage.

Mattie caught her breath as we clomped up the steps to the entrance to the hotel. "That man is a lunatic."

"Go inside and help Martha get the quilt judging under way. I need to make a quick call to the sheriff before I go in."

She nodded and ran into the hotel.

Before the door closed, I had my cell phone out and dialed.

"Mitchell speaking," the sheriff's rich official voice came over the line.

I tried to catch my breath from the sprint across the hotel grounds in the icy air. "Hey, Sheriff—"

"Good morning, Angie."

"So I'm at the Swiss Valley Hotel, and um, I just witnessed Jasper Clump destroy the swing from the play with a sledgehammer right on the barn stage."

There was a pause. "What were you doing in the barn?"

"Let's not focus on such a silly detail like that."

"Angie . . ." His voice trailed off.

"Anyway, I'm sorry to say the swing is toast. I hope you got your fingerprints off it when you could. Oh, and Jasper is crazy. So I'm sorry to report you have two crazies in this case, Jasper and nutso Nahum Shetler. At least one is English and one is Amish. It's always good to be evenhanded with the two groups in this county."

"Angie, take a breath," the sheriff ordered.

"Okay," I said, exhaling.

"That's not the swing," he said.

"Yes, it is. I was there. Mattie too. We saw him go all gladiator on it. All that's left are splinters, maybe a few larger pieces of wood, but mostly splinters. He's got a wicked arm for such a small guy. I guess the last name Clump fits after all."

"It's the backup swing. The swing Eve fell from is in my evidence room. Do you really think I would have left evidence there? The stagehands and actors will be in and out of the area all day. I can't have them tampering with things."

"They will be in and out all day. Does that mean the play will go on?" I asked, shoving my cold hands into the pockets of my coat.

"Yes. Farley made it very clear that show must go

on. A lot of revenue both for the hotel and for Rolling Brook is at stake. We got everything that we can from the scene. Now it's down to the interviews and leg-work. That's what's going to crack this case."

"I would still talk to Jasper. The man has a lot of rage and was broken up over Eve's death. There's more to the story there."

"Angie, I'm talking to everyone involved. It's my job. It is *not* your job. Your job is to sell quilts."

I felt myself bristle at his tone. "Is there something wrong with selling quilts?"

"Of course not. I wish you'd stick to it though." He sighed. "I'll send Anderson over there to check out the damage."

"A lot of good that will do."

"Please go back to your quilts and stop getting involved in my investigations." He hung up.

Ryan may have been preoccupied at times when we were together, but he never told me what to do, not like Mitchell had just done—and had done on many other occasions. I pointedly ignored the fact he had said please. Ryan Dickinson was looking better and better.

Chapter Ten

Of course, Mitchell was right. I had no business asking people about Eve's death. I had helped Mitchell with his investigation in the past but never with his blessing. I just couldn't get Eve's face out of my head. I knew that we had only met a few hours before her death, but she was a bright and beautiful girl with so much talent and so much promise. How could I not wonder about what happened to her?

I sighed and stepped into the hotel.

In the sitting room, Martha glared at me. She was going to hold it against me that I wasn't there when the judging began. I knew it.

I sidled up to Mattie. "How is it going?"

"Okay," she whispered. "The judges had already begun when I got here. Martha hasn't said two words to me."

No surprise there.

The five judges moved around the room as a group. They were each holding a clipboard with a scoring sheet attached to it. One of my closest friends in Holmes County, Jessica Nicolson, smiled at me. She owned an antiques shop in Millersburg called Out of Time. She wasn't much of a quilter herself. She was learning and taking classes at Running Stitch, but after years of working with antiques, including quilts, she could recognize good craftsmanship when she saw it. Plus, I needed another judge, so I played the friend card and made her do it.

One of the judges walked over to me. It was Austina Shaker. She was a librarian who ran the bookmobile throughout the county. Most of the patrons she serviced were Amish. She knew every back road in Holmes County and could maneuver the bulky bookmobile on every last one of them. I had seen the woman parallel park that monster on Sugartree Street between a buggy and a station wagon. She got it on the first try. It was a demonstration of beauty.

She pushed her wire-rimmed glasses up the bridge of her nose. "Angie, I was surprised that you weren't here when I arrived."

Martha stepped up behind me. "Ya, where were you?"

I glanced back at Martha. "I'm so sorry about that. I was over in the barn."

"Whatever for? Are there more quilts over there?" Austina asked.

"No," I said, hoping to leave it at that.

The other judges gravitated toward us.

She clicked her tongue. "Wasn't it terrible what happened to that poor Eve Shetler? She was such a sweet girl. I always thought so."

"You knew her?" I asked.

"I know all the children who come to my bookmobile. There are many, but some I remember better than others. Eve was one of those children. You know she grew up Amish right here in Rolling Brook."

I nodded.

"She made her choice to leave the community," Martha said.

Austina nodded. "Yes, and I wasn't the least bit surprised when she left Holmes County. I can always tell when one of them is going to leave during their *rumspringa*."

"How's that?" I asked.

"Their reading choices. For example, Eve was fascinated with biographies about actors and actresses. She would ask me specifically to find as many as I could for her, but to hold them behind my desk on the bookmobile so that no one else knew about her reading habits. A librarian never tells."

"How did she even know about those people to ask for books about them?" a member of the school board, who was also a judge, asked.

"The Amish aren't as sheltered from the media as they once were."

Martha frowned at that comment.

Austina sighed, bringing us back to the sad subject at hand. "Now that Eve's gone, I suppose I don't need to keep my silence about her favorite books any longer. When I heard that she left Rolling Brook to pursue a career in acting, I wasn't the least bit surprised. What surprised me was that she came back."

"I heard her sister, Junie, told her about the part and encouraged her to return to try out," I offered.

"Ahh, Junie." Austina nodded. "I knew she would stay Amish by her book choices."

"What were those?" I asked.

"I can't tell you. Junie is still very much alive, and that would be breaking patron-librarian confidentiality."

Oh-kay.

"The whole thing is just too awful for words," Jessica said. "Eve was such a sweet girl. What do you plan to do about it, Angie?"

"What? Me? Nothing. I'm not going to do anything." I felt Martha watching me again.

"This is not good for tourism. Mark my words," Austina said. "I know it will be all the talk of the county when I take the bookmobile out on my rounds later today."

"You drive that monster in this snow?" Jessica asked.

"Absolutely. I'm like the postal service with books. Nothing will keep me from my patrons."

"Can we get back to judging here?" one of the other judges asked. "I have to pick my grandson up from pre-K at eleven."

"Fine, fine," Austina said.

The woman circled a Rolling Block quilt made by a conservative Mennonite woman living in Sugarcreek. It was one of the most beautiful quilts in the show. I wouldn't be surprised if it took top honors. In addition to the quilts being judged, I had a couple of my aunt's best pieces on display. Those were disqualified from the contest since they came from my shop.

After the women finished judging, they handed the clipboards in to Martha. Mattie would tabulate the scores, and the winning ribbons would be posted on the quilts by the time the quilt show officially opened for the day at ten in the morning. Jessica hung back and milled around the quilts until all the other judges turned theirs in and left the room.

Martha handed the stack of clipboards to Mattie, and my assistant sat on a love seat and started counting. Martha sat next to her, checking her work. I shook my head. I had hoped that the quilt show would be the start of some kind of peace between Martha's shop and mine, but it wasn't looking like it would be.

Jessica placed her clipboard on the love seat next to Mattie and grinned at me.

"What?" I asked.

"Is *he* here?" Her eyes crinkled at the corners.

"Who?" I said, walking away from Martha and Mattie. I didn't want Martha to overhear our conversation.

Jessica followed me. "The infamous Ryan."

"Oh, *ya*, he's here. I met him yesterday at Running Stitch," Mattie said, looking up from her numbers. "He's very handsome."

I shot an irritated glance at my assistant, and she dropped her eyes to the clipboards.

Jessica clapped her hands. "When do I get to meet him?"

"You want to meet him?" I wrinkled my nose.

"Yes." She lowered her voice. "I want to meet the jerk who broke your heart."

"That jerk is right here," Ryan said from the doorway.

Ugh. I smacked the heel of my hand onto my forehead.

Jessica's pale Irish complexion morphed from white to pink to red to purple in a matter of seconds. "I—I—I'm so sorry."

"Don't apologize," Ryan said smoothly. "I am a jerk when it comes to Angie, so the title is well deserved. She just won't let me apologize or admit that."

"I'd let you admit that," I muttered. I cleared my throat. "Jessica Nicolson, this is Ryan Dickinson. Ryan, Jessica."

Ryan held out his hand to shake Jessica's. She stared at it. I nudged her with my knee.

Jessica's hand shot out, and she shook Ryan's. "I've heard so much about you."

"I bet," Ryan said good-naturedly, looking at me.

"Now that we have all met one another, Mattie and I have to finish up here and get over to the shop to open up," I said.

Ryan frowned. "I was hoping that I could talk to you today."

"Talking is good," Jessica said dumbly. Ryan's polished appearance and chocolate brown eyes had Jessica under his spell. Me, not so much.

"If you want to drop in at Running Stitch later today, that would be just fine. We can talk there."

"Won't there be other people there?"

I nodded. "We have our last quilting class of the year

today. They're making quilted snowmen, so the store will be pretty busy. You are welcome to sit in. Maybe try your hand at quilting."

Ryan frowned. "I wanted to talk to you alone."

"Why don't you let Mattie and Anna handle the class, Angie?" Jessica said without taking her eyes off Ryan. "Ryan is only here for a few days."

"We can handle it," Mattie called from the sofa.

Traitors, rang out in my head.

"I would prefer to be there for the last class. The shop will be closed tomorrow and Christmas Day. Ryan and I will have plenty of time to talk after today."

Jessica looped her arm through Ryan's. "If you have nothing to do, why don't I show you around town?"

"Jessica," I said through gritted teeth, "don't you have to get back to Out of Time?"

She waved away my concern. "I have my new intern working in the shop today. Between him and Cherry Cat, the shop will be well covered."

Ryan looked down at Jessica. "I could use a tour guide to pass the time, and you would keep me out of Angie's way. You'd like that, wouldn't you, Angie?" His gaze held a challenge.

"Sure," I said, my voice shooting up two octaves. "It's a great idea. Jessica will be a terrific tour guide."

Jessica dropped her arm from Ryan's and scooped up her coat hanging over the arm of a sofa. "Let's go."

"Okay," Ryan said. "We'll see you later, Angie."

I forced a smile. "Bye," I said with as much cheer as I could muster while hiding the tic in my right eye. "Have fun."

After they left, Mattie said, "Are you okay?"

"Okay? Yes, I'm okay. Why wouldn't I be okay? Ryan can do whatever he wants with whomever he wants to do it."

"Are you lying?" Mattie studied me. Maybe she saw the tic.

"I hope not," I said honestly. "Because if I am, I'm afraid of what that might mean."

Chapter Eleven

The quilt show winners were chosen, and I left Mattie and Martha to adorn the winners and runners-up with the appropriate ribbons.

"How's Oliver doing?" I asked Bethanne as I crossed the lobby.

"I think he's all right." She smiled.

I leaned over the counter and found Oliver holding on to a ham bone with his paws and gnawing on it with the side of his mouth. "He looks pretty content to me. You're an excellent pet sitter. Can I give you a call if I ever need one?"

Her face lit up. "I would like that."

"I should warn you first. I also have a kitten name Dodger. He's a little more rambunctious than Oliver."

"I don't mind. I love all animals. When the vet comes to the farm, he always lets me assist him."

"I will keep you in mind, then." I paused. "I know you said she wouldn't be in until later, but have you seen Junie yet today?"

"Actually, I have," Bethanne said. "She is in the dining room. Most of the guests are finished with their breakfast now. Junie is clearing the tables."

"Thanks." I slapped my thigh. "Come, Oliver. Let's go say good-bye to Junie before we leave."

Oliver shot one round brown eye at me. The other's concentration remained pointedly on the bone between his paws.

I put my hands on my hips. "You can't take the bone with you. We have a quilting class going on in the shop today. We can't have the smell of old ham bothering the ladies while they quilt their snowmen."

Oliver wrapped his legs more tightly around the bone. I hoped this didn't turn into a wrestling match.

Bethanne leaned over and took the bone from the Frenchie. Oliver didn't fight her for it, but he gave an audible sigh when his physical contact was broken.

She smiled. "I will keep it here behind the desk for him."

Oliver is such a charmer. Now he had young girls hiding treats for him.

I smacked my leg again. "Come on, you old Casanova."

He grinned and trotted after me.

The French doors opened into the dining room. The long table where I had seen the cast and crew eating breakfast more than an hour ago was empty. A few of the smaller tables had guests sitting at them, perusing the newspaper while they savored their coffee. Junie moved around the long play table with a dishpan. As she collected cups and plates, she added them to the pan. A metal cart sat to the side. It had even more dishes on it. Drama must make a person hungry, because the cast and crew could certainly eat.

I picked up an empty bin from the cart and started collecting silverware. Oliver followed me around the table, most likely thinking I would drop a crumb or two for him to gobble up.

Junie's head snapped up. "What are you doing?"

"Cleaning up. Boy, those actors sure enjoyed their breakfast, didn't they?"

She set the bin at the end of the table. "You can't. You're a guest. I will get in trouble if it looks like I asked a guest to do my job for me."

"I'm not a guest." I placed a serving spoon in my bin.

"But you don't work here."

"I do, in a way, at least as long as the quilt show is going on. Besides, I need to talk to you, so you might as well put me to work while I am at it."

She started gathering coffee mugs again. "Me? Why would you need to talk to me?"

"I want to know more about your uncle Nahum."

She dropped the coffee mug she was holding onto the table. Luckily, it didn't break, but the remnants of the coffee inside splattered across the white tablecloth. Her face turned red, and she dabbed at the stain with a wet rag. "Why? What would you want to know about him?"

A man three tables away pointedly rattled his paper, which caused Oliver to wriggle under the long table.

I lowered my voice and moved closer to her. "Where

can I find him? I want to talk to him." I paused. "About Eve."

She gnawed on her bottom lip so much that there was a small dot of blood right at the crease. "You can't want to talk to him. He's crazy."

"I have to. He has a motive."

She dropped the rag onto the silver cart. "A motive for what?"

I gave her a look. "A motive for Eve's accident."

Junie dropped her eyes to the table. "I don't think it's a good idea if you talk to him. It will make him angry."

I took that as a gross understatement. "Just tell me where I can find him, and I will be the judge of that. Do it for Eve."

She swallowed. "If I tell you, do you promise not to go alone?"

That sounded ominous, but I wanted the information, so I said, "I won't. Do I look stupid?"

She didn't say anything for a full minute. Finally, she said, "He lives in a cabin in the woods on the outskirts of Holmes County. It's almost in Wayne County."

"What's the name of the road he lives on?"

"If he's still there, and I'm not certain that he is, it's called Yoder Bend. The cabin is not exactly on the road, but that's the closest road to it. I've never been there myself, but I heard my father describe it. He had gone there before to try to talk some sense into my uncle and ask him to rejoin our community."

"Yoder Bend," I repeated to commit it to memory.

"Junie, why isn't that table cleared off already?"

Mimi said as she stepped through the French doors. "Guests have checked out and their rooms need to be turned."

I found Mimi's reaction a bit harsh, especially considering Junie's sister just died under suspicious circumstances.

Junie lowered her eyes. "I am sorry." She started to pile the last of the dishes on the cart with abandon.

"It's my fault," I said, jumping in. "I was offering Junie my condolences on the loss of her sister."

Mimi's face softened. "Yes, it has been terrible for all of us."

Interesting, I thought. Mimi seemed to be speaking on a more personal level than I would expect her to use with one of the actors.

Junie threw the last of the dirty napkins on the metal cart and wheeled it toward the kitchen without a backward glance.

"Did you know Eve well?" I asked Mimi.

To my shock, the hotel owner burst into tears.

The man with the rattling newspaper was really giving the sports section a workout. I wrapped my arm around Mimi's shoulder and led her across the dining room to the French doors, which led into the swimming pool area. Oliver waddled in after us and made a beeline for a lounge chair. Shades and a towel were all he needed to be ready for a day at the pool, which looked pretty enticing right then.

I guided her to a small table near the deep end and farthest away from the door. The whirlpool bubbled a few feet away, and the smell of chlorine burned the inside of my nose. There was no one in the pool room, and the whirlpool would cover our conversation if anyone were to step inside.

Mimi whipped at her eyes, and her heavy layer of mascara melted and smeared onto her cheek. "I'm sorry," she muttered through her tears. "I should have better control over myself."

I rifled through my monster purse and came up with a crumpled packet of travel tissues. "Don't be silly. Eve's death has been a shock for all of us." The tissues appeared to have been stepped upon by an elephant, but they were clean. I handed Mimi the package.

She accepted it and removed a tissue from the plastic. "Thank you." She blew her nose.

Oliver hopped off his lounger and licked Mimi's hand. The hotel owner smiled. I could always count on Oliver to mend wounds.

Overhead, snow gathered on the corners of the atrium's glass ceiling. Inside the pool room, tropical plants flourished, and the warm humid pool air felt lovely against my dehydrated winter skin. It was all I could do not to throw myself into the crystal blue water.

"How did you know Eve? Was it from her life here before she left for New York?" I asked.

She nodded. "She was like a daughter to me."

Involuntarily, I felt my eyebrows pop up.

Mimi wiped tears from her eyes with one of the mangled tissues. "She was such a sweet girl. I don't know how anyone could do this to her, especially her own family."

I leaned back in my chair. "Her family? Do you mean her uncle Nahum?"

"I wouldn't limit it to just him." There was an edge to her voice.

"What do you mean?"

"Nahum may have been the most outspoken against Eve's return to Holmes County, but her whole family has treated her poorly since she returned. People think that the Amish are kind and caring. They usually are, but they can be cold too. They treated Eve like a leper, even her own father."

"What's her father's name?"

"Noah Shetler. He and his brother, not Nahum, own Shetler Tree Farm in Berlin. They are very well off for an Amish family. They supply many of the greenhouses and nurseries with trees and shrubs in Holmes, Wayne, and Stark Counties."

"Tree farm?" I asked. "What about Christmas trees?" I asked with an idea sparking in the back of my brain.

"Oh yes, this is a great time for business for them. Even though the Amish won't have Christmas trees in their homes, it doesn't mean they won't make money off the English who will."

"Do you include Junie in that number of relatives who have been unkind to Eve?"

Mimi placed her hands on the table. "Junie is confused. She wanted Eve to come back to Holmes County, but when Eve arrived, Eve told me that Junie had hardly spoken to her. I know she was hurt when her sister left, but now was her chance to make amends. That chance is gone now. She will never get it back."

"Did you meet Eve through Junie?"

She shook her head. "I met Junie through Eve. Eve

started working for me the summer after she finished school."

Oliver stared into the whirlpool. I hoped that he didn't get any ideas about going for a dip.

Mimi twisted the packet of tissues in her hands, and the plastic crackled. "Eve was a star employee, and I put her on the desk most of the time. She was so charming, and guests loved her. Everyone loved her. Junie is a year younger, and I gave her a job as a maid because Eve asked me to. Junie is a good worker, but she didn't have the special sparkle Eve did."

I wondered how many times Junie's quiet nature was compared to her sister's lively spirit. Something told me that wouldn't stop, even now that Eve was dead.

"I don't want you to get the wrong idea. I'm happy I have Junie working here. She's dependable."

Eve was special, and Junie was dependable. The two compliments didn't have the same ring to them.

"Eve's the reason I turned the barn into a playhouse. I wasn't using the barn for anything more than storage. She always said it would be the perfect place to put on plays, and she explained how much business it could bring me."

I kept one eye on Oliver as he sniffed around the edge of the whirlpool. I really didn't want to get wet this morning.

"So you knew about her dream to be an actress when you hired her."

"No, but not long after she started working here, she told me about those career aspirations. She knew she would have to leave the Amish to become an actress." She pressed the tissues into the tabletop. "I encouraged her to follow her dreams, and when she did leave, I gave her a place to live here at the hotel until she was ready to make her move to New York.

"I helped her get her social security number, driver's license, even her birth certificate. When Amish children are born, they have none of those things. It's like they don't even exist, at least as far as the English world is concerned." She sighed. "She left Holmes County two years ago. It was hard to let her go, but I was so proud of her. She had to overcome a lot to make her dream come true."

The question was, had Eve's dream really come true? Yes, she moved to New York, but she was struggling as an actress, so much so that she was willing to come back to Holmes County to star in a small production.

I wrinkled my brow. "Did Eve stay in touch with you after she moved to New York?"

"From time to time she would send me a letter about her life in New York. She had a dream to perform on Broadway, but it's difficult for any young child, especially a former Amish child, to break in. She worked at a deli to pay her portion of the rent for a tiny one-bedroom apartment that she shared with six other roommates."

I grimaced.

"She wasn't a wild child in New York," Mimi said. "She worked hard and was practical. She knew it would take time to achieve her dreams. *An Amish*

Christmas was really just the beginning. She was going to be a star."

"How did she even hear about Broadway? That's not something most Amish children know about."

"When she was a child, one of her English friends used to let Eve sneak over so they could watch DVDs of musicals. Eve fell in love with the theater"

"What's this friend's name? Where can I find her?"

"I think her name is Amber. Junie would know."

But would she tell me? Junie wasn't as forthcoming with information as I would hope her to be.

"Did her family know you helped her leave their district?"

She nodded. "Her father came and talked to me twice about her."

"And they didn't mind Junie working here? Weren't they afraid you'd convince Junie to leave too?"

She shoved the used tissues into the pocket of her suit jacket. "No one is afraid that Junie will leave the Amish. I need to get back to work. You will need to forgive me for breaking down like this. You see, I was never able to have children of my own, so this hotel was my child in many ways until Eve came into my life."

I reached across the table and squeezed her hand. "There's nothing to forgive. Someone you loved died. Cry as much as you need to."

Tears appeared in her eyes again. "When she told me that she was coming back here to be a part of the play, I was thrilled, but now . . . now, I wish she had never come."

As I was about to ask her if she knew Junie asked her to return for the play, a large crow landed on the glass roof above. It tapped its long black beak on the windowpane. Oliver's neck snapped up, and his eyes bugged out of his head. He yipped in terror and ran straight into the pool with a giant splash.

"Oh my word," Mimi shouted.

Without a moment's hesitation, I kicked off my boots and jumped into the pool. Oliver was only a foot away from where I landed in the water. I wrapped an arm around Oliver's torso and hugged him to my chest.

The pool was only five feet deep, so my head was well above the waterline.

Oliver kicked and panted.

"Shh, shh. You're okay."

"What happened? Did something bite him?"

I waded through the shallow water to the pool steps. "No. He's afraid of birds. The crow on the roof gave him a scare."

"I've never heard of a dog afraid of birds."

"Most people haven't, but my dog seems to like the special attention." I set Oliver on the ground and wrung out my sweater.

Above, the crow flew away. It may have just been me, but I thought I heard amusement in its squawk.

Chapter Twelve

In the car, I turned the heat up to full blast. Oliver pressed his pushed-in face up against the vent.

"Don't hog all the warm air. I'm freezing over here."

He cocked his head at me.

I tugged on a batlike ear. "You're worth it, buddy. You are always worth it."

He gave me a drooling grin. How could a mother not love that face?

Back at home, I let Oliver and myself inside the house, and struggled out of my boots in the entranceway. My wet socks squished on the tile. I hate wet socks almost as much as Oliver hates birds.

My parents, bundled up in scarves, hats, winter coats, and gloves, looked like they were ready for a polar expedition.

My mother's mouth fell open. "What happened to you?"

"Oliver fell into the pool at the hotel. I jumped in for the rescue."

"Oh my!" Mom covered her mouth.

Dad squatted next to my Frenchie. "You poor boy. You could have drowned."

Oliver gave him his very best poor-me face.

Dodger wriggled out from under the couch. The kitten stood on his hind legs and licked his brother's cheek.

"Where are you off to?" I asked.

"Since you don't have time for us today, your father and I thought we would go do a little Christmas shopping and maybe drop in for lunch at one of the restaurants in the county."

"That sounds like fun," I said, ignoring my mother's jab.

While my family comforted Oliver, I went upstairs for my second shower of the day, and it wasn't even ten o'clock in the morning yet.

Dry and warm, Oliver, Dodger, and I headed to Running Stitch. Anna and Mattie must have been wondering what happened to me.

I parked my little SUV in the community lot across from the mercantile. I tucked Dodger's soft-sided carrier under one arm and held Oliver's leash in the other hand.

The three of us were strolling up the sidewalk when we saw Rachel running toward us. Her black cloak flew behind her like Supergirl's cap.

"Angie!" she cried.

I skidded to a stop. "Rachel, slow down. You are going to fall. What's gotten into you?"

She gulped air. "Is it true?"

"Is what true?" I asked.

She patted her prayer cap. She wasn't wearing a bonnet.

One-handed, I unwrapped the scarf from my neck and wrapped it around Rachel. "You're going to freeze out here."

She accepted the scarf. "I'll be fine."

"What did you want to know about?"

"I heard Eve Shetler"—her eyes got big as she paused for a moment—"died."

Dodger yowled from inside the carrier. He wasn't one for the cold. I started walking toward Running Stitch again. "Yes, that's true. It happened during the play last night."

Color drained from her face. "I'd hoped that it was just a rumor."

"Did you know her?"

"Eve is my cousin."

I stopped dead on the sidewalk. "Your cousin?"

She nodded. "Shetler is my maiden name."

Snowflakes landed on my eyelashes, and I brushed them away. "Why didn't Mattie tell me?"

"She may not have remembered. Shetler is a common name, and I speak very little of my own family," she said barely above a whisper. "I wanted to catch you before you went into the shop to ask. I didn't want to talk about it in front of the other ladies."

I held up my gloved hand. "Wait, wait. If Eve is your cousin, who are your parents?"

"Nahum." She swallowed. "Nahum is my father. My mother died when I was small."

I blinked at her. "What?" Since I had lived in Holmes County, I had considered Rachel my best friend. I thought I knew her well and knew all her vital information, but this came as a shock. But now that I thought about it, Rachel never spoke about her parents or about any brothers or sisters. Whenever she spoke of family, it was always in reference to the Millers, Aaron's family.

Oliver walked around me and wrapped the leash around my legs. I stepped out the tangle. "You've never mentioned your dad."

"I haven't spoken to my father in nearly ten years."

The snow began to fall harder, but I ignored it. "Why not?"

She glanced back at the bakery. "Aaron is a *gut* man, but he wouldn't like it. My father has made many enemies within the Amish community. It is best to separate myself from him for my husband and children."

"What about the rest of the Shetler family? Do you speak to them?"

She twisted my scarf in her hand. "I can't tell you how much it breaks my heart to live so close to my cousins and aunts and uncles and have so little interaction with them. I never knew who would speak to me from the family, so I stopped trying." She bowed her head. "I know that was wrong. I should have kept trying. That is what *Gott* would want me to do."

It was difficult for me to believe that anyone would not want to be friends with Rachel. She had the sweetest spirit of any person I had ever met.

The door to Running Stitch opened, and Anna

stepped out. Her wire-rimmed glasses slid to the tip of her nose, and she shoved a fist into her side. "Angie, the class is already here. We've been waiting for you. Mattie has been back from the hotel for more than an hour."

"I'm sorry, Anna." I looked back at Rachel.

Rachel touched my arm. "Go. We will talk later." She handed me my scarf.

I chewed on my lip. "I'll stop by the bakery after class, okay?"

She nodded and crossed the street to Miller's Amish Bakery.

Anna held the door open for me. "Is something wrong with Rachel?"

"Eve Shetler was her cousin."

Anna put a hand to her cheek. "That's right. Rachel is a Shetler." She watched as Rachel stepped into the bakery. "This must be so difficult for her. After the class, we must discuss how we can help."

When she said "we," I knew that Anna meant the entire quilting circle.

She looked at the cat carrier in my hand. "Did you have to bring that little troublemaker?"

"You know how Oliver feels when I leave Dodger home alone. He worries."

She snorted.

Inside the shop, I removed Oliver's snow boots and unhooked his leash. He immediately went over to greet the class, which consisted of a group of ladies who sat in a circle of chairs in the middle of the shop. Last night, before I left for the play, Mattie and I had set up for the class. We pushed the heavy cutting table to the back of the shop beside the large quilting rack so there'd be space for everyone to sit.

Metal clamps tethered a half-finished Ohio star quilt to the rack. It had been pieced by a woman living in Columbus, and quilting it was the quilting circle's latest project. It would be done in early January, if Anna could resist taking apart the client's clumsy piecing stitches and redoing them.

Lois, a middle-aged woman from Millersburg and a quilting class regular, patted Oliver's head. "I wondered if you would show up."

I opened Dodger's carrier, and the kitten galloped forward.

"He is just precious," another member of the class said.

"Keep your eye on him," Lois said knowingly. "He's a handful."

"Ain't that the truth," I said. "I'm sorry I'm late, everyone. I got held up at the quilt show at the Swiss Valley Hotel." When I hung up my coat on the peg on the wall, I saw Sarah Leham standing behind the counter. "I didn't know you planned to be here today, Sarah."

Sarah adjusted her glasses on her nose. "I stopped in to see if I could lend a hand to the class."

"That was nice of you. We can always use the help," I said.

Anna snorted without looking up from her snowman. "Don't let her fool you. She's here because she wants to hear all about Eve Shetler's death."

"That's not true, Anna Graber. I do want to help

with the class." Her face broke into a grin. "But if I hear a word or two about the goings-on at the Swiss Valley Hotel while I'm helping, is that my fault?"

"You are going to have to wait for that," Anna said, nodding to the women waiting for class to begin.

I tucked my purse under the counter. "Anna's right. We'll have to talk about this later. I don't want to discuss it in front of the class."

Mattie carried a tray of cookies and hot cocoa and coffee around to the seven women in the class. Lately, our classes had been larger with nine to ten students, but I was still happy with the turnout because it was close to Christmas. Beside each lady's chair, there was a tray table she could use for her refreshments and her quilting supplies.

Shirley, another regular, took coffee only. "Those cookies look scrumptious, but I'm on a strict diet until after my daughter's wedding on Christmas Eve. Christmas Day can't come soon enough. But the coffee will certainly take the chill off. I can't believe what a cold winter we've had so far."

"It's just the beginning, Shirley. There are still January, February, and March to get through."

Shirley sighed. "Please don't remind me. My daughter and future son-in-law are going to Puerto Rico for their honeymoon. How I envy them."

Mattie filled some more plain white mugs with coffee. Sarah set Danishes on small paper plates, placing them on the tray tables beside each woman's chair.

"Angie?" Anna said, watching me. "Are you ready to begin?"

I blinked. "Yes, of course. Welcome, ladies. I'm so glad you were able to make it out in this cold weather and so close to Christmas too. I know you must all be very busy preparing for the holiday." I smiled at Shirley. "Especially you, with your big wedding coming up."

Shirley sipped her coffee. "I couldn't miss class. Besides, it gives me a chance to get out of my house. Between Christmas and the wedding, I have twenty people staying with me. It's impossible to find a moment's peace."

Anna stepped forward. "We are taking a break from our lap quilts for a small project today that we thought you would enjoy."

"What's that?" another woman asked.

Anna held up the quilted snowman she had made earlier in the week. "By the time you leave class today, you will all have one of these to either give as a Christmas gift to someone you love or keep for yourself."

The women ooooed and ahhed.

"That is just the most adorable thing I have ever seen," Shirley said.

With the class starting on a new project, I was happy Sarah was there after all to lend another pair of hands. Between the four of us, we were each able to help two of the students.

I handed Lois pillow stuffing for her snowman and heard her say, "Terrible shame about Eve Shetler. She was talented. It was a big surprise to think of a child from Rolling Brook making it on Broadway."

"Especially an Amish child," Shirley said.

"It seems everyone in Holmes County knew Eve," I said.

Lois nodded. "She was the kind of girl you took notice of."

"She had a special flare," Shirley agreed. "It makes the loss that much greater."

"There was a lot of gossip in town when she left her Amish life and moved into the hotel full-time." Lois pushed stuffing into the head of her snowman.

"Moved into the hotel?" Sarah asked. Her eyes sparkled with interest.

"Right after she left the Amish and before she moved to New York, she lived at the Swiss Valley Hotel with Mimi and her husband until she got on her feet."

I had already heard this from Mimi, but I let Shirley continue the story. It would be interesting to hear it from a second perspective.

"Mimi treated her like she was her own daughter. It might have been because her own girl would have been Eve's age."

"Her own girl?" I asked. "Mimi had children?" Hadn't Mimi told me she couldn't have children?

"She had a daughter," another woman said.

Shirley nodded. "She was stillborn. Mimi never really recovered. . . ."

"How terrible," I said. "Poor Mimi. How awful to lose another person she loved. I can't even imagine."

Sarah wiped a tear from her eye. "She didn't have any other children?"

Shirley shook her head. "She said that she couldn't bear taking the risk of losing another child she loved.

She and her husband divorced not long after they lost the baby."

"Eve seemed to have many close ties to the English. Did she have other English friends?" I asked.

Shirley thought for a moment. "I suppose she had. She had so many friends, both Amish and English. She was the kind of girl who attracted attention. It was clear that she was meant for something bigger than our little town."

"Do you know any of their names?" I asked.

The ladies shook their heads.

"Does the name Amber ring a bell with you?"

"The only Amber in Rolling Brook I know who would have been close to Eve's age would be Amber Rustle."

"Rustle?" I asked. "Is she related to Trustee Jason Rustle?"

Shirley nodded. "That's her father."

That was interesting. I didn't know Jason well, but I had been in countless meetings with him since I was sworn in as a township trustee.

"Amber works at the Millersburg library," another woman piped up. "I just saw her on my way here. I was there picking up a book on hold and she checked me out. She is such a sweet girl. Now that you mentioned it, she was a little red about the eyes. I thought she had a cold, but maybe it had to do with Eve."

It sounded to me like I needed to make a stop at the library.

"Ladies," Anna said, "look this way. I'm about to show you how to create the bodies of the snowmen."

Anna wrapped thread around the snowman's neck like a noose. I rubbed my throat as I watched.

My cell rang. Head Trustee Caroline Cramer's name appeared on my screen. "Will you excuse me for a moment?"

No one heard me. They were too engrossed in Anna's demonstration.

I stepped behind the register. "Hello, Caroline."

"Angie, I'm glad I caught you. We are having an emergency trustees' meeting tonight at Willow's tea shop. Be there at eight," she said, assuming that I would drop everything and be there. At least the former head trustee, Farley Jung, had asked me if I would like to join.

I leaned on the counter. "What's the meeting about?"

"The situation at the hotel. What do you think? We have three more groups of progressive diners scheduled to move through Rolling Brook over the next two weeks. The next tour is on December twenty-six. We need to decide how to handle the situation."

"Is there a possibility that the progressive dinners won't go on? The play won't resume?"

"That's what we are trying to avoid. The township can't afford giving refunds back to guests with reservations. We have to make this work."

I felt eyes boring into my back. This wasn't the time and place to question Caroline any further. "I will see you at the tea shop."

"Who was that, Angie?" Sarah asked.

I inwardly groaned. Couldn't Sarah have at least waited to ask me until after the quilting class left? "Caroline Cramer," I said. "We have a trustees' meeting to-night."

"I bet it's about Eve Shetler," Shirley said. "And I couldn't help overhearing something about the progressive dinner. I hope you all aren't thinking of canceling it. I have reservations for myself and five of my family members for the dinner and play on December twenty-six. I would hate to miss it. Worse yet, if it's canceled, I will have to think of another way to entertain all of those people until they go back home."

"The progressive dinner is not in danger of being canceled," I said even though I wasn't nearly as confident as I sounded.

A last-minute trustees' meeting wasn't all bad. It would give me an opportunity to speak to Jason about his daughter and Eve, but first, I wanted to speak to his daughter myself.

Chapter Thirteen

At the end of class, the women packed up their be-longings. Each had a quilted snowman tucked away in her bag. During the demonstration, Anna made a few extra, so she tucked those in the window display.

Mattie closed the front door after Shirley, the last student to leave.

As soon as the door was shut, I said, "Mattie, why didn't you tell me that Eve was Rachel's cousin?"

Mattie stared at me. "I—I guess I forgot. Rachel never talks about her family. I was still in school when she and Aaron married." She chewed on her lip. "How is Rachel?"

"Upset," I said as I carried one of the class chairs to the back of the shop.

Anna clicked her tongue. "It's a shame."

"Nahum is Rachel's dad?" I asked, because I still couldn't believe it, even though Rachel told me that herself.

Anna nodded. "He went crazy after his wife's death and said all kinds of terrible things against his bishop at that time. He was asked to leave the district. This was when Rachel was a baby."

"Where did Rachel go?" I asked. My heart hurt for my friend.

"She lived with her aunt and uncle from her mother's side of the family." Mattie started folding up the other chairs from class. "She thought of them as her parents, and I always thought of them as her real parents too. We didn't talk about Nahum in our house. I guess over time I forgot who he was, at least in relation to my sister-in-law."

"This just makes me want to find out what happened to Eve more." I braced myself on the back of one of the chairs. "Maybe it will bring some peace between Rachel and her father's family if I do."

Anna shook her head. "I understand your wanting to help, but that wound goes very deep."

I frowned. "Mattie, can you watch the shop for a couple of hours? I think I'm going to stop by the library."

Sarah cocked her head, much like Oliver would. "To talk to Amber."

I laughed. "Is it that obvious?"

Anna placed a hand on my arm. "Please just be careful, Angie. Nahum is Rachel's father, but that doesn't make him a *gut* man."

I shivered.

I left Dodger with Mattie, which my assistant grumbled about. My cat and helper rarely saw eye to eye.

Oliver followed me out of the shop, and it was nice to have the company. On the sidewalk in front of Running Stitch, I looked across the street into the bakery. Rachel was wiping down the counter. A light snow began to fall, and it was like watching my friend through a snow globe.

Rachel had had a difficult year. In October, the trustees disputed her husband's bid to build a baked goods factory at the end of Sugartree Street, and she had been a prime suspect for murder. Neither set of circumstances was typical for an Amish woman to find herself in. And now she had Eve's death and her father's possible involvement to contend with.

Down the street, work was yet to begin on the factory. When the snow began to fall, any hope of breaking ground before spring was lost.

I waited for two buggies to cross our path, and then Oliver and I walked across the street.

Rachel looked up from cleaning the counter when Oliver and I pushed through the door.

She smiled and reached under the counter for the container of dog biscuits that she kept there just for Oliver. My dog wasn't spoiled or anything. She tossed him one.

Delicately, the Frenchie picked it up between his teeth and carried it over to the small café area. He snuggled by the cooler, holding the biscuit between his paws and began to lick it. Apparently, the Frenchie was determined to make the treat last. Even though he had no reason to, Oliver always worried about his next meal.

Rachel wrapped up a loaf of pumpernickel bread for the last customer waiting to be served. When the Amish man left, she stepped around the counter. "Let's sit in the café."

I poured two cups of coffee from the carafe the Millers always kept on a warmer near the café tables.

Rachel accepted one of the mugs. *"Danki."*

I poured a generous helping of cream into my coffee. "Anna told me a little bit about your family history."

She smiled. "Anna knows something about everyone in the township."

"I'm sorry. And I feel like a jerk. How many times have you heard me complain about my mom, and you . . ." I trailed off.

"Don't apologize, Angie. I'm the one who didn't tell you. I should be the one to say I'm sorry."

"When's the last time you saw your father?"

She stirred her coffee and was quiet for a long moment, so long I thought she wasn't going to answer. "It was well over a year ago. I saw him in Millersburg. I was picking up supplies for the bakery, and there he was, walking down Main Street. I almost didn't recognize him. He'd changed so much. He looked wild."

"Did you say anything to him?"

She shook her head. "And it's not because he's shunned among the Amish or because Aaron would not want me to. I stopped because—"

"Because why?"

"He didn't know who I was or pretended he didn't. He looked right through me." She concentrated on her mug.

I couldn't imagine my father pretending that he didn't know me. "That must have been very painful."

She nodded. "I should be grateful though. My aunt and uncle were wonderful parents to me, and now I have Aaron, the boys, and Mattie. They are my family now. They are all I need."

It sounded to me like Rachel needed closure with her father, but the Amish don't give much weight to pop psychology, so I didn't say it.

"What about your uncles and cousins on that side? Why don't you speak to them?"

"I don't know. They have never been interested in me. It wasn't until I was married that I even knew that Noah Shetler's family was related to me. Shetler is a common name in the county."

"How did you find out?"

"My *aenti* told me not long before she died. I went to the tree farm my uncles owned to talk to them, but they weren't interested in speaking to me."

I frowned. It seemed to me that a trip to the tree farm was in order for a couple of reasons. Firstly, I wanted to meet Eve's father, and secondly, I now was motivated to for my friend.

Rachel looked up from her tea. "Angie, you don't plan to do anything reckless, do you?"

"When do I plan to do anything reckless?"

She laughed lightly. "I suppose you never plan it, but you won't do anything that might put you in danger, will you, especially where my father is concerned? He's a very angry man. If . . ." She paused. "If he hurt you, I would never forgive myself."

I grinned. "Don't worry about me. Don't I come out okay every time?"

"There are burn marks on your palms from this past summer. Does that mean you've come out okay?"

I flipped over my hands and looked at the faint scars. They faded more and more with every passing day. "I'd say so. I came out of that barn alive and so did Oliver."

The Frenchie lifted his head from his biscuit.

"I am going to talk to your father, but I won't go alone."

"Please don't mention me when you do."

"Rachel—"

"Please, Angie. I could not bear it if I thought that he would acknowledge me, but then in the end ignore me. It would be too painful to go through again." She wrapped her tiny hand around my wrist. "Please promise."

I swallowed. "Okay. I promise."

Twenty minutes later, Oliver and I were on the road to the main library in Holmes County in Millersburg.

Fresh snow crunched under the tires of my SUV as I turned into the library parking lot, which I had reached via an access road. A long hitching post dominated the left side of the space. A lone horse and buggy waited patiently for the owner to return. I made Oliver a nest in the backseat of my car with the blankets I kept in there. "I won't be long," I promised. The temperature held at thirty, so I knew he would be okay for the few minutes I needed to speak with Amber.

Since moving to Millersburg, I had been in the library countless times. I had the stack of books and movies in my house to prove it. I stepped around the open stairwell and went to the main desk. I smiled at the young man at the desk, who was checking in books off a cart. "Is Amber here?"

Without asking who I was or why I was asking, he pointed back toward the fiction section. People in Holmes County were certainly trusting. If I'd asked something like that at the main library in Dallas, I would have been interrogated as to why I needed to know.

An Amish woman sat in an armchair, leafing through an issue of *Food Network* magazine. In the children's section a few feet away, two Amish children played with puppets while an English child played a spelling game on the computer.

The library wasn't very big, so I found Amber quickly. She was shelving books in the Western section. Her cart was piled high with books adorned with pictures of cowboy boots and Stetsons. I looked down at my ugly snow boots, missing my cowboy boots back home. Maybe I should give Westerns a try. Maybe they would remind me of home, at least in the descriptions of the clothing.

Amber stood on a rolling library stool, trying to reach the top shelf with a book. She was a petite girl, I would guess just shy of five feet tall, so she had to stand on her tiptoes to reach the top shelf. She kind of tipped the book into place and pushed it in with her index finger.

"Amber?" I asked.

She yelped, and the book tumbled to the industrial-carpeted floor with a bang. I threw out my hand to steady her. "Careful!"

She hopped off the stool and scooped up the novel, holding it to her chest.

"I'm sorry I startled you," I said.

"It's not your fault. I was too focused on what I was doing." She gripped the book even harder.

I smiled. "I'm sure you have to pay attention to make sure all of the books get in the right spots."

She shrugged. "Can I help you find something?"

I swallowed. "Actually, I was looking for you."

"Me?" She paused. "Do I know you?"

I shook my head. "I knew Eve, and—"

Amber burst into tears.

Sheesh, I was beginning to believe that every time I mentioned Eve's name, someone would start to cry. I took the book from her hands and wrapped my arm around her shoulder. "Shh!" I couldn't believe that I was shushing someone in the library.

She wiped at her eyes with the back of her hand. "I'm sorry."

"There's nothing to be sorry for."

"It's just been so hard. I've been in a daze ever since I heard. The littlest thing can set me off."

I handed her the book. "Because Eve was your friend."

She nodded, replacing the book on the cart. "She was my best friend. She was like a sister to me."

I felt the corners of my own eyes itch. True, Aunt Eleanor had been gone for several months now, but Amber's open grief reminded me about the acute pain

I'd felt right after my aunt died. "Maybe you should go home?"

She shook her head. "I'll be all right. The library will be closed for Christmas, and I can't afford to miss work. I need the money for school."

"Are you in college?"

She nodded. "How did you know Eve?"

Ahh, that was a tricky question. I hadn't really known Eve at all. I had sat beside her for a little more than an hour, but in that time I had liked her. I was sorry she was gone. However, that would not impress her best friend.

"I own Running Stitch. It's a quilt shop in Rolling Brook."

"Across from the bakery?"

"That's right. I'm a Rolling Brook trustee too."

"So you know my father."

I nodded. "And I met Eve at the progressive dinner."

"Yesterday? The day—the day she died."

"Yes."

She stared at the floor. "I wasn't there. I was supposed to go, but I told Eve that I would see it another time. I had to work late at the library. She said I should have called off." She sighed. "The last time that we spoke, she was mad at me. The last thing she said to me was I didn't care enough about her to see her on opening night."

My heart broke for the girl.

"It wasn't true. Eve was my best friend. Even after she moved to New York, we never lost touch. I couldn't believe it when she took the job at the play here. I was so excited. Since she moved to New York, I had only seen her in person once. She didn't want to come back here, and I don't have much money to travel."

"Junie told her about the part in the play," I said.

Amber nodded. "Eve told me that. To be honest, I was a little surprised. Eve and Junie weren't that close. At least Eve made me think they weren't." Amber shrugged. "But Eve was away from home for almost three years, so she must have missed her sister and family. She couldn't talk to them as easily as she could have spoken to me. We talked on the phone or texted every day. You can't do that with an Amish person."

No you couldn't, I thought.

"It's weird to speak to someone every day of your life, and then one day it just stops, like all those conversations were a figment of your imagination. Sometimes I replay the conversations that we had and things that made us laugh in my head. I'm starting to wonder if the memories are true or if my mind is twisting them in some way to make them better or worse than they really were. There's no one to ask to know for sure because I am the only one left who remembers."

I squeezed her hand. "They are your memories. I think you have a right to remember them any way that you can."

She slid the stool out of the way of her book cart with her foot and then rolled the cart down the aisle. "I hope you're right."

"Did you see Eve after she came back?"

"I saw her almost every day except"—she swallowed—"except for the day she died."

"Was anyone upset that she came back?" I took a step after her.

"So many of the Amish were, but they wouldn't hurt her. They just ignored her. That was painful enough." She ran her fingers along the spines of the books on her cart.

"What about her uncle Nahum?"

She chewed on her lip. "Well, Nahum is different, but Eve always said he was crazy but harmless. She told me to just ignore him." Amber picked up a stack of novels and began sorting them by author's last name. She did this quickly and without thinking. It must have been something that she had done a thousand times before.

"Do you think he's harmless?"

"I don't know. The guy is definitely nuts. Eve's old Amish district even kicked him out. That had to have made him mad, but what does that have to do with Eve?"

Good question. Why was Nahum so upset with Eve for leaving the community when the community wanted nothing to do with him?

"Did she ever say anything about her cast mates during the play?"

Amber began to shelve books. "She said Lena was angry for being passed over for Eve's part. I guess Lena had been part of the theater company for a long time. She wasn't very nice to Eve, but after three years in New York, Eve said that she was used to diva actresses."

It was interesting that Eve would call Lena a diva

actress. I certainly needed to have a conversation with her, and then with her leading man, Ruben Hurst.

"Can you think of anyone who might have wanted to hurt her?"

She straightened several books, building a new stack to shelve. "Yes, the person who was threatening her."

Chapter Fourteen

My pulse quickened as I realized that Amber was about to tell me something critical about Eve's death. "Who was it? What do you mean?"

"I know she was having some trouble with someone. The problem is Eve and I didn't know who." Her shoulders sagged.

"Trouble? What kind of trouble?"

"She was getting threatening cards and notes at the hotel. Every morning when she woke up, she would find one had been slipped under her door. She even tried to stay up all night to see it happen. She wanted to catch the person in the act. She said she must have dozed off around three because when she woke up again, another note was just inside the door."

I shivered. "Was she afraid?"

"I don't know. Eve may have grown up Amish, but she was not a timid girl. I was the more reserved one between the two of us." She shelved two books. "I think she was more irritated by it."

Amber's description of Eve was what I experienced. Of all of the people at the progressive dinner, she was the last I would have suspected of growing up Amish.

"I was more upset by it than she was. I offered for her to stay with me, but she said that it would be too much trouble. Up until the opening day, their rehearsals were going on until after midnight. I would have needed to pick her up late each night, which I had no problem with, but she kept turning down my offer, saying she'd never know when the rehearsals would be done. Eve didn't know how to drive even if she had access to a car. She never learned because she grew up Amish, and she didn't need to learn to drive to live in New York. The actors here didn't have much time to prepare for the production since the hotel added the performances before Christmas. The original opening day was the day after Christmas."

I raised my eyebrows. "I hadn't known that." I made a mental note to ask the trustees why a day was added before Christmas. "Did she show you any of the notes?"

"She showed me one a few days before she died. It was awful. I told her to take it to the police, but she refused. She said she didn't want whoever was doing it to think he had any power over her. That was a big thing with Eve—she didn't like people controlling her. I think that was why she was never comfortable being Amish."

"What did the note say? Do you remember?"

"It said 'Break a Leg or I will break it for you.' That was it. It wasn't signed or anything."

I shivered again. Did the sheriff know about this? The notes had to be related to Eve's death. "Did you tell the sheriff about these notes?"

"No. Do you think I should?"

I wanted to scream "Yes!" but instead, I merely nodded. Amber was grieving. During a time of mourning, it was difficult to wake up in the morning, much less have your wits about you to know what to do. I was impressed she had the determination to come into work the day after her best friend was murdered. I didn't think I would be able to do that. In fact, I knew that I wouldn't. "What did it look like?"

"What do you mean?"

"Was it handwritten, typed, or were the letters cut out of a magazine?"

She wrinkled her nose. "You mean the way a serial killer sends a note? That would have been really scary."

As if the situation weren't already scary enough.

"It was typed," she said. "You know, on regular paper."

"With a computer."

"I guess. What else would a person use?"

"There is a typewriter in the library," I reminded her. I knew this because Mattie used it from time to time when she was in the library to type up letters to her friends in Lancaster County.

"It wasn't from a typewriter. If it had been, I would definitely think the person was Amish. Who else uses a typewriter nowadays?"

I wasn't so sure. A savvy Amish person could use a computer if they had to, but could they without drawing attention to themselves? They wouldn't have one in the privacy of their homes, and for such letters, would they risk using a public computer at the library? In any case, I couldn't completely rule them out, but it did make the culprit that much more likely to be English.

She licked her lips. "I should get back to work."

"Do you want me to shelve this book?" I asked, picking up the one she dropped when I first arrived.

She took the book from my hand. "You don't have to. It's not your job."

"Let me. I worked in my college library. I think I can handle it." I held out my hand for the book. "It's the least I can do for almost making you fall."

She relented and handed me the book.

I slid it into its spot.

"Thank you." She chewed on her lower lip and didn't look more than ten, but if she was Eve's age, she was closer to twenty. "Can I ask you a question?"

"Sure."

"I've been afraid to ask anyone else. I mean anyone I know."

I tensed. "Ask me whatever you want."

"Do you think it hurt when she fell? Do you think she felt a lot of pain?"

I gave a sharp intake of breath. I suspected the impact onto the stage hurt a great deal, but Eve died on impact, so it was short-lived. Maybe less than a second. Even so, I couldn't tell her friend who loved her so much that. I shook my head, trying to suppress the tears gathering in my eyes. "No, no, I don't think it hurt."

She gave a great sigh. "That's good. For some reason, that's what I have been thinking about the most. I couldn't bear it if I knew she had been in pain even for a moment."

"She died on impact," I said.

New tears started to fall from Amber's eye. "Thank you for telling me. I have been afraid to ask because I was afraid to know." She began sorting the books on her cart again.

I turned to go.

She stopped me. "Can I ask you one more thing?"

I spun on my heels. "Sure."

"If you find out who did this to Eve, can you come back and tell me why? I need to know why. That's the second thing I think about most."

I nodded. "Okay."

"Thank you," she murmured, and returned her attention to her cart.

I left the library, itching to call the sheriff and tell him about the threatening notes Eve had been getting. Did he already know about them? Was it worth giving myself away as a meddler to tell him? I knew the answer was yes. Even if the sheriff already knew, the information was too important to keep to myself.

"What are you doing there, staring off into space?" a jovial voice asked.

I found Jonah smiling at me from beside the book drop. Instead of his typical black felt hat, he wore a black stocking cap. He opened the book drop's hatch and slid four books inside.

I pushed thoughts of the sheriff away. "Are you surprised to see me at the library?"

"*Nee*, but I didn't expect to see you here today. Shouldn't you be visiting with your parents?"

I was grateful he didn't mention Ryan, although I suspected that he was thinking it. "I dropped by to talk to Amber Rustle."

"Trustee Rustle's daughter? Why did you talk to her?" Jonah thoughtfully pulled on his dark blond beard.

"She was Eve Shetler's best friend."

Jonah dropped his hand from his beard, and his face clouded over. "And that is important to you because?"

"I had some questions about Eve."

Jonah groaned. "Does the sheriff know about this?"

"No." I pulled my gloves up over my wrists. "But he probably suspects I'm poking my nose where it doesn't belong. Why should I be the one to disappoint him?"

Jonah shook his head. "I know you won't pay me any mind, but I don't think you should be talking to anyone about Eve."

"You're right about the 'not paying you any mind' part." I adjusted my bag on my shoulder. "Why do you feel so strongly about it?"

"We don't know those theater people. They could be dangerous. On cases you've looked into before, the people involved were all people I knew. We don't know anything about these new folks, and they are actors. They can lie right to your face, and you won't even know it."

He did have a point about the lying. I would have to take everything that they said to me with that in mind, but then again, I have had Amish lie directly to my face. You didn't have to be an actor to be a great liar, especially when you were trying to protect your own hide.

"Speaking of investigating, I need your help."

Jonah pushed a book through the slot. The book fell to the bottom of the book drop with a thud. "I don't think I am going to like whatever you have to say next."

"You need to take me to Nahum Shetler's shack."

"I'm right. I don't like it." He turned and started strolling toward his buggy, which was hitched to the post.

I trotted after him. "Come on, Jonah. You have to." I knew I sounded just like I had when I was seven when I tried to convince him to go to the pond on his farm and catch frogs when he should have been mucking stalls for his father. He said yes to me that time, and I knew he would say yes to me again this time.

He glanced over his shoulder as he walked across the icy parking lot. "*Nee*, I don't. And you shouldn't talk to Nahum Shetler. He is an unstable man. Haven't you learned anything after all the trouble you've been in?" He pointed at my gloved hands, reminding me of the burn marks there. Would my friend ever be able to forget that?

"I've learned that I can help." I ran after him, holding my arms out for balance as I slid across the slick layer of snow on the blacktop.

He snorted and unwrapped his horse Maggie's reins from the hitching post.

"If you don't go with me, I'll go without you."

"You don't even know where Nahum lives."

"Sure, in the wood cabin off Yoder Bend." I fished my key out of my purse and made like I was going to my car.

He grimaced. "Sadly, I know that's not an idle threat."

"So?" I gave him my most hopeful eyes.

"*Ack.* All right. But I can't take you today. I have much work to do."

"When?" I asked.

He thought for a moment.

"It has to be soon. It's for Eve," I said.

"Fine. Tomorrow. Meet me on Yoder Bend near the crossroads with Kepler Street at first light."

"Why so early?"

"It is the best time to catch Nahum."

"What about—"

"So many questions." He threw up his hands. "I have told you I will go. Let's leave it at that."

"Okay. First light at Yoder Bend near Kepler Street. I'll be there."

He climbed into this buggy. "I know you will. I hope I don't regret this later."

I closed his buggy door for him. "You won't."

"*Nee*, you are wrong. I already do," Jonah said as he flicked the reins on Maggie's back.

Chapter Fifteen

I drove back to Running Stitch, mulling over my conversation with Amber and still debating whether I should call the sheriff about the threats Eve had received.

The bell over the door rang as Oliver and I stepped into my shop. Two English women dressed in matching oversized parkas perused the fabric bolts, which were organized by color and pattern along the wall across from the register.

Oliver went straight for his dog bed, where Dodger was napping. The Frenchie snuggled down next to the kitten.

Anna was no longer there, but Sarah sat in the rocking chair next to the large picture window. She was quilting another snowman. "Sarah, I didn't expect you to still be here." I glanced around the shop. "Where's Mattie?"

"She saw me shopping at the mercantile and asked me if I could mind the shop while she went and checked on a friend."

"That's not like Mattie," I said. I couldn't remember Mattie ever leaving the shop without checking with me first. She knew my cell phone number and could have used the shop phone to call me. "It's nice of you to cover for her, Sarah."

"Oh, I don't mind." Sarah rocked on the chair.

"Did she tell you where she had gone?"

"Nee." She smiled. "And you know that I asked."

I certainly knew that.

"I wonder if I should go back to the hotel."

"Whatever for?" Sarah asked.

"I think I'd like to talk to Junie again." I told her what Amber shared with me about the threatening notes Eve had received.

Sarah held a hand to her face. "Oh my. *Ya*, you should go to the hotel and ask her if she knew about the notes. It's essential intel for the case."

I cocked an eyebrow at her. "Intel?"

She grinned. "I've picked up a word or two since we have solved some murders."

That I didn't doubt. I was single-handedly teaching my quilting circle murder investigation. Mitchell must be so proud.

"I saw Junie there this morning at the hotel, but I didn't know about the notes then to ask her." I shook my head. This morning seemed like so long ago. "I was surprised to see her so soon back at work."

"It's not the Amish way to stay home and cry. Busy hands keep the mind busy and off your troubles," Sarah said, sounding just like Anna.

I wasn't sure I'd agree with that. A good crying fit

after such a loss sounded like a better course of action to me, but then again, everyone deals with grief in a different way. If working helped Junie, that was what she needed to do, but from the sound of it, it didn't help her that much.

Sarah made a shooing gesture with her hands. "Go. Go."

I shook my head. "I can go after Mattie returns. I don't want to keep you from your family any longer."

"You aren't at all. In fact, I'm happy for the distraction. My husband's family is here from Geauga County for Christmas. I need a break from my mother-in-law. It seems I can't do anything right where she is concerned." She wrinkled her nose, and her glasses slid down to the tip of it. "This morning she said that my biscuits were passable. Can you believe that? Passable? My husband and children have never found fault with my biscuits."

I smiled to think even Amish had unwanted visitors at Christmas. "All right, then. Thank you for helping me! I will be back as quick as I can." I glanced at Oliver, who had just fallen asleep. "Ollie, we are leaving."

The Frenchie opened one eye and sighed. Slowly, he stood.

"Now, go. I'll organize a quilting circle meeting while you are gone," she said firmly.

That sounded ominous.

As I drove back to the hotel, my cell phone rang. I winced when I saw my mother's face on the screen. I wasn't being a very good daughter. Mom and Dad had come a long way to spend Christmas with me, and I had yet to even have a meal with them.

"You're father and I had a nice day shopping. When are you coming home?"

"The shop closes at four today." I wasn't at the shop, of course, but she didn't need to know that.

Mom sighed.

Remembering Rachel's story about her own parents, I said, "I'm sorry. How about we meet for an early dinner? Can you meet me at the Double Dime Diner at five?"

Mom sighed. "I suppose we can if that's the only way that we will be able to see you today. I hope you will spend more time with your family on actual Christmas."

"I will," I promised. "Today is just a crazy day between the quilt show and the quilting class." And because of Eve's death, but I didn't say that. "So I will see you there. Do you know where it is?"

"I know where it is," Mom said. "That place has been in Millersburg for decades. I can't believe it's still open."

"See you there," I said, and hung up as I turned into the hotel parking lot.

Before I went inside the hotel, I called the sheriff. The call went directly to voice mail. That was just as well.

"Hi, Mitchell. Just wanted to let you know that I spoke with Amber Rustle, Trustee Rustle's daughter, in case you didn't know. She's Eve's best friend here in Holmes County. She said Eve was receiving threatening notes in her hotel room. Talk to you later."

As I slipped my phone into my mammoth purse, I

imagined Mitchell grinding his teeth as he listened to that message.

"It can't be helped," I told Oliver.

Oliver huffed and followed me into the hotel. Instrumental renditions of Christmas music played lightly over the hotel's loudspeaker in the lobby.

Bethanne was no longer at the desk. Instead, I found Junie dusting the counter.

Her face fell as I approached the desk. "Oh, it's you."

"Were you expecting someone else?" I asked.

She was about to say something and then thought better of it.

"I came here looking for you."

"Me?" she squeaked.

"Did you know about any threatening notes that Eve had been getting?"

She swallowed. "Notes?"

I nodded.

Her eyes flitted around the room. "*Nee.* I don't know about anything like that. My sister didn't tell me if she was in trouble."

"I met Amber today."

Junie resumed her dusting.

"Did your sis—"

"A pox on you, sir!" someone shouted from the sitting room.

Oliver ducked behind the registration desk, and an elderly couple reading and drinking coffee beside the Christmas tree fled.

There was a squeal, and then Blake, the stagehand,

leapt into the lobby. He held a quilt rod in his hand. "Stand back or I will run you through."

A second teenager appeared, holding a second quilt rod. "Prepare to meet your Maker."

"Whoa! Whoa! Whoa!" I said, sounding much like Jonah when he was trying to pull Maggie to a stop.

Both boys froze, with quilt rods held at the ready to strike.

"What in the world are you doing?"

Blake lowered his arm. "Um."

I held out my hands. "Give those to me!" I made a gimme sign with my hand.

The nameless second actor with the goatee scowled. "Why should we?"

I stared him down. "Because they belong to me. You took them from the sitting room, am I right? Where is the quilt that was on this?"

Blake blushed. "Kyle, give it to her. We're really sorry."

"My name is Angie, and you had better hope for your sake none of the quilts were damaged. They are worth a lot of money."

Kyle snorted. "Why? They are just blankets. I can buy one at Walmart for ten bucks."

I glared at him. "For your information, these are handmade Amish quilts and worth much more than ten dollars. They are worth more than your paycheck."

He handed me the rod. "Geez, there's no reason to get all bent out of shape over it."

I held my hand out to Blake.

He placed the rod in my palm.

I frowned. "You can't tell me that swordplay is part of *An Amish Christmas*."

Blake's blush faded, making his freckles more pronounced. "We were just messing around. Practice has been canceled for the rest of the day. There's not much to do around here."

"Especially if you don't have a car," Kyle grumbled. "We might as well be trapped on a desert island."

"Polar ice cap," Blake corrected.

"Why's practice canceled?"

Kyle narrowed his eyes. "Who are you to ask?"

I tapped the two rods on the floor. "I'm just curious."

Blake pushed Kyle lightly. "Don't be so uptight." He looked at me. "The director said he had business to take care of this afternoon. Practice will resume after dinner."

"Man," Kyle complained. "I hate that. We will practice late into the night. I need my Zs. I'm exhausted just thinking about it."

"What kind of business?"

Blake frowned.

Kyle eyed me. "You ask a lot of questions for a quilt lady."

"So I've been told." I leaned on the rods as if they were canes. "I don't remember seeing the two of you in the play. I was there last night."

"Yeah, we didn't even get to my scene before Eve fell," Kyle said.

"Hey, man, show some respect."

Kyle shoved his friend. "Blake thought he had a chance with her. Everyone knew she was off-limits."

I straightened up. "Did she have a boyfriend?"

Kyle shook his head. "Don't know. She made it clear she wasn't interested in anyone. She said she was focusing on her career."

Blake shoved his hands into the pockets of his jeans. "I know Ruben had his eye on her too. He probably didn't take it well when she turned him down cold."

"I wish I could have seen that. Just because he has an accent, he expects women to fall to his feet. Some do, like Lena."

"I hope Lena didn't know he asked Eve out. She would poke Ruben's eyes out with a butter knife. The girl is vicious."

Jealous girlfriend. I mentally rubbed my hands together. Tailor-made suspect.

"What has she done?" I asked.

Blake folded his arms. "The female lead of our last production broke her arm when she fell down the stairs at the theater we were performing at."

"Oh yeah," Kyle said. "I remember that. It was the gig in Des Moines. Everyone thought Lena pushed the girl down the stairs, but she insisted she tripped, and nothing happened to Lena. The girl went back home to Kansas or wherever she was from. Everyone thought for sure that Lena would have the lead in our next production, and then one day Wade shows up with Eve.

"I thought Lena was going to go all jungle cat on Eve the moment she stepped into the room. I mean, the girl had *hate* in her eyes."

Interesting. Very interesting. Lena was looking better and better as a prime suspect for the murder. And there was the matter of the notes too. Could she have been behind them also? The two events had to be connected. I wished I could get my hands on at least one of those notes, but Amber had said that Eve destroyed them the moment she found one.

Kyle gave me a wide grin. "Hey, you should come to another performance to see me in action. I'm pretty good."

His friend snorted. "Yeah, you do an awesome job playing farmer number one and the love-struck Amish boy."

"You will regret saying that when I accept my Oscar someday."

The two young men strolled away, laughing and pushing each other.

I returned the quilt rods to the sitting room. At least Kyle and Blake had had the decency to fold the quilts before they took off with the rods.

When I returned to the lobby, Junie was gone. She must have made her escape from me while I had been speaking with the actors. In fact, there was no one at the registration desk. An old-fashioned guest book sat in the middle of the desk.

Thanks to Kyle and Blake's antics, they had scared off the only other guests in the room. It was a golden opportunity. One little peek wouldn't hurt.

My finger slid down the registry of guest names and stopped at "Shetler, Eve. Room 215." The check-in date was a week ago Monday. The checkout date was left open. I supposed, to be accurate, yesterday's date could have been entered there.

What would I do with this information? I knew I should return to the shop to let Sarah go home. I still needed to find out why Mattie ran off without telling me in the middle of the afternoon.

The second floor was just at the top of the staircase. I could dash up there for a quick look. Undoubtedly, the room would be locked and that would be the end of it. However, it might be good to know where Eve's room was, because that was where the threatening notes were dropped each night.

I stepped around the registration desk to Oliver's hiding place. "What do you think, Ollie?"

He set a white paw on my boot. He knew as well as I did that my mind was already made up.

Chapter Sixteen

I carried Oliver up the stairs. The grand staircase opened onto the second-floor sitting room. A grand piano stood quietly in the corner. A lone man sat in the corner of the room, talking on his cell phone.

If play practice was postponed until evening, where had the actors gone? Didn't Blake mention they were here without cars? Were they taking a collective nap in their various rooms?

Oliver padded behind me over the flowered carpet on that floor of the hotel. He stopped to smell the legs of a coffee cart piled high with Christmas cookies.

"Oliver, those are for the guests."

With a sigh, he followed me into the hallway.

Room 215 was halfway down a long corridor. Light shone from the doorway. I slowed my pace. The door was open.

I squatted next to Oliver. "Sit," I whispered. "And stay."

The Frenchie wagged his front paw at me in protest.

I pointed to the ground. "Stay."

He lay down on the flowered carpet with his head on his paws.

I crept the rest of the way to room 215. As I suspected, the door was ajar. My pulse quickened. I heard movement inside. With both hands, I pushed the door open and it banged against the wall.

Junie covered her face and screamed.

"Junie! Junie! Calm down. It's just me."

Oliver galloped into the room. His bat ears perked on high alert. He skidded to a stop next to me in the doorway. Frenchie to the rescue.

Junie dropped her hands a fraction of an inch. "You gave me the scare of my life."

I winced. "I'm sorry. I thought—I don't know what I thought." I took a breath. "This was Eve's room, wasn't it?"

There was a pile of clothes on one side of the king-sized bed. Next to the clothes two large suitcases sat open.

"You're packing her things," I said.

"It has to be done. The room must be turned. Mimi asked me to do it. She wanted someone who knew Eve to do it." She picked up a T-shirt and folded it with such precision, she put a teenager working at the Gap to shame. "She wasn't up to doing it herself. She's broken up over Eve."

Mimi was too upset to do it but asked Eve's sister to do it? I wondered. And wasn't Junie equally broken up over Eve's death, if not more?

Her brow furrowed as if she were trying to read my

thoughts. "And the sheriff said that was all right. The police were here last night. Mimi would not ask me to pack Eve's things if it wasn't allowed."

"No, of course not." I scanned the pile of clothing on the bed. "Did the police take anything from her room? Did you notice anything missing?"

"I would not know what was missing among her *Englisch* things."

"Of course," I said. I knew Mitchell's deputies would take anything that might be remotely related to her death. That put my chance of finding one of the threatening notes at zero.

Even with that in mind, I asked, "Care if I have a look around?"

She shrugged and kept folding.

I knelt and peered under the bed. No note. Junie had already emptied the closet and the dresser of Eve's clothes. I wandered into the bathroom. Eve's cosmetics stood in a line on the bathroom counter. They were many. The right side of the counter was her everyday toiletries, but the left side was covered with stage makeup.

I poked my head out of the bathroom. "Did Eve do her own makeup for the play?"

Junie shrugged. "I don't know. I suppose she did."

That wasn't too surprising, considering the size of the production. How many stagehands had Mimi said there were? Four: Jasper, Blake, and the two teenagers from Millersburg, doing it for school credit.

I sat on the desk chair. "Do you know if she had a sweetheart?"

"A—a what?"

"Did Eve have a boyfriend?"

"She never said anything about anyone from New York. I told you we didn't talk much since she's been away. Eve doesn't like to write letters, and I don't have access to a telephone."

"This hotel is full of telephones." I pointed to the one on the nightstand.

She folded a pair of jeans. "I can't make long-distance calls from Mimi's phones."

"That's a good point. If Eve didn't have an English boyfriend, did she have an Amish one before she left?"

Silence. She folded three more shirts during the quiet.

I spun the desk chair in her direction. "Junie?"

She played with the edge of her apron. "There was a boy, but it was so long ago. I wouldn't give him another thought. He's married to another girl now. He married right after Eve left."

I leaned forward. "Is it a happy marriage?"

"I think so. They have two children now."

"What's his name?"

She scowled, taking her frustration out on an I LOVE NYC hoodie. "It's bad enough that you come here and pester us with your questions. I won't let you bother him."

"Is he a friend of yours?"

She paused. "He was. A long time ago. His name is Nathan Eby, and I am only telling you because you will not leave me alone until I do."

At least she understood that about me.

"Was it serious?" I opened the closet door. There were a few pairs of jeans and a couple of dresses hanging there. Three pairs of shoes sat at the bottom. They were sturdy and dependable; none of them were that expensive. If her possessions were any indication, Eve lived on a very tight budget.

"They went to singings and on buggy rides. It was a way Eve could pass the time while she decided what to do with her life. I knew nothing would ever come of it."

If Junie wouldn't tell me about this mystery boy, maybe Amber would.

Junie wrapped her arms around her waist just above the band in her apron as if she had a stomachache. "I have much work to do. I think you should leave now."

I stood. "Don't you want to know what happened to your sister?"

She didn't say anything.

I turned. "Don't you?"

Tears welled up in her dark eyes. She removed a white handkerchief from the pocket in her apron. "Finding out what happened won't bring Eve back."

I gripped the back of the desk chair. "Junie, we can't let whoever did this get away with it."

"The actors will be gone within the week. Let them go and let us forget." She dropped her gaze back down to the pile of laundry.

"You think this will be over when they are gone. Do you think one of them is behind it?"

"They are all jealous of one another. Look at Lena."

"You think it's Lena?"

"I didn't say she did it, but what does it matter in the

end?" she argued. "It's better to grieve and let *Gott* do the rest."

Mimi had been right. There was no doubt that Junie was destined to stay Amish. Her Amish beliefs were cemented in forgiveness and the justice of God.

Junie was right too; I should leave the room and return to Running Stitch. If there were any notes, the sheriff's department must have already found them. I wondered if Mitchell had heard my voice mail and how that went over.

"Did Eve say anything to you about feeling afraid or threatened?" I asked.

"Nee." She zipped up the larger of the two suitcases and put it on the floor. "Eve didn't have a care in the world."

That I didn't believe. I shut the dresser drawer. All I learned from searching Eve's room was that she was really a struggling actress. All of her things were well cared for, but she didn't have many of them. Many of the clothes had been mended. The only way I knew was I had an eye for seams and thread as a quilter. It made me terribly sad.

"What will happen to her things?" I asked.

"I guess we will give them away. My parents are handling her funeral arrangements. It will be small and not as noteworthy as it would have had she remained Amish."

"That is kind of them," I murmured.

"My mother loves—loved Eve." She wouldn't meet my eye and continued folding.

"She must have missed her terribly when she left the community," I said.

"It broke her heart. My father told her to forget Eve, that it would be easier if she did." She dropped a pair of socks into the second suitcase. "But you can't help who you love. It's not always who you are supposed to."

"What do you mean by that?" I asked.

"Nothing. My father tells me I should not give in to idle musing. I should focus on the here and now. Eve was the only one with daydreams." She studied me. "Are you going to marry the nice man from Texas?"

I tripped on the rug and had to brace myself on the side of the bed so that I wouldn't fall to the carpet. "What? No, of course not. He's a family friend."

Her eyes narrowed. "He is very handsome."

"He is, but I'm still not marrying him."

"And he loves you."

I stepped back from the bed. "He might have at one time, but not anymore."

"You are wrong on that count. He still loves you. You are all he's spoken about since he got here." More underwear and socks went into the suitcase.

"You've spoken to Ryan?"

"He's nice and likes to chat. I'm only being kind to a customer of the hotel."

I bit my tongue to hold back the questions about what Ryan said about me. It didn't matter what Ryan said about me; that wouldn't change anything. At the end of the week, he would go back to Dallas, and I would remain here with my quilting circle, Running Stitch, and the sheriff.

Her face darkened. "It must be nice to choose who you want to love because everyone loves you back. Eve was like that. Everyone, even Nathan, knew that Eve was going to leave the Amish life. I think he was just hoping he could talk her out of it. You couldn't make Eve do anything that she didn't want to do." She said it like someone with experience. "So you see, Eve was just like you. She was the one who got to make the decision to walk away and break someone's heart. Not all of us have that chance."

I didn't bother to argue with her or tell her Ryan dumped me, not the other way around. So it wasn't true. Sometimes the person I loved did not love me back.

Chapter Seventeen

When I got back to Running Stitch, Anna, Mattie, and Sarah were all waiting for me. The only member of the quilting circle not there was Rachel, which was telling. The quilt frame was in the middle of the room, and the three women sat around it, adding stitches. Dodger curled up on the counter between the register and a large picnic basket.

After I removed his boots, Oliver padded over to check the condition of his young charge.

"What's going on?" I asked, hanging my coat on the peg on the wall.

"Have you eaten anything?" Anna asked, ignoring my question.

"Not since breakfast, but I'm meeting my parents for an early dinner at the Double Dime Diner after the shop closes for the day."

Dodger jumped off the counter, and he and Oliver chased each other around the store.

"You still need to eat something now." Anna licked

the tip of her thread before pushing it through the eye of the needle. "There is vegetable soup in the thermos in the hamper there. It's still good and hot."

I opened up the picnic basket and found the promised thermos of soup, plus fresh bread, bowls, and spoons. "Do any of you want some? There is plenty here."

"We already ate while waiting for you," Mattie said.

I filled one of the bowls with soup, grabbed a spoon, and sat in my chair at the quilt rack. "Now, can you tell me what you are all doing here? Shouldn't you be home making last-minute preparations for Christmas?"

Anna pulled her thread through the fabric. "Christmas preparations are all but done, and as a quilting circle, we have pressing business."

"Does this have something to do with Eve's death?" I blew on my spoon. Anna was right, the soup was hot.

"Yes, it does, and with Rachel. The poor girl. She doesn't need this last incident bringing up old feelings from her childhood," Anna said. "She's had a hard-enough year as it is."

"Do you know more about her family?" I asked, feeling a little guilty for going to Anna for the information when I knew I should talk to Rachel herself.

Anna pushed her glasses up her nose. "They've always been an odd bunch. Part of the district but very standoffish. My husband used to say it was because of the family tree farm. The Shetlers thought that they were better than everyone else in the district because the farm is big enough for all three boys to work there, and they did until Rachel's father, Nahum, went off the deep end."

"What happened to Nahum? Why did he go crazy?" Sarah asked. "I don't think I have ever heard the story."

"If you haven't heard it," Anna said, "then it's been kept a close family secret."

With deft fingers Sarah tied a quilter knot at the end of her thread. "Very funny. Is it my fault people tell me things?"

"The great mystery," Anna said, "is why they do."

Sarah frowned.

I set my empty soup bowl on the small tray table between Mattie and me. "Okay, okay. Back to the Shetler family, please."

Anna began a stitch. "From what I have heard and have not repeated until this moment"—she gave Sarah a pointed look—"Nahum did not agree with a ruling the bishop made. It may have had to do with the death of Rachel's mother. At least that was what everyone else assumed because there didn't seem to be anything else that would have made him so angry."

"Do you think Rachel knows?" I asked.

Anna frowned. "I'm not certain. She was very young. And since she lived with her mother's sister and brother-in-law, she had very little interaction with her father or his family."

"But she's still upset about Eve, even though she didn't know her well," Sarah said. "I mean, she seems more upset than an average person would be about the death of a young girl. It seems strange."

"She is," I said. "But you know how sensitive and caring Rachel is." I picked up a needle and threaded it. We worked in silence for a moment.

"Angie, you promised to tell me about your visit to the library this morning, and I would like to hear about your trip back to the hotel this afternoon too." Sarah peered at me over her glasses.

I told the ladies about my conversations with Amber and with Junie. "So, there is reason to believe because of the notes that someone was threatening Eve. The question is who, and whether that person was the one who actually cut the rope."

Mattie shook her head. "It's just so terrible."

When Mattie spoke up, it reminded me of her absence earlier that day. "Mattie, why weren't you here when I got back from the library? I was surprised to find Sarah filling in for you."

"I—I had some business to take care of."

I frowned. "Sarah said you needed to speak with a friend."

Mattie frowned at Sarah. "*Nee*, it was just an errand for Christmas. I hope you don't mind."

"Of course I don't mind, but please tell me when you leave the store."

She ducked her head. "I'm sorry."

I tied a quilter's knot at the end of my thread. "It's fine, Mattie, really," I said, but I knew there was more to the story. I trusted my assistant. Mattie would tell me when she was ready. Then again, that didn't mean I wouldn't try to get to the bottom of it.

Anna stuck her needle into an apple-shaped pincushion. "Our only choice is to find out who cut the rope, not just to solve the murder but to help Rachel make peace with her past."

Easier said than done.

"I'm going to see Nahum tomorrow morning. The best way to find out why he left the Amish and why he had such a problem with Eve is to go directly to the source."

All three Amish women cried out at once. Sarah was the loudest. "Angie, you can't do that. It's too dangerous."

I stood and carried my empty bowl back to the picnic basket. "I'm not going by myself. Jonah is taking me."

Anna snapped the lid of her sewing box shut. "My son should do no such thing."

I smiled. "Don't blame Jonah. I didn't give him much of a choice. I told him if he didn't go with me, I would go myself."

Anna shook her head. "It's foolish. Wait until you can see Nahum on neutral ground. Don't go to his home, because then it will be on his terms."

"The decision has already been made. I'll be fine. I'm even more eager to go now that I know he's Rachel's father." I looked at each of them in turn. "Don't any of you tell her that I am going. . . ."

Anna and Sarah reluctantly nodded, but Mattie stared at the quilt in front of her.

I walked over to my assistant's chair. "Mattie? Are you going to tell Rachel?"

She removed her needle from the quilt and slid the thread out the needle's eye. "I won't tell her."

It wasn't until I was driving to Millersburg that I remembered Ryan had gone off with Jessica that morning. It was best not to dwell on why I found that irritating. After a quick stop at home to drop off Dodger, I rolled by her store on the way to the Double Dime Diner. At the last second, I swerved into a parking space in front of it.

The driver in the minivan behind me made angry gestures and shouted something indecipherable out of his window.

Oliver hopped right out of the car when I opened the door. He was always happy to visit Jessica's shop. It was where he met Dodger for the first time and fell in love with his feline brother.

Before I even stepped into the shop, I saw Ryan and Jessica through the window. Ryan laughed at something Jessica said, and she put her hand on his arm.

I clenched my jaw and was about to turn away when Jessica saw me and waved me inside.

"We need to be on our best behavior, Ollie," I said before opening the door.

He cocked his head at me as if to ask when he had ever not been on his best behavior. Truth be told, he really didn't want me to recite the list.

Inside the shop, I spied Melon, Jessica's ginger-colored shop cat, snoozing on top of a bookshelf. The big cat opened one eye, saw it was Oliver and me, and went back to sleep. Melon and Cherry Cat, Dodger's mom, were the only two I had ever seen. Jessica had claimed to have a third cat, but I had never seen it. I was convinced it was a ghost.

I edged around Sir Richard, Jessica's suit of armor standing guard at the front door. Oliver gave Sir Richard a wide berth. He'd run into the suit of armor one too many times and almost got chopped with Sir Richard's ax.

"Angie!" Jessica beamed at me. "Come in from the cold. Ryan and I were just having a cup of cocoa. Would you like some?"

"Angie is always up for chocolate," Ryan said with a smile.

"That's true," I admitted.

Jessica spun around to the electric kettle on the back counter to make my cocoa.

Cherry Cat, a sleek, solid, silver gray beauty, sat on the counter and peered down at Oliver. My Frenchie wagged his stubby tail in greeting. The pair's relationship had much improved ever since Oliver and I took in her son, Dodger.

"What were the two of you up to all day?" I asked, trying to sound casual but failing miserably.

Ryan stirred his hot chocolate with a teaspoon. "Jessica has been kind enough to give me a tour of the county. We drove through Berlin, Sugarcreek, and Rolling Brook. I was shocked with the number of Amish I saw. I can see why you like it here. The scenery is very picturesque and charming. Jessica was the perfect tour guide. I'm sure I got a much more thorough tour of the county than those poor folks stuck on those tour buses we kept seeing. I can't see traveling like that as being comfortable."

Jessica blushed. "Ryan was very curious about the county. We even stopped at one of the cheese shops where he could get samples."

"I sent a huge cheese basket home to my parents. It won't make up for my missing the big Dickinson Christmas, but it will at least make my father happy."

I moved a candelabra from the top of a dresser and perched it on the dresser's top. "The county is beautiful, but Texas is pretty too."

Ryan perked up. "Do you miss it?"

"Of course, I miss it sometimes, but I know I can always go back since my parents are there." I paused. "I'm glad Jessica was available to show you around."

Ryan frowned.

Jessica handed me the mug of hot chocolate, but she wouldn't meet my eyes.

"Thanks." I sipped from the Flintstones mug. "I was just about to head over to the Double Dime to meet my parents for an early dinner. It's a bit early, so I thought I would stop in and see how the two of you were."

"The Double Dime?" Ryan asked.

"It's the diner across the street," Jessica said as she stirred her hot cocoa. "The food is really good traditional diner fare. It's especially nice if you need a break from all of the Amish restaurants in the county."

"Care if I join you?" Ryan asked. "I've used up too much of Jessica's time as it is. I know she must have work to do."

"No," Jessica said a little too quickly. "I don't have anything pressing." She blushed. "But if you want to join Angie and her parents for dinner, please go ahead. Visiting with them is the reason you are here."

It seemed that Jessica liked Ryan a lot, but how could I tell her that she had no chance? Ryan would never move to Rolling Brook. He would have to leave his high-powered career in Dallas. He was a Texas guy through and through.

But what was I doing begrudging her a little distraction? I was being absolutely ridiculous. Jessica was my friend. So what if she had a crush on Ryan.

Regardless, I knew inviting Jessica to dinner too with my parents would be a bad idea. My mother would hit the roof if she saw Ryan with another woman, especially one so taken with him. But I had an alternative. I took a deep breath and said, "Jessica, what are you doing on Christmas Eve?"

"Oh," she said. "I planned to go to Midnight Mass, but other than that, I will be wrapping gifts and baking. My extended family celebrates on Christmas Day."

"Why don't you come with us to the Grabers' farm for Christmas Eve dinner? It will be at three, so you will have plenty of time to finish everything you need to for Christmas Day beforehand and to go to Mass afterward."

Ryan's eyebrows knit together as if he didn't like where this conversation was going. Too bad for him. He should have thought about that before he spent the entire day with my friend.

She ran her hand along Cherry Cat's back as Dodger's mother pranced across the counter. "Are you sure? Won't that be one person too many for Anna and Miriam?"

"Anna would love for you to come." I laughed. "And Jonah's wife is always put out about something. One more person won't make a bit of difference with how she feels about the entire affair. Besides, the dinner is at Anna's little *dadihaus*, so Miriam can't argue much."

"A *dadihaus*?" Ryan asked.

"That's what the Amish call the home that the grandparents live in on the farm," Jessica explained. "When one Amish generation turns over the family farm to the next, the older generation usually gives the new generation the big house and moves into a small home on the property. It's translated as 'grandpa house.'"

I nodded. "But in the Grabers' case, Anna lives there alone because she is a widow."

Oliver was lying across Ryan's shoe. I tried to suppress the grimace. It shouldn't bother me that Oliver was so enamored with Ryan. Ryan had always been kind and taken great care of my dog. Jessica watched Ryan with rapt attention. Oliver wasn't the only one taken with the Texas lawyer.

"So, do you have room for one more at your dinner table for today?" Ryan asked.

"Sure," I said through my teeth. "I know Mom would like to see you. She and Dad have been sightseeing today too. You can compare notes."

Chapter Eighteen

As we crossed the street, Ryan, Oliver, and I met my parents, who were just climbing out of their rental car in front of the Double Dime Diner. The bell over the door rang as the four of us went inside the diner. Since I had discovered it a few months back, I had become a regular. Linda, the head and, as far as I could tell, only waitress in the diner, wiped down the Formica counter.

Her face brightened when she saw me. "Angie, choose any seat that you'd like. I'll be with you in a jiffy." She clicked her tongue at Oliver. He abandoned me for the promise of bacon. I was onto their secret code. Although Linda never let Oliver into the kitchen, I found rules were much more lenient about dogs in restaurants in Holmes County than they had been in Dallas.

I led my parents and Ryan to a booth by the front window. It was my favorite spot and gave me a clear view of the county courthouse. The statue of Lady Justice jutting out from the side of the building held her scales high in the air. Her head, scales, and shoulders were weighted down by heavy snow, while even more began to fall.

"Angie," my mother said as she slipped into the booth, "where did Oliver go? I'm surprised you allowed him to wander off like that. You usually watch him every minute."

I picked up my menu, even though I knew what I would order. I could use it as interference if need be. "He and Linda—that's the waitress—are buddies. I'm sure he's getting his choice of bacon right now."

"Do you come here often?" Ryan asked.

I smiled. "Probably more often than I should. The food is great, but you'd be hard-pressed for a salad here."

My mother wrinkled her nose. To her, salad was a mainstay. To me it was a necessary evil. Perhaps that would explain the difference in our sizes.

It wasn't until everyone was seated that I realized my miscalculation. Why had I chosen a booth? My mother was quick to sit beside my father, which meant I was left next to Ryan. Would it look bad if I pulled up a chair to the end of the table? Probably. I slid into the booth and sat on the very outside corner. I was sitting so far on the edge that a light breeze would have knocked me right off my seat.

"I'm not going to push you out of the booth," Ryan said barely above a whisper.

I felt my face grow hot. Of course he wouldn't do that. For all his other faults, Ryan was a perfect gentleman.

He smiled at me as I sat properly in the seat.

Mom picked up her menu. "Ryan, what have you been up to all day? We haven't seen you at all. I hope you aren't too bored up here."

"Not at all." Ryan gave Mom his best smile, which would have been charming enough for a pageant judge, unlike mine. "Angie's friend, Jessica Nicolson, showed me around the county. It was nice to see the area from a local's perspective."

My mother frowned at this, but Dad said, "How nice of Angie's friend to show you around while Angie Bear was working."

"I've told you about Jessica, haven't I, Mom? She is the one with Out of Time, the antiques shop here in Millersburg." I pointed out the window. "In fact, that's her shop right across the street. You and Dad should check it out. You would love it. There is a suit of armor named Sir Richard that she's placed right at the entrance to the store. It's in great condition."

My mother closed her menu. "I don't have any need for more antiques."

"I've always wanted a suit of armor," my dad said. "Think of how nice that would look in the foyer of our home, Daphne."

"I certainly will not."

"Maybe I will go over and have a peek at it. It would be a bear to ship back to Dallas, but it's worth a look." Dad winked at me over his menu.

Mom frowned harder, looking as if she had just swallowed an eight-ounce glass of grapefruit juice in one gulp.

Linda trotted over in her circa 1950 waitressing uniform. "Angie, it's so good to see you. Merry Christmas! I wasn't sure you'd come back in before the holiday."

"Hey, what about my order?" a man in the next booth asked. "I was here first."

"Oh hush," Linda said. "I will get back to you in a minute."

The man grunted but didn't bother to argue. If you wanted to eat at the Double Dime, you did what Linda said.

"Who do you have with you?" Linda peered eagerly over the table.

"Mom, Dad, this is Linda O'Neal. Linda, these are my parents, Kent and Daphne Braddock."

My mother gave her a tight smile. "How do you do?"

"Can't complain. I can't tell you how much we like Angie in this county. She's a breath of fresh air. She's smart as a whip too. She's solved two m—"

I kicked Linda, stopping her in the nick of time from uttering the "m" word, "murder."

"Ouch." Linda rubbed her shin.

"Sorry—foot slipped." I smiled sweetly. "And this is our family friend, Ryan."

Ryan flinched when I introduced him as a family friend.

"Ryan?" Linda asked. "Is this *the* Ryan?"

Ryan's smooth brow wrinkled. "I seem to be getting that a lot in this town."

Linda straightened up to her full height. "Well, you go and break our Angie's heart, that's what you are going to get. I have half a mind to kick you out on the street this very second."

"Linda," I said, "Ryan is here for Christmas, visiting with my family as a friend. There is no reason to chase him out of the diner."

"Well, I'm going to burn his meal," she muttered only loud enough for me to hear.

As much as I would enjoy that in the moment, I hoped she was just kidding.

Linda passed menus all around. "I'll give you a minute to look it over, and then I'll come back for your order."

"How was your sightseeing?" I asked.

"It was nice to see the old haunts," my father said.

"I wish you would have come with us, Angie. We are only here for a short while," my mother complained.

"I told you I would be working during part of your stay." At least I had been for part of the time. "And the trustees just scheduled a meeting that I have to go to later this evening."

"Angie, you are just like your father. You work too hard. All you talk about is work. It's Christmas." Tears gathered in my mother's eyes.

"I'm sorry, Mom. But I have a great idea to make up for today. I don't have a Christmas tree at my house."

"I know," my mother said. "It's quite depressing."

"So let's change that. Let's go find a Christmas tree tonight. Together."

"All of us?" Dad asked, nodding to Ryan.

"Sure," I squeaked. I hadn't thought to include Ryan, but it wouldn't be fair to exclude him. "I know just the farm to go to. There's an Amish place where we can purchase the tree. It's called Shetler Tree Farm, and it's in Berlin."

"We've never had a real Christmas tree before," Dad said, warming to the idea. "And it would help us feel more in the Christmas spirit."

I knew I would regret what I said next, but I said it anyway. "We can go right after we eat and pick out the tree, and since I don't have any Christmas decorations, Mom, I will put you in charge of décor for both the house and tree."

My mother sat up straighter in her seat. "Really? You would let me do that? You never let me touch your apartment back in Dallas, even though I offered on numerous occasions."

"I do have to work tomorrow, and this will give you something to do while I'm gone. And you're right; the house does need a little TLC."

Mom clapped her hands. "I will start making a list as soon as we get back to the house."

Yep. I was going to regret this. If I really hated the decorating choices that my mother made, I could just change them when she was back in Dallas. I couldn't back out now; this was the happiest that I had seen her since she arrived in Ohio.

"What kind of work do you have to do tomorrow?" Ryan asked. "I'm not much for decorating, but maybe I can help at the shop."

I blinked. "I'm working on new flyers for January quilting classes and quilting pattern designs that can be printed by class members from their computers. It's nice to be able to use my graphic design background."

"I should say so. Since you threw away your career," Mom said.

Okay, maybe my suggestion for the tree farm visit hadn't fully made up for my MIA status today.

I ignored my mother's comment. "It shouldn't take me very long, and I will be minding the shop. You would be bored. I don't expect much business."

"I could keep you company," Ryan said.

"Mattie will be there most of the day," I said, hoping that he would take the hint.

Ryan opened his mouth to say something, but fortunately Linda returned with our drinks. As she set them on the table she asked, "Are you ready to order?"

Ryan appeared concerned as he perused the menu. Nothing on it was within his meal allotment of calories.

Dad rubbed his hands together. "I'll have the left side of the menu, please. If that goes well, I will finish off with the right."

Linda grinned. "You're my kind of diner."

"Kent, don't tease the woman. Why don't you have the chicken breast, hold the gravy, and instead of potatoes, can he have the vegetable of the day?"

"That would be green beans."

"Plain green beans?"

"With ham." Linda knocked the eraser end of her pencil on her order pad. "Why would anyone bother to eat plain green beans?"

I had spent a good portion of my childhood asking the same question.

Mom sighed. "All right. Green beans with ham will have to do. Kent, you can pick the pieces of ham out."

Dad frowned. "Daphne, I am perfectly capable of ordering my own meal."

She opened her mouth to protest.

"I'll have the chicken potpie with a side of mashed potatoes and gravy." Dad handed Linda his menu.

Linda took his menu.

"Kent, that's not part of your diet."

"You said it yourself. It's Christmas. I deserve to indulge. You will get to redecorate Angie's house, and I will get to eat something that doesn't taste like cardboard. Everyone wins."

My mother shook her head. "Well, I will have what I previously ordered for my husband."

Ryan spoke up. "I will have the same that Mrs. Braddock is having."

I handed Linda my menu. "BLT with fries and extra bacon."

Dad reached over the table and gave me a high five. The diet-war battle lines were drawn.

"Well," Mom said, "I see that we have two very different views when it comes to food. I do hope our taste won't be that different as I work on your house, Angie."

I knew it was a given. "Just leave the kitchen alone. That's all I ask. I love that kitchen."

Mom wrinkled her nose. "With all those outdated appliances."

"I appreciate their charm. As for the food, it is Christmas," I said. "We will all eat better after the holidays."

"Or at least aspire to," Dad said with a chuckle.

"Were you at the shop all day?" Ryan asked.

"Actually, most of the day I was at the hotel because of the quilt show," I said quickly. I didn't want Ryan or my parents to know about my dabbling into amateur-sleuth territory. All three of them knew about my run-in with the law during the summer. A dead body had been found in the stockroom of my quilt shop, so my involvement in that investigation had been impossible to keep secret. However, I had been able to avoid telling them everything since then, and I planned to keep it that way.

"See the sheriff while you were there?" Ryan asked.

My head snapped up, and I met Ryan's gaze. "Why would you ask that?"

"I assume he would be investigating that poor girl's death."

"Oh, right." I examined my water glass.

Linda returned with our food. "Are you talking about Eve Shetler?"

I nodded.

Linda set my BLT in front of me. "I heard about that. It's a real shame. Eve was a sweet girl."

"You knew her?"

"'Course I did. She and her friend used to meet here at least once a week. They always got the pancakes."

"Amber Rustle?" I asked.

"Yep, I think that was her name. It was hard to remember whoever Eve was with because she was such a standout. Even in her plain clothes. I knew she would never stay Amish. I've known so many Amish kids in my day. Most of them never stray, but I can always pick out the ones that leave. There's just something different about how the kids hold themselves."

I removed the toothpick from a quarter of my sandwich. "Did you see Eve since she came back?"

"I did. About a week ago the whole cast came here for dinner. We had to move most of the tables together so they would all have a place to sit, and I even had to turn some regulars away because there wasn't enough room for them to eat. You can imagine how that went over."

"Did you overhear any of their conversations?" I asked.

"Oh, you know I don't eavesdrop," Linda said defensively. "But then again, if someone talks too loud and I can't help but hear, that's another thing altogether and not my fault in the least."

"Of course it's not," I agreed.

"Can't say they said anything of importance, but Eve was definitely the belle of the ball. Everything seemed to revolve around her, including the men. The other girl actress, maybe a year or two older, did not like it. Every time she heard Eve speak, she would squish up her face like someone put too much salt in her soup."

"Lena?" I asked. "Was that the other girl's name?"

"If you say so. I never heard her name said."

"Linda," another customer called, "I need a warm-up."

Linda sighed and went to that table.

"Angie," Mom hissed after Linda moved to the next table, "why are you asking all those questions about that girl?"

"Just curious," I said evasively. "It's just so tragic. Everyone in the county is curious about it."

"I hope you don't have any silly plans to get involved. That isn't your place. You have no idea what your father and I went through when you were a murder suspect during the summer. Ryan too."

I glanced at Ryan. "Ryan too?"

He nodded. "I was worried about you. Please, Angie, don't do anything stupid."

I gritted my teeth. Ryan had no claim to tell me what to do. I moved the conversation back to Christmas decorations and hoped that they would all forget about it.

After the meal, I said, "Y'all can head out and I'll just grab Oliver."

Mom, Dad, and Ryan went through the main door. I found Oliver behind the counter. Linda was giving him little bits of bacon.

As my parents walked through the door, Linda called, "Come back soon!" She dropped the last bit of bacon on the floor. Oliver gobbled it up before I could grab it from him. Linda yanked on my sleeve when the bell rang their exit. "You never said how good-looking he was."

"You were defending my broken heart early. It shouldn't matter what Ryan looks like."

She snorted. "That always matters. What are you going to do?"

I pulled Oliver's boots out of my hobo bag and knelt beside my dog. "What do you mean?"

"Clearly the man came all this way to profess his love to you and whisk you back to Texas."

I struggled to get Oliver's boots onto his feet. "I don't think—"

She put her hands on her hips and stared down at me. "So he gave up Christmas with his big fancy family in Texas to visit Amish Country? You can't be that naïve. In fact, I know you are not. You're in denial."

I knew Linda was right, but I didn't want to admit it, not even to myself. I stood with Oliver tucked under my arm like a football.

"What will you do?" She repeated her question.

"I will deal with it if the conversation comes up," I said, surprising myself. Why hadn't I immediately said, "I will say no"? I didn't want to leave Rolling Brook, my quilting circle, Running Stitch, or Mitchell. Did I?

I left the diner more confused about my personal life than I was over Eve's death. Considering I was nowhere near finding the killer, that was a scary thought.

Chapter Nineteen

I exited the diner to find my parents and Ryan chatting with Mitchell and his son, Zander, under a street-light. While we had been inside the Double Dime, the sun had set. Mitchell's Boston terrier, Tux, was also with them. Oliver yanked at his leash in his excitement to see his best buddy.

The two dogs touched pushed-in noses and wiggled their stubby tails.

My mother stared at the dogs as if their interaction told her something she didn't like. It probably did and revealed much more than I wanted her to know, at least while Ryan was standing just feet away.

My mother sniffed. "We were just telling the sheriff how sorry we were about the poor girl at the play. It's terrible when someone so young is lost."

"Who do you have with you there?" my father asked.

"This is my son, Zander. Say hello, Z," the sheriff said.

"Hello," Zander said. He had his father's trademark blue-green eyes. He'd be a lady-killer, just like his dad. "Angie, I just asked Dad this morning when you were going to come over again. I want to show you the new Lego set I got from my grandma for Christmas. You are the only adult I know who likes to play with Legos."

"You play Legos together at the sheriff's house?" my mom asked. Her question asked much more than that.

Mitchell tapped his son on the top of his stocking hat. "Z, we will talk about that later."

I glanced over at Lady Justice hanging above the courthouse. There was a spotlight at her feet, giving her an eerie glow in the early-evening darkness. Was it me, or was she smirking at this awkward moment? At least someone was enjoying it, other than Tux and Oliver, that is. The dogs touched noses again.

Mitchell cleared his throat. "How did you all enjoy the Double Dime? It's our favorite place in the county."

"The food was excellent," Dad said. "I could go for another piece of pecan pie right now."

Mom arched her eyebrow. "'Our'? Who's 'our'?"

She didn't miss anything.

"Oh." Mitchell blushed. "Z's and mine, of course."

My mother pulled her leather gloves farther up her wrists. "What about his mother? Does she like it there?"

"No way!" Zander hopped from foot to foot. When he moved, the red light on the back of his boots lit up. The dog crouched and watched this with rapt interest. "She always says all I do is eat junk when I'm at my dad's house. She thinks the Double Dime is a heart attack on a plate." He said that last part as if quoting his mother.

My dad grinned and patted his belly. "But what a way to go."

"Your dad's house?" My mother would not be derailed.

The inquisition was getting out of hand. "Mom, the sheriff is divorced. That's what you want to know, isn't it? His ex-wife, Hillary, is a really nice lady."

Mitchell grinned. "She likes Angie. Me, not so much."

Ryan spoke up for the first time. "Everyone likes Angie."

"Yes, they do," Mitchell said, giving him a level look.

Okay, it was time to break this up.

"Gosh, it's cold out and getting darker by the second," I said. "And we want to get to the tree farm before it's fully dark. So . . ." I trailed off.

Dad wrapped his arm around my shoulder. "That's right. Angie, I will take your mom to the house so we can get warmer clothes for the Christmas tree hunt. How about we meet you there?"

"I'll just go back with you, Mr. and Mrs. Braddock," Ryan said. "It will give Angie and the sheriff time to talk."

Mom looked ready to protest but shut her mouth quickly when she and Ryan shared a look. What were those two up to? I was probably better off not knowing.

I kissed both my parents on the cheek. "I'll see you back at the farm."

My mother eyed Ryan before she, my father, and Ryan crossed the street on the green light and disappeared around the side of the courthouse where Dad had parked their rental car.

Zander knelt in the snow and played with the dogs. I nodded at Mitchell to join me a few feet away.

"How was dinner with Ryan?" he asked with mischief in his eyes.

"Tolerable."

"I will certainly be glad when he's gone."

"You and me both."

"Glad to hear that." The corner of his mouth perked up. "So when *are* you coming over to play Legos with Z?"

"Not until after my parents are gone." I chewed on my lower lip.

Mitchell noticed because his cop eyes narrowed. "Do you have something to tell me?"

I nodded.

"And does it have to do with Eve Shetler?"

"Yep."

He sighed. "What is it?"

I told him about the day's events. I left out the part about asking Jonah to take me to Nahum Shetler's shack in the woods. That wouldn't end well, and Mitchell would try to talk both of us out of it or forbid it altogether. I didn't think he would go as far as throwing us in a jail cell to stop us, but I wasn't going to chance it.

"You have been busy," Mitchell said, not sounding too pleased about it.

"So what do you think about this business with the threatening notes? I assume you got my call."

"I did, and the tip about the notes is credible. We found an unopened one in Eve's hotel room when we searched it last night. It was right inside the door as Amber described."

My pulse quickened. "So Eve never saw it."

The snow let up, and the sun peeked through the clouds for a brief moment.

Mitchell squinted. "Apparently not."

"What did it say?" I asked, trying to sound nonchalant.

He frowned. "Enough to make us concerned, and to give us more proof that Eve's death was no accident."

"How were the letters written?" I wrapped my arms tightly around myself. The temperature fell with each passing second. I didn't know how Zander could kneel on the cold sidewalk so long.

He sighed, glancing back at his son and the dogs, who were happily romping in the snow. "They were done with a laser printer. It will be difficult to trace, but as we narrow down the suspects, of course we will determine whether they had access to such a printer, and then maybe, just maybe, we can match it. Printers aren't quite as easy to match as old typewriters. I'm betting whoever did this was smart and would use a printer we will never find."

"It was premeditated." I swallowed.

"Since the moment I saw the cut rope," he said, "I've never doubted that Eve's death was planned from beginning to end."

I shivered. Why would someone what to hurt such a young talented girl? Was it her youth and her talent that got her killed? "Did you learn anything from them? Did you have the letter tested for fingerprints, DNA, and whatever else?"

His brow furrowed. "Yes, of course we did all of that. The DNA test will have to be done in the state crime lab. We don't have that kind of equipment."

"I'm sorry. I know you are doing all you can. This case is playing with my head."

"It doesn't have to. It's not your responsibility. You have enough going on with Mr. Dallas in town." He gave me a sideways smile.

I chuckled at the nickname. "Maybe you're right, but I liked Eve. I sat by her at the progressive dinner just an hour before she died. She was so vibrant and full of life. It's hard for me to go on like nothing happened. And every time I think of everyone she loved losing her this close to Christmas, it breaks my heart."

"I know." He placed a hand on my shoulder.

"I feel the worst for Junie, her sister. She's like a lost puppy."

"You have a thing for taking in strays."

"Maybe I do, but I want to help her."

"You drive me nuts, but I admire you all at the same time. You and Oliver had better get going. I heard you are looking for a Christmas tree." He smiled.

"Mitchell, have you thought about Nahum?"

He nodded. "We won't know for sure if Nahum was on the property at the time until we check the time stamp that Blake recorded. Those ropes could have been cut anytime between the safety check and when Eve climbed on the swing."

"Assuming it is accurate."

"Yes, assuming that. Now, go on. I don't want your mother to get the wrong idea about why I held you up."

"Okay, okay," I said. "One more question."

He rolled his aquamarine eyes. "I doubt it's the last one."

"What are you doing for Christmas Eve?"

"I'm working."

"And Zander?" I glanced at his son.

The sheriff's face fell. "He will be with his mother and her family. He spends Christmas Eve night with her, and I will get him late afternoon on Christmas Day."

"That must be hard waking up Christmas morning without Zander there." I reached out and rubbed his arm.

He frowned. "It is, but this will be our fourth Christmas like this. Z is comfortable with the arrangement, and that's the most important thing."

"Will you have any free time during the day?"

He grinned down at me. "I might. Why do you ask?"

I swallowed. "Why don't you come with us to Christmas Eve dinner at the Grabers'?"

His face brightened but just as quickly fell again. "Won't it be awkward? I don't want to cause trouble between you and your mother."

"It won't. At least it won't cause any more trouble than I am already in with her." I smiled and gave him a hug. "Of course it will be awkward with both you and Ryan there, but I can't stand the idea of you alone on Christmas Eve."

"Angie, that's very sweet, but—"

"You have to come. Anna invited us to her home for Christmas Eve dinner along with the Millers. You know Rachel and Anna both always make enough food to feed the Roman army."

He laughed at my description. "I wouldn't want to intrude."

"You're not intruding. If Anna found out that you were alone on Christmas Eve and I didn't invite you, she would never forgive. Besides, I already invited Jessica on Ryan's behalf."

"Oh?"

I smiled. "She took him on a tour of the county today."

"I've always liked Jessica." He glanced at his son and saw Zander was facing away from us as he talked to the two dogs. Quickly, the sheriff leaned over and brushed my lips with his. "You are a hard one to argue with. All right, I'll come. Text me the time, and I will be there. But I hope Anna won't mind if I'm late or have to leave suddenly. I never know what will come up, especially on a holiday." He clapped his hands. "Z, it's time to go. Come on, Tux."

I smiled as he left. But then my smile faltered when I saw Ryan watching me from across the street.

Chapter Twenty

I snapped Oliver's leash on his collar. The act gave me a moment to collect myself before facing Ryan.

I pulled on Oliver's leash. "Come on, Ollie. Let's go."

The little Frenchie sighed as he watched his canine pal fade into the distance.

Oliver and I waited for a buggy to cross our path, and then we jaywalked across the street.

Ryan waved. "Does the sheriff know that you don't always use the crosswalk?"

"He probably suspects. I thought you left with Mom and Dad," I said, relieved he said nothing about the kiss between Mitchell and me. With any luck, he never saw it.

"Your parents wanted to go home and change before the tree cutting. I think your mother has a special outfit in mind for the event."

I chuckled. "I don't doubt it. I guess we will meet them there. Where's your car?"

"It's still at the hotel. Jessica drove all day."

"Okay, come with me. I can drop you off at the hotel when I head to the trustees' meeting."

Oliver hopped into the backseat of my SUV.

I closed the driver-side door as Ryan buckled his seat belt. "I can't believe that you have the same car."

"Why?" I asked, starting the engine.

"Because so much has changed in your life, I expected this to change too."

"It's a good car, and I can't afford a new one, even if I wanted one, which I don't." I turned the key in the ignition.

"The cost of a new car doesn't have to be a problem for you."

I ignored that comment as I turned onto Route 39, the most direct route from Millersburg to Berlin.

We drove in silence for a couple of blocks until I turned out of town and onto a country road.

"Did you and Mom plan that we'd ride together?" I finally asked.

He laughed. "Is it that obvious?"

"Yes." I smiled. "Is Mom really changing her outfit to buy a Christmas tree?"

"I think so."

I smiled. "Honestly, I don't doubt it."

He wrapped his hand around the shoulder harness of his seat belt. "Angie, we need to talk."

I gripped the steering wheel. "Ryan, we just had a nice dinner with my parents, and now we are going Christmas tree shopping. Why ruin it?"

He turned to face me. "I'm sorry."

I concentrated on the road ahead. There was no traffic and the snow had stopped coming down. It didn't need my undivided attention. "That's a good start. You should be sorry."

"I made a mistake. I got scared."

"Scared? Yep. I'm really scary."

"Not of you."

Oliver stuck his head between the two front seats.

"You're making Oliver frustrated. He likes to sit shotgun."

"Angie, please. Stop trying to avoid this. I came a long way to have this conversation with you."

"Why didn't you call? I'm *sure* my mother would have given you all my phone numbers."

"You would have hung up on me."

"Probably," I admitted. "Okay, what do you have to say?" I kept my eyes on the road.

He took a deep breath. "I wasn't afraid of you. I knew you. I was afraid of marriage and commitment. I don't have a good reason for it, but that's why I broke it off. It was stupid, and I know what an enormous mistake it was."

"At least you know that." I gripped the steering wheel. "We were together seven years. I would call that commitment."

"Marriage is different."

"It is and it's not."

"Angie—," he began.

"You said what you came here to say. I listened to it, and I forgive you. I don't blame you for your decision. You made the right one. I wouldn't be here in Holmes County without it. I am grateful to you for that." I paused. "*Now*, anyway. I wasn't at first, but I am now."

He opened his door. "I don't want you to be grateful because you are here. I want you to come home."

"This is my home." I sighed as we joined the long line of traffic on Main Street in Berlin.

He was silent for a moment.

An Amish family wagon pulled out in front of me in the road. Berlin's Main Street was the most congested in Holmes County. It was the number one stop in the county for tour buses and tourists, and it made Sugartree Street in Rolling Brook look like a ghost town in comparison. Amish and English shops and businesses lined both sides of the street. The Shetler Tree Farm was on the other side of it, and Main Street was the most direct way to get there. Now that I was stuck in Amish Country traffic, which included automobiles, trucks, buggies, and tractors, I wished I had gone the long way. The traffic jam only trapped me in the car longer with Ryan. At the moment, that was the very last place I wanted to be.

"It's because of the sheriff," he said as if his mind were made up.

"Sheriff Mitchell?" Playing dumb might not be the best strategy, but it was the best I had at the moment.

Five cars ahead of us, the light changed to red. I was never getting off this road.

"I saw him kiss you." He sounded hurt. That was just too bad.

I tapped my fingers on the steering wheel. So playing dumb was not going to cut it. "I care about the sheriff. He's my friend, but he's not the reason I'm staying here. My quilt shop is the reason."

"I'm not telling you to give up the shop if it means that much to you. I'm sure one of your Amish friends would manage it for you, and you can visit as much as you like."

I ground my teeth. "Gee, thanks for allowing visitation rights with my own business. How kind of you."

"I didn't mean it like that."

"That's exactly how you meant it, and whatever your intention was, it doesn't matter. Running Stitch was my aunt's and now it's mine, and I want to run it. I can't do that from Texas."

"If managing your shop was the only thing that you were doing."

I whipped my head to face him. "What does that mean?"

"You're meddling in the investigation into that Amish girl's death, aren't you?"

"How?" I let the word hang in the air between us.

"I knew it as soon as you said you spent most of the day at the hotel. Yesterday you said the quilt show judging was in the morning, and today you spent most of the day there. Why would you need to be there that long?" He folded his arms. "Also, anytime the conversation veers toward Eve's death, you perk up. I can almost see the wheels in your head spinning."

"That's ridiculous."

"*Shetler* Tree Farm. Of all the tree farms there must be in their rural county, that is the one we are going to today, the day after Eve *Shetler* falls to her death at the performance of *An Amish Christmas*. I know they are related, and I know that your sudden need for a Christmas tree was motivated by the crime investigation."

Ryan was a winning attorney because he was excellent at details. I would have to give him that.

"Angie," Ryan said, using his serious attorney voice. I suddenly remembered how much I'd hated it when he spoke to me in that tone. "You should not be involved in a criminal investigation. You could get in trouble."

"Ryan, you are a corporate lawyer."

"I may be that, but I still took criminal law in law school. You could get in major trouble if you mess with a police investigation." He paused. "Whether or not the sheriff is your *friend*."

The wagon in front of me turned off a side street, and I finally cleared the end of Main Street. The road widened into two lanes, and the car picked up speed. In the dark, I saw the entrance to the tree farm ahead lit by gas lampposts.

My tires crunched on the ice and hard-packed snow. As the parking space lines were covered, some visitors to the tree farm had parked creatively. Vehicles came to a stop in every which way in the parking lot. Amish men helped English families tie evergreen trees to the top of their cars with rope, bungee cords, and, as I suspected, prayer. Some of those trees looked like they would blow off with a stiff wind. I squeezed my little SUV between a minivan and a pickup truck. "We're here." I opened my car door.

Ryan reached across the seat to me and caught my

hand before I could escape. "I'm here for five more days. I'm not giving up that easily."

I pulled my hand away but said nothing.

Dad and Mom's enormous rental SUV turned into the parking lot.

I clipped on Oliver's leash. I didn't want him getting away from me in all the confusion.

Mom stepped gingerly through the snow toward me. "Angie, are you sure this is the best place to buy a tree? It's a zoo."

"It's the only tree farm I've heard about," I said, which was completely true.

Beside me Ryan snorted.

"If you tell my parents what you suspect," I said under my breath, "I'll make the rest of your vacation miserable."

He smiled. "Don't worry, my love."

I flinched.

Dad clapped his gloved hands together. "Angie Bear, this was such a wonderful idea. I haven't chopped down a real tree since I was a boy. It's something that Dad would do with us when we were young right here in Holmes County. Of course, we went to an Amish farm too. They grow the best trees."

Mom pursed her lips. "Kent, do you think this is wise?"

"Oh, I remember the basics from when my father did it." He marched across the uneven parking lot. My mother had to jog to keep up with him. Ryan, Oliver, and I fell into line behind.

A seven-foot-tall fence surrounded the tree farm on

all sides. The acreage was impressive, and eventually the chain-link fence disappeared from view, making you think that the tree farm went on forever. Families and Amish workers went in and out of the gate carrying freshly cut trees.

A large hand-painted sign, saying ENTER HERE, pointed to a large barn to the right of the open gate leading into the trees.

The noise from the excited English families there to pick out the perfect tree for their living rooms was deafening. Mom winced at the noise. Her kind of shopping took place at high-end clothing stores where everyone spoke in reverent tones.

We huddled in the doorway, unsure where to go, until an Amish man, who appeared to be anywhere between forty-five and sixty, waved to us. "Come on in."

He was the same height as Nahum, and his deep-set features were close enough to Nahum's for the pair to be brothers. While Nahum's beard had been grizzled and wild, this man had a solid gray beard, which was neatly trimmed and hung just two inches below his chin. He had to be one of the Shetler men who ran the business.

"What can I do for you today?" the man asked.

"We are here about a tree," Dad said. "We need the best Christmas tree that you have for my daughter's house." He pointed at me. "This is my daughter, Angie."

The Amish man nodded at me. "Then you've come to the right place. We have the best trees in the area."

Ryan held out his hand to shake the man's. "I'm

Ryan and this is the Braddock family. What's your name?"

My pulse quickened.

"Nehemiah Shetler. My brother Noah and I own and operate the tree farm."

"How nice to own a family business," my mother said.

"Have you been in business for a long time?" Ryan asked.

"We are fourth-generation tree farmers. We've been doing fruit trees and broadleaf trees for nearly that long. My brother and I were the ones who expanded the business to Christmas trees."

"Is your brother here?" Ryan shoved his hands into the pockets on his long wool coat. "It would be nice to meet him too. It's always nice to know the owner of the business where you buy things."

Nehemiah's face fell for just an instant. "*Nee*, he's with his family today."

"It seems like a busy time of year to take off work," Ryan said.

The Amish man's eyes narrowed. "He has a *gut* reason."

Dad cleared his throat. "It seems the Christmas tree business has been a good decision."

"It has, no matter what anyone else might say." Nehemiah bent over and patted Oliver's broad head. "Who is this little guy?"

"Oliver," I said. "Are dogs allowed in with the trees?"

"Sure. But keep an eye on him. We aren't responsible if a tree topples onto him."

Oliver whimpered and hid behind my legs.

"If you are ready to pick out your perfect tree, follow me." Nehemiah took an ax down from the wall.

I stepped beside Ryan. "I don't need your help," I whispered.

Ryan smiled at me as we followed Nehemiah out of the barn and into the tree yard. "So you admit that you are investigating the girl's death."

I glared at him and caught up with my father.

Chapter Twenty-one

Nehemiah led us down a long line of trees. All around us, English couples and families chopped at trunks with axes just like the one on Nehemiah's shoulder. The Amish tree farmer glanced over his opposite shoulder. "What kind of tree are you looking for?"

"An eight footer," Dad piped up. "An extra full."

"Whoa." I stepped ahead of my father. "Dad, my ceiling is just at eight feet."

"Aww." He slung his arm around my shoulder. "We'll make it fit."

"I have just the tree for you," Nehemiah said, and quickened his pace.

The Amish farmer led us on a winding path through the tree farm. Evergreen after evergreen—any of them looked fine to me. I couldn't distinguish any differences between one and the next. As we went, we got farther and farther away from the other English families looking for trees. Suddenly, Nehemiah turned and disappeared down another row. We scrambled to follow him. He came to a stop in front of an enormous tree, which rose several feet above my dad's head and was twice his girth.

"Yikes," Ryan whispered.

My thoughts exactly.

Nehemiah patted the tree. "Isn't she a beaut? She's a Douglas fir, and the best one I have. I hate to see her go, but it's time. No farmer can become too attached to his crops or livestock. The end result will always be the same."

I stared up at the tree. "Um, are you sure that's only eight feet tall?" I asked. "I think it's eighteen."

"Actually she's ten, but by the time we trim her down to get onto your car roof, she will be eight."

My mother placed her hand on Dad's arm. "Kent, maybe something more modest would be better."

The tree was the size of a bus. There was no way it would fit in my living room.

"What about this one?" I asked, pointing to a similar tree, but one that was just a few inches taller than my height of five foot nine.

Nehemiah turned. "That is also a Douglas fir."

Dad sighed. "It will be your tree, Angie Bear. If you want the smaller one, I suppose that will be okay."

I smiled. "Thanks, Dad. I think that with this one, we'll actually be able to sit in the living room and open presents on Christmas morning. With that one"—I pointed at the huge tree—"the chances of our fitting in the room with it are slim."

"All right," my father said. "The smaller tree it is."

Nehemiah handed my father the ax. "Here you go."

Mom, Ryan, and I instinctively backed up.

"Mr. Braddock, have you ever used an ax before?"

My father hefted it into his hands. "It's been some time, but it's like riding a bike. You whack the blade end on the tree's trunk easy as pie."

"In my opinion," Mom said, "making a pie is rather hard. Nehemiah, perhaps you could show my husband the proper technique before we have a casualty."

The Amish man laughed and accepted the ax when Dad handed it to him. "I can show you."

Crack! The ax cut into the trunk of the tree. Immediately, twittering erupted from the branches. Three starlings burst out.

Oliver froze in sheer terror, and then he was off like a ball from a cannon.

"Oliver!" I ran after him.

"Angie!" Mom cried.

I waved at her. "It's okay. Keep chopping down the tree. I'll get him."

Oliver was running at full speed, and he wasn't easy to spot in the trees since the sun had now completely set. The moonlight and the occasional gas-lit lantern hanging from a post were all I had to guide me.

I turned to see Ryan running behind me. I clenched my jaw. I wished he would just leave me and my dog alone. We were doing just fine without him in our lives. Now he was back and causing trouble.

Oliver paused in a fork in the path either to contemplate his options or catch his breath. In any case, I took my opportunity. I dove and tackled the Frenchie to the ground. He fought against me. "Shh . . . shh . . . Ollie."

Ryan's boots skidded to a stop just beside my ear. He bent over to catch his breath. "I forgot how fast the two of you could run."

I struggled to a sitting position with Oliver in my arms.

Ryan offered me his hand. I tucked Oliver under my left arm and took Ryan's hand with my right hand.

I stood and he held on to it for a little bit too long. I pulled my hand away and suddenly got a fit of giggles.

Ryan's face broke into a smile, and he started laughing too. Soon we were both doubled over in near hysteria.

"I don't know what is so funny," I said, gasping.

"Neither do I," he said. "I haven't laughed this hard since we broke up."

The laughter died on my lips.

Ryan frowned. "I ruined the moment, didn't I?"

I pulled Oliver's leash out of my coat pocket and clicked it onto his collar. "You killed it dead."

He sighed.

I looked around; we were surrounded by trees, hundreds of dense pine trees, and long shadows.

Uh-oh. "Um," I said. "Do you know the way back?"

Ryan fished in his pocket for his smartphone.

I rolled my eyes. "Your GPS is not going to get us out of here. We are off the grid."

"Oh, right." He put the phone back in his pocket. "Should we call your parents?"

"Not yet." I pointed in the direction that we came.

"We ran through fresh snow. We can just follow our trail out."

"Wow, you are like a Girl Scout now. What other mad survival skills have you picked up in the country?"

"Shut up," I said, but I was smiling.

Ryan chuckled.

We walked in silence for a few dozen yards.

"It's hard to believe little Oliver ran this far," Ryan said. "But I'm not complaining. I always enjoy time alone with you."

I glanced over my shoulder at him and narrowed my eyes. "Don't start and don't get any ideas."

"Angie, I don't think—"

Whatever Ryan was thinking was cut off by an angry shout. "I told you to leave!"

"Wha—"

A muffled, clearly angry reply came back.

Ryan pulled me into the thicket between the trees. The spiny branches pulled at my winter coat and scratched my face.

"What are you doing?" I hissed.

"Shh," Ryan breathed into my ear.

I swallowed. He was too close to me.

"I won't, not without an answer!" a second voice shouted.

The voices came closer and sounded angrier with every step. Soon two men appeared on the path and trampled the footprints that Ryan and I had been following back to my parents.

They were two Amish men, two brothers. Nehemiah

and Nahum. Now that they stood face-to-face, there was no doubt they were related. They had the same deep-set eyes and bushy hooded brow, which made them appear angry, even when they were not. However, at that moment, I thought it was safe to say that they were both very angry.

"Nahum, get out of here," Nehemiah said through clenched teeth.

"You bring a curse on our family with this business." Nahum's face was bright red. "You sell out your soul to make a dollar from the *Englischers*. Selling Christmas trees." He spat. "What would our father say at such a thing? Christmas trees for the *Englisch* and the *Englisch* only."

"It is no different than any of the Amish factories that make motor homes or electric tools for the *Englisch* to use. We have to adapt a little so that our culture won't be lost."

"You believe we have to adapt." Nahum sneered. "I am loyal to the Old Order way."

"The Old Order way?" Nehemiah spat. "You aren't even part of a district. You can't be Amish and not be part of a community. That's what it means to be Amish. You are the one who would be a disappointment to our father."

"I am more of an Amish man than you can ever pray to be."

"I told you to leave." Nehemiah's voice was measured, threatening. If I were Nahum, I would have run for it. Nehemiah added something back in Pennsylvania Dutch.

Nahum scowled. "That is the reason Eve left. It is the reason she is dead."

I gasped, and Ryan covered my mouth with his hand.

I yanked it away.

Nehemiah closed his eyes. "You are no longer my brother. Leave. You made your choice. You are not my family. You will never be welcomed back."

Nahum's chest moved up and down as he stared at his brother. "Why would you even think I would want to come back?" He stomped toward Ryan and me.

Ryan pulled me back deeper into the brush.

Nehemiah stood there for a moment, and then walked in the opposite direction from his brother. I listened to the crunch of his footsteps in the snow until they faded away into nothing.

Ryan and I stayed in our hiding place for two more minutes. Oliver tugged at my pant leg with his teeth, and I stumbled out of the trees.

I brushed pine needles off my coat. It was no use. They stuck to the wool like Velcro. Ryan's coat was even worse, but I wasn't going to tell him that.

Ryan plucked a stick off my stocking cap. "The man Nehemiah was speaking to is clearly insane."

"That's his brother Nahum. They are both Eve's uncles." I stamped my cold feet. "He's also my friend Rachel's father."

"Rachel from the bakery?"

I nodded. "I just wish he had said that part about whatever had caused Eve's death in English. The answer was right there, and I didn't understand a word of it. Maybe Jonah and I will find out tomorrow." My shoulders drooped. "If Jonah had been here, I would already know the answer."

"Wait." Ryan watched me in the dim light. "How will you and Jonah find out tomorrow?"

"Never mind. Let's go this way." I took two steps up the path. Nehemiah would be heading back to the barn entrance.

Ryan grabbed my arm. "Tell me."

I yanked my arm away from him for the second time that day. "I wish you would stop doing that. We have to get moving. I don't know about you, but I don't want to be lost in the trees in the dark."

"Are you going to talk to Nahum?"

"Ryan, let's go." I started walking again.

"I'm not leaving until you tell me. I'll stand here all night."

I spun around. "What? Are you twelve?"

He folded his arms. It would have been comical if it weren't so ridiculous.

"You will freeze to death."

He shrugged.

"Suit yourself." I headed up the path with Oliver in tow.

I made my way, following the footprints Nehemiah had left behind. The tracks were clear and easy to follow in the moonlight as if the Amish tree farmer had been stomping his way back to the entrance. Considering how angry he had been with his brother, it was certainly possible that he had been stomping.

Oliver stopped and started pulling on his leash and nodding back in the direction that we came.

"Oliver," I complained.

He wiggled his batlike ears at me.

"Ryan made his choice. This is just one of *many* poor decisions he's made in his life."

Oliver barked.

"Ugh. Okay, okay. But I don't agree with this."

Oliver wiggled his hindquarters like he always did when he knew he had won an argument. Sadly for me, this happened more often than I would like to admit.

Oliver and I trudged through the snow, back to the place where I had left Ryan. When I appeared through the trees, Ryan grinned. "I knew you would come back."

"You have Oliver's kind heart to thank, not mine."

"So?" He arched one eyebrow.

"Fine. I don't know why you care, but Jonah and I plan to pay Nahum a visit at his cabin in the morning." I waved him on. "Now, let's go already."

Ryan started to follow me. "I'm coming with you," he said. His mind was made up.

I stopped this time. Now the light was all but gone. However, we were close enough to the entrance that I could see lanterns moving in the trees and hear the sound of people talking and laughing. "Ryan, I'll be with Jonah. I'll be fine."

"Okay." He reached into his coat pocket again and came up with his phone. "I'll just give Sheriff Lover Boy a call and let him know what you have planned. If he doesn't throw you into the county jail for your own protection, I would be surprised."

I closed my eyes for a moment and counted to ten in Pennsylvania Dutch. "Fine. You can come, but it will be early. I will swing by your hotel at seven to pick you up."

He smirked. "Excellent."

Chapter Twenty-two

"Put your back into it," Dad cried as we tried to push the six-foot-tall, still-way-too-big-for-my-house tree through my front door. Mom and Dad were on the inside pulling on the tree, and Ryan and I were on the outside pushing.

"Getting a real tree was such a great idea," Ryan muttered.

"On the count of three. One. Two. Three. Push!"

Ryan and I pushed with all our might. The tree didn't budge, but then there was a crack from one of the branches, which had been snagged on the door-frame, and the tree flew forward.

Mom yelped from the other side, and I sprawled spread-eagle on top of the Douglas fir.

"Huzzah!" Dad crowed. "We did it!"

I rolled off the tree and onto the hardwood floor with a thud. "Ow."

Ryan gave me a hand up. This time I dropped his hand immediately.

Mom, fortunately, was safely all the way across the room. Oliver's eyes bugged out of his head from behind her leg. He couldn't bear to get any closer.

It took another half hour to get the tree upright in the stand that Dad had thought to stop and buy on the way home from the tree farm. Finally, it was up. It looked huge, completely dominating my tiny living room.

"It makes a statement," Dad said.

"Fire hazard," Ryan murmured.

I tried very hard not to smile at the comment but failed, and by his smile, Ryan noticed.

Dodger stared at the tree as if he were Indiana Jones seeing the Holy Grail for the very first time. His thin pewter-colored tail whipped back and forth in anticipation.

Ryan pointed at Dodger. "That's going to be a problem."

I didn't doubt it.

"Okay," I said. "It's time I took Ryan back to the hotel for the night. I'll drop him off, and then I have my trustees' meeting. I should be back in a few hours. I never know how these meetings are going to go."

Dad walked around the tree, examining every angle. "Sounds good, Angie Bear."

"I'll start working on a color scheme for the tree," Mom said.

"Terrific," I replied, and headed for the door. At least the new project would keep my parents occupied.

Oliver had had a long day, which included a bird encounter, so I decided to leave him at home with my parents. I also hoped that he would keep an eye on Dodger, because Ryan was right. Dodger and the Christmas tree were a dangerous combination.

I was thankful that Ryan was quiet on the ride back to the hotel. I think we were both too worn-out from wrestling with the tree to have any conversation about our relationship status. That was fine with me. As far as I was concerned, that door was shut, and Dodger hid the key.

As we drove up the long hill that led to the hotel, I had to marvel at how pretty the place looked with the twinkle lights in the trees and the dozens of windows giving it a warm yellow glow. What had Eve felt after seeing it again for the first time after spending difficult years struggling in New York? Had she found the scene welcoming, or had she suspected trouble instantly? Was the trouble here already in Holmes County from one of her family members, or had she noticed it around her in the acting troupe?

I pulled my car into the hotel's circular front drive.

Ryan opened the door. "You certainly keep it exciting, Angie."

"I try."

He climbed out of the car and held on to the door before closing it. "Don't forget me tomorrow morning."

"You are probably going to regret wanting to tag along." I examined his expensive wool coat, which was still decorated with pine needles from our leap into the trees. "A word of advice—wear something more country tomorrow. From what I hear, Nahum's cabin is way back from the road."

"I'll country it up for you, Miss Braddock. Don't you

worry your pretty little head about that." He slammed the door shut.

Ugh.

As I turned my car around, I passed the barn. The place was lit up, and then I remembered Blake's saying play practice had been postponed until that evening. I parked in an open spot next to the barn. The trustees' meeting would just have to wait.

I entered the barn through the main doors. No one noticed me when I stepped inside, because all of the attention and energy were focused on center stage, where Lena stood in Eve's Amish costume, holding back tears.

Wade marched back and forth in front of her. "No, no, no! That is so off-key!" the director bellowed from the foot of the stage. "Can't you get it right just once? That's all I ask. This production is going down in flames. I will be ruined. First I lose my star, and now I have to deal with an understudy who can't even find middle C!"

"It's not like anyone will notice. This isn't Broadway," Jasper muttered from the wings. "Not even close."

The director jumped on the stage in one leap and got into Jasper's face. "I don't care if this is Broadway or not. We treat every production like it is our last. In your case, it very well might be. If you had secured your set, we wouldn't be in this mess. Eve would still be here, and I wouldn't have to contend with a second-rate soprano."

Ruben, also in his costume, which for his role as an English young man, consisted of a business suit and tie, stepped off his mark. "Wait just a minute, Wade. You know Lena could have outsung Eve any day. In fact, she should have had the lead in the first place. Instead, you gave it to a nobody, and we are all suffering because of it."

Wade's complexion went from white to flaming tomato in two seconds flat. "Hold your tongue. That girl was a better actor than you and your sweetheart have any hope to be. She was destined to be a star."

Lena left her mark and joined Ruben. She whispered something to him.

Ruben frowned at his girlfriend. "I won't keep quiet. It's the truth." He turned back to Wade. "Maybe you should take a minute to notice you're pushing Lena too hard. She can't sing when you are screeching at her. She's just tired and is under too much stress. Give her a break so that she can collect herself. You've been yelling at her, at all of us, for more than an hour. It's a wonder we are able to get through a single scene."

Wade folded his arms. "I have a better chance of going hoarse than she has a chance of hitting the right note."

Lena wiped a tear from her cheek. "I know I can do better, Wade. Just show me you believe in me."

The director threw up his hands. "I don't have any other choice but to use you. We have another performance in three days." He held up three fingers. "Three. Do you know what that means? It means we practice twice every single day before the performance until we are ready."

"What about Christmas?" one of the other actors dressed up like an Amish man asked.

"You all know that you gave up Christmas when you signed up for this play. That hasn't changed."

"But we weren't supposed to have practice on Christmas," the man grumbled.

Wade glared at him. "Well, my star wasn't supposed to die in the middle of the performance either." Wade pointed at Lena. "She's the reason we have practice on Christmas. Now, everyone take five. Lena, this is the role you wanted, and you are wasting it. At this rate, I will have to cancel all the performances if you can't pull it off."

The other actors slunk offstage. Many of them gave Lena accusatory looks for being the reason for practice on Christmas Day. I wouldn't want to be in Lena's position within the acting troupe.

Lena's face turned bright red. "I can hit the notes, Wade. I just need a minute." She covered her face and ran offstage. Ruben followed in her wake.

Jasper strutted into center stage with his hands in his pockets and grinned at Wade. "You are grasping at straws, man, and at a lost dream. I know it must be hard to be back in the small time when you've already seen your name in lights."

Without warning, Wade decked Jasper. The stage manager staggered backward and then catapulted himself at the director. The two men fell onto the stage floor with a bang. They threw punches and kicks at each other as they rolled across the dusty floor. Cast and crew flooded the stage, apparently with the goal of pulling the two men apart. Blake got ahold of Jasper, but he was soon thrown off and landed on his backside a few feet away. No one else dared get that close again. They stood and watched with their mouths hanging open.

I ran toward the stage. "Someone do something before they kill each other."

Collectively the cast and crew turned to me as if I had appeared out of nowhere, which as far as they were concerned, I had.

Jasper and Wade continued to pummel each other and rolled closer and closer to the edge of the stage. Finally, they rolled so close to the edge, they fell off onto the hard pinewood floor.

I winced.

However, the jar of the fall didn't stop them from beating on each other.

I rummaged through my massive purse and came up with a full water bottle. I could always count on my purse in a moment of crisis. I opened the bottle and dumped the contents on the two men.

"What the—," Wade cried.

Jasper crawled away from him. There was a cut over his eyebrow, and his lip was split open and bleeding. Wade didn't look much better. The director had two black eyes and a bloody nose.

Jasper struggled to his feet and looked intent on jumping Wade again. Blake jumped off the stage and took ahold of his boss's arm. "Hey, man, calm down. Calm down."

"I'll kill him," Jasper warned. His pointy, ratlike features twitched.

A chill ran down my spine. Jasper spoke like a man

who had followed through on that promise in the past. Had Eve been the victim last time?

Two young actors helped their director to his feet. Wade wiped the back of his hand across his face, smearing blood across his cheek in the process. He shook the men off him. "This is the end for you, Jasper. I will ruin you." The director turned and half walked, half limped from the floor entrance to the backstage.

"You can't ruin me," Jasper yelled, stomping in the opposite direction.

"What do we do now?" one of the actors asked.

"Um, I guess, take a fifteen-minute break," Blake said.

The cast and crew wandered off the stage, grumbling under their breath. Blake sat at the foot of the stage and spotted me. He hopped to the ground. "What are you doing here?"

I walked down the aisle like I had every right to observe their play practice. "I met you earlier in the lobby when you were playing swords."

Blake's ears turned bright red. "I remember."

"I didn't mention then that I'm a township trustee." I held out my hand, and he shook it. I resisted the urge to wipe my hand on my coat after the handshake. "I dropped in, representing the township trustees' board. We have a meeting tonight, and I wanted to be able to report back how well rehearsals are going."

He flicked his long bangs out of his eyes with a jerk of his head. "Not very well. Everyone is on edge. I guess you might have seen the fight between Jasper and Wade."

"I did," I said, happy he brought up the subject so I

didn't have to. "Do you know what the argument is about?"

He shrugged. "They've known each other forever, longer than I've even been alive."

I eyed him. "How old are you?"

"Nineteen, but I'll be twenty next month," he added quickly.

"You're not much older than the stagehands they hired here in the county."

Blake straightened up to his full height, which was an inch or two shorter than me. "They are just hired help to assist with the heavy lifting. I'm the assistant stage manager, and I have many more responsibilities than they do. Jasper depends on me to keep the show running."

"Like he depended on you to check the swing's ropes before Eve went onstage."

He finger combed his bangs. "How do you know about that?"

"I told you I am a township trustee. We have to know this information in order to better serve the community."

Blake's brow wrinkled as he thought about what I had just said. I hoped he wouldn't think too hard on it. "Do you want me to get Wade for you?"

"No," I said a little too quickly. "I mean, he seems to be very upset. I can talk to him later. You will all be here through Christmas, so I'll have lots of opportunity to see him again."

Blake kicked the leg of one of the padded folding chairs in the audience seating section. "I can't believe

I'm spending my Christmas here. I should quit and go see my parents in Chicago. But I only joined because of Wade in the first place."

"Because of Wade?" I asked.

He stopped kicking the chair. "Don't tell me you don't know who Wade Brooklyn is."

I shook my head. "I don't really follow Broadway."

"He was, like, one of the most famous stage directors in New York. He directed productions on Broadway for nearly twenty years. Everyone wanted to work with him. Bette, Meryl, the entire A-list."

"What happened? Why is he here instead of in New York?" I shifted my bag on my shoulder. I should really take some stuff out of it. It always got heavy by the end of the day.

"That's the mystery. No one knows for sure . . . at least no one I've talked to."

"So Bette and Meryl might know," I joked.

He gave me a withering look. "All I do know is it involved a young actress, and I heard whispering about something being settled out of court. I don't know the actress's name. She wasn't famous or anything. She kind of disappeared after that."

Involved a young actress? I couldn't help but think of Eve.

I tapped a finger to my cheek. "So after whatever happened with Wade and the young actress." I grimaced as I thought of the possibilities. "Then what happened? Wade was kicked out of Broadway?"

"From what I heard, no one asked him to leave. He just did. He disappeared for nearly twenty years, and then an advertisement appears in the trade journals for this production he's directing in Holmes County, Ohio. I applied right away. I wouldn't have another chance to work with such a genius."

I frowned. "So you were willing to spend Christmas away from your family to work with Wade in Ohio, even though he is no longer respected by the Broadway community?"

"Of course. We all were. If this is the beginning of Wade's comeback, he'll take us with him. The man is a genius."

"And Jasper? You said they know each other from way back. Did Wade hire him?"

Blake wrinkled his nose and nodded. "I know he is my supervisor, but I don't know why Wade chose him as the stage manager. He has such a sour disposition." He lowered his voice. "Some of the other crew members say Wade hired him because Jasper knows whatever caused the director's ruin all those years ago. I can't help but think that must be true. No one likes Jasper." He shrugged. "Maybe Wade's just giving someone from his past a chance." He jumped onto the stage without using the stairs and walked to a broken chair. Frowning, he said, "I'm going to try to fix that."

"What happened to it?" I asked, standing just below the stage.

"Wade threw it across the room."

I made a face. "Yikes."

Blake shrugged. "At least he didn't throw a person."

"He throws people?"

"Not yet."

I wanted to ask why Blake assumed Wade would throw a person, but it might have seemed too inquisitive. So instead I asked, "Are the actors afraid of him?"

Blake spun the chair leg in his hands. "I don't think so. I mean everyone is used to a yelling director. You wouldn't make it very far in this business if you weren't."

"Where do you think Wade went?"

Blake frowned. "To smoke. He does that when he's angry. He's been doing it a lot lately. You can probably find him just outside the backstage door."

I thanked Blake and went in search of the play director.

Chapter Twenty-three

The back door had been left open a crack, and I heard angry voices. I peeked out just long enough to see Wade and Jasper glaring at each other. Each man had a lit cigarette in his hand.

"Listen to me. You mess with me and I will expose your story. That wouldn't look too good to the police if they knew. They'd throw you into prison so fast, your head would spin."

I took another look to catch Wade's reaction.

Wade blew smoke out of the side of his mouth. "Fine. But after this production, we're through. Do you hear me?"

Jasper's lips curled. "Loud and clear."

My heart beat faster. I should call Mitchell right away. He needed to find out what the two men were talking about. Why would it land Wade in trouble with the police? Did it have something to do with the young actress twenty years ago? What I really wanted to know was whether it related to Eve's death.

A day ago, I didn't know who could possibly kill the rising star. Today, I had more suspects than I knew what to do with. There were Jasper, Wade, Lena, Ruben, and Nahum, to name a few. How many more suspects would surface before the investigation was over?

I waited a few more beats until I knew Jasper was gone and had stepped outside. I cleared my throat. "Hello, Wade."

"What are you doing here?" he snapped.

"Representing the township; I was just checking to make sure everything is on track." I gave him a bright pageant smile. "And to offer any assistance if you need it."

He took a long drag from his cigarette. "Can you sing? Can you dance? Can you act?"

The wind whipped snow across the field that divided the barn from the main hotel. In the dark, yellow light from the barn's open back door reflected in the snow as it swirled in our faces.

I pulled my stocking cap down over my ears. "Um, no."

"Then what use are you to me?" He waved me away. The wind caught ashes from his cigarette.

"Well," I said, "the township is very sorry for your loss. I was here the night of her performance. Eve was very good." I paused. "How did you discover her?"

He blew the smoke out through clenched teeth. "She found me. She came to my office in New York and auditioned. I knew she was destined to the part, and *not* just because she grew up Amish, although that certainly helped. I don't know how she knew about the production. Most of my advertising for roles had been well off Broadway." He grimaced as if he were reluctant to admit that.

"Her sister told her about the play. I gather she heard about it because she works here at the hotel."

Wade dropped the still-burning cigarette onto the ground and stomped on it with his boot. "A sister. Eve never told me that she had a sister working in the hotel. Of course I knew she was from here, but I didn't know her family was that close to the production." He shrugged. "In any case, she was destined to be a star. I can always tell which kids have it and which ones don't."

I took a step backward, closer to the entrance to the backstage, before I asked my next question. "Is that what you thought about the actress twenty years ago?"

He stepped into my face. "Who told you about that? Was it Jasper?"

He leaned in so close, I could smell the tobacco on his breath. "I paid enough money never to answer that question. I advise you to never ask it again."

My hip hit the side of the barn. The open door was just one step behind me. "I'm sure the sheriff will be curious to find out."

"Listen to me, little girl. You don't want to get involved with this. If you poke your nose in where it doesn't belong, you might lose it altogether."

I resisted the urge to touch the tip of my nose to make sure it was still intact. "I don't scare easy."

He smiled and stepped back. "That's your first mistake."

Instead of slipping into the barn, I stepped around Wade and retreated to the safety of the hotel. I felt the director's eyes on my back throughout the long cold walk. I was so preoccupied with what I had witnessed in the barn and the conversation with Wade, I didn't see Junie materialize out of the snow until it was too late and I collided with her.

I was twice the girl's petite size, and she bounced off me and fell into a snowdrift.

"Junie, are you all right?" I gave her my hand. "I'm so sorry."

Junie rolled back and forth in the drift for a moment, trying to find her footing, but finally, with my help, she stood up.

"I am sorry," she murmured as she brushed snow off her sleeve. "I wasn't watching where I was going."

"Where are you going?"

"The barn. Mimi asked me to tell the people working on the play that supper is ready for them, and then I'm headed home. It's been a very long day."

I couldn't agree more about the length of the day. It felt like I had seen Junie at the hotel three weeks ago instead of just that morning. So much had happened between then and now.

I grimaced. "Right now might not be the best time to deliver the message, at least not to Wade or Jasper."

She wrapped her arms around her waist. "Why not?"

"A small misunderstanding," I said.

If you can call an open brawl in the middle of the stage a misunderstanding.

"I'll just tell Blake, then."

"You know Blake?" I asked.

She blushed, or at least I thought she blushed. I wasn't certain because of the darkness. "I know all the people from the production. I have been tending to their needs for more than two weeks."

"But Wade didn't know that you and Eve were sisters."

She frowned. "If she never told him or any of them, that was her choice. I had no reason to tell them. I barely saw my sister while she was here at the hotel. That's why you are here at the hotel tonight, isn't it? It's about my sister again. I wish you would let it go. *Gott* will sort it out for us all."

I didn't answer, but with Wade's threat ringing in my ears, I was more determined than ever to find out how Eve fell from that swing.

Junie continued on her way to the barn.

"How do you plan to get home?" I asked.

She glanced over her shoulder. "I will walk. It's less than two miles."

The temperature hovered in the single digits. "It's too cold for you to walk home tonight. Let me give you a ride."

She bit her lip. "I can walk home."

"Don't be silly. I can drop you off on the way to my meeting."

"All right. I will just tell Blake about dinner, and we can go." Junie disappeared into the barn.

I marched in place to fight back the cold. I was just thinking about going into the barn to look for her when Junie reappeared. "Did you find Blake?" I asked.

"*Ya,*" she said, but a strange pinched expression washed over her face. The expression came and went so quickly that I didn't know if I imagined it or saw it at all. The only light on the snow-covered walkway between the hotel and barn came from the windows of both buildings.

I shook off the uneasy feeling creeping up my spine. "Let's go."

Snow began to fall, and she opened the car door. "*Danki.*" She gave me directions to her home.

"Work must have been tough today without Eve around."

Junie stared out the window at the snow-and-rain mix pelting the glass.

I bit the inside of my cheek, deciding whether I should press Junie about her sister's death. One question still bothered me: Why did Junie tell Eve about the play? It seemed even stranger, now that I knew that the sisters barely spoke to each other in the two weeks Eve lived in the hotel where Junie worked.

It was a large hotel by Rolling Brook standards, with more than sixty rooms, but it wasn't so big that the sisters wouldn't see each other, especially since Junie seemed to be a jane-of-all-trades in the building, doing everything from waiting tables in the breakfast room, to being a maid, to being a fill-in receptionist. But maybe I was pushing the girl too far when I asked her for information. Junie couldn't be more than nineteen.

"I'm sorry if I keep bringing up Eve."

She continued to stare out the window. "I know you're trying to help." She took a shuddered breath.

"But I still think it is best if you leave this alone. *Gott* will claim his justice. Of this I am sure."

I turned off the main road onto a long country lane. The car bumped on the deep cuts made by buggy wheels in the snow. The back roads were always the last to get plowed. Living in Ohio during the winter has never made me so grateful for my little SUV. I never knew what it was capable of in Dallas.

Junie pointed to a black mailbox ahead, sitting under the soft glow of a lantern. "That's my home. You can stop at the end of the driveway to let me out. *Mamm* always leaves a lantern burning for me at the end of the driveway when the weather is poor. She says that it's to guide me on my way, but I know she watches it. I will blow it out to let her know that I have made it home."

The car rolled to a stop at the end of the drive. I looked up the very long driveway. The house seemed so far away. "Jump out and blow it out, and I will drive you up to the door."

"I can walk from here." She opened her car door. Rain and snow blew into the car's interior.

"Don't be silly. Your driveway is a sheet of ice. I can't let you break your ankle. Plus it is sleeting. You will be frozen by the time you cross the threshold."

"All right." She hopped out of the car, blew out the lantern, and brought it back into the car with her. "*Mamm* will know I am home now."

My car bumped the rest of the way up the uneven driveway. Junie's family must have been in and out of the house often through the winter. The buggy wheel ruts were much deeper here than they had been on the road. "I'm sure your parents will be happy you made it home safe and sound. And your brothers and sisters too."

"Eve was my only sister."

"Oh, I'm sorry. I shouldn't have assumed you had other siblings."

"Because I am Amish, you thought I came from a large family, but my family is very small." She paused.

I watched the house grow bigger in my windshield as the wiper blades moved back and forth on the glass. The farmhouse's front door opened, and a petite Amish woman with a thick wool cape wrapped around her body stood in the doorway, holding a lantern identical to the one in Junie's lap.

I shifted the car into park.

"Thank you for the ride," Junie called as she hopped out of the car before I could reply.

In the light of the lantern, the woman, who I could only assume was Junie's mother, stopped her daughter from dashing into the house by touching her arm. The pair spoke for a moment before Junie went into the house. Instead of following her daughter inside, Junie's mother held the lantern high as she approached my car.

I powered down the passenger side window.

"Guten Nacht," she said as she peered into my car. I was shocked by how much Esther looked like Eve. I could almost see the girl in her mother's face. There was no resemblance between her and Junie. I wondered if the younger Shetler sister took after her father. "I am Junie's mother. Please call me Esther. *Danki* for

bringing Junie home on such a terrible night. Please come in for a cup of *kaffe*."

I hesitated. If I accepted her offer, I would certainly be late for the trustees' meeting, and I was already on thin ice with Head Trustee Caroline Cramer for tardiness in the past. Then again, this might be my only opportunity to speak with Eve's mother.

I unbuckled my seat belt. "I would love a cup of coffee, especially on such a frigid night like this."

"*Gut*. You can leave your car right here. We don't expect any visitors tonight." She turned and headed back to the house, fully expecting me to follow, which I did.

My ugly boots crunched in the snow as we crossed the yard.

Instead of going in through the front door where I saw her waiting with the lantern in vigil for her younger and only remaining daughter, she led me to a side door.

Chapter Twenty-four

By the way the snow was packed down in this part of the yard, I could tell that the side door was the commonly used entrance. The door opened directly into the kitchen. A round kitchen table sat in one corner of the large room. On the table a chain of popcorn and cranberries was under construction, and two bowls of each sat on the table.

"I used to love making those with my aunt when I was a child," I said.

Junie's mother removed her cloak and hung it on the peg by the kitchen door. I did the same with my ski coat.

"I haven't made any in years, but I was at the mercantile this morning and saw the cranberries," she said. "I could not resist. Evie—"

"*Mamm.*" Junie touched her mother's arm.

"*Nee*, I am fine, Junie. Why don't you check on the cornbread in the oven? It should be just about done. We are having a simple and late supper tonight. Your *daed* went to the tree farm not long ago to lend a hand to your uncle."

Junie dropped her hand. *"Ya, Mamm."*

Esther fell into her seat. "I was inspired to make it because it was Evie's favorite Christmas decoration. She always liked decorations since she was a very small child. I should have known then that she wouldn't remain Amish."

I removed my gloves and stuck them into the large pockets of my coat. "Do you make them to hang inside your house?"

Esther sat at the kitchen table and gestured for me to do the same. "Sometimes, but more often we make dozens of them and hang them on the pine trees in the yard to feed the birds. It can be hard for them to find food during the winter, and it is especially hard during a winter this harsh." She picked up a plump cranberry and rolled it back and forth in the palm of her hand. "I thought it would be a good remembrance for Evie this Christmas to do it again. I don't tell my husband this is why. He would not understand." She dropped the cranberry into the bowl and threaded a needle. "My husband didn't understand anything when it came to Evie."

Junie silently moved around the kitchen during our conversation. She was so quiet that I forgot she was there until she set a steaming mug of coffee in a plain white cup in front of me on the table.

Esther slid a pincushion, thread, and bowl of popcorn across the table to me. "Since your aunt gave you Running Stitch, I assume that you are good with a needle. You can start a new string."

"I'm not bad," I said as I removed a needle from the cushion and snipped off a long piece of thread.

She laughed and stuck her needle through a cranberry. "I knew your *aenti* very well. She was a *gut* woman, a pillar of the community. She came to see me after Eve left. She assured me that Eve must choose her own path that *Gott* wanted for her."

I could see Aunt Eleanor doing that. Even in the darkest pit of her cancer, she encouraged and comforted others.

Esther bent over her popcorn and cranberry chain and shook her head. A large tear landed on one of the cranberries like a drop of rain. "I don't know how being an actress was part of *Gotte's* plan for my elder daughter. It went against everything we were or wanted for her."

I placed a handful of popcorn and another handful of cranberries in front of me on the tabletop, not knowing what to say to comfort her.

When I was silent, she continued. "Everyone in the district loved Eve before she left. That was why it was so heartbreaking when she made her decision to go. I think of the life she could have had. She could have done so well here. She had the pick of the young men. She would have had children and been happy and alive."

I stabbed a piece of popcorn with my needle. "But she wanted a different kind of life."

She strung three pieces of popcorn in silence. "One I couldn't give her."

"Junie said that you would still be handling the funeral. I'm glad for that."

"It will be at the gravesite as soon as the sheriff . . ." She took a breath. "As soon as the sheriff releases her body to us. Since Evie was no longer Amish, our bishop and elders won't preside over the burial. A minister from the Mennonite meetinghouse offered to come and give prayers for the quiet service. Only Junie and I will be there."

"Your husband?" I asked.

She shook her head. "*Nee.* Noah won't attend. It would be too difficult for him. You have to excuse my husband. He is as distraught as I am over Eve's passing." She dabbed at the corner of her eye with a dish towel. "But to him she was lost years ago when she went to New York. I held on to the hope that she would come back. My *mamm* said the secret of the home is women were always tougher than their husbands. I believe that now."

"May I come?" I asked. "I would like to come. I didn't know Eve long, but she made an impression on me during that time." I paused. "And I think her friend Amber would like to come too."

She nodded. "I will have Junie tell you when it is time. I guess you will know how to tell Amber, as we . . ."

"I do." I stabbed two cranberries with my needle and squirted myself in the eye with cranberry juice.

Esther handed me her handkerchief with a sad smile, but she did not comment on the cranberry juice.

I wiped at my eye and chuckled. "I'm used to working with fabric. There's no juice in fabric."

She offered me the tiniest of smiles. "*Nee*, I suppose there is not."

I folded the handkerchief and placed it on the table. "Were you happy when you heard of Eve's return to Holmes County?"

She nodded. "I was so happy to see her, but I knew it would be difficult too." She sighed. "Part of me hoped that when she got back, we could start again. Maybe she would remember what she gave up for her *Englisch* life and want to return to our way. If she did, all would be forgiven. She would be welcomed back into the community like a long-lost daughter. That is why Junie mentioned that play was coming to the hotel. I told Junie to write to her sister and ask her to join the play."

I glanced at Junie, who was focused on the task of drying and putting away the dishes. "Why didn't you write her yourself?" I asked.

"I couldn't do that. Eve left the community. My husband was very angry when she left and forbid me to contact her. He never told Junie directly that she couldn't speak to her sister, which is why I asked Junie to write the letter about the play to Eve. I know it was wrong that we disobeyed the spirit of my husband's order, but I so desperately wanted to see my elder daughter again. It was the only way. I would never travel into her world in New York City." She held the dish towel to her chest. "When she wrote us two months ago to tell us that she got the part, I was so happy. Now I wish I never asked Junie to write. At least then I would know she was alive and had a chance to return to our ways one day." She dabbed at her eyes with the towel. "I am sorry."

Without a word, Junie refilled the white coffee mug in front of her mother. The girl wore a pained expression. I had to look away. The grief, both mother's and daughter's, was too stark.

"I'm so sorry for your loss." My voice caught. "Anyone who met her knew Eve was special."

"She was," Esther said. "She was."

I wrapped my hands around the plain white mug. "So you didn't see Eve when she returned to the county?"

"I did once. I went to the hotel to see her. She didn't know I was there. I peeked into the barn when she practiced her songs for the play. Had my husband known, he would have been so angry with me, but I had to see her. My only regret is that I didn't speak to her, didn't get the chance to tell her I loved her. But I could not; it is not our way."

What I was going to ask next would be uncomfortable, but I pressed on. "But she had to know many Amish weren't happy she returned to Holmes County. Nahum Shetler made his disapproval of Eve's return known."

"Nahum is my husband's brother." Esther pinched a piece of popcorn so hard in her hand that it crumpled into a dozen tiny pieces on the table. "I do not care for him. He's wild and can't be trusted."

I selected another piece of popcorn. "Do you think he would hurt Eve? Did he have any reason to?"

"Does anyone have any reason to hurt another person? As Amish, we are nonviolent, and we would say no."

True, the Amish were nonviolent in their teaching, but if my life in Holmes County had taught me anything, it was that some of them fall short in the practice.

"Whatever he might call himself, I don't consider Nahum to be in my Amish family any longer," she added. "But I don't believe my brother-in-law is capable of hurting Eve. I know it was one of those theater people."

I was beginning to agree with her, especially after overhearing that conversation between Jasper and Wade. I hoped that the sheriff had been able to check into Wade's background by now.

Water sloshed out of the pot that Junie carried onto the floor. Junie cried out as some hot water splashed her ankles.

Mrs. Shetler snapped at her daughter in Pennsylvania Dutch.

I jumped out of my seat. "Are you burnt?"

Junie replaced the kettle to the stove with shaky hands. "*Nee*, the water wasn't that hot. I was startled, that was all."

I grabbed a dish towel from the handle on the oven door and wiped at the floor.

Junie squatted next to me. "You should go," she whispered. "*Mamm* is upset."

I stood and handed her the towel. Junie was right. "Thank you for the coffee."

Esther smiled. "Thank you for coming. It was kind

of you to stop and chat. It's not often I am able to speak so freely about Evie. I'm afraid others in my community like to pretend that she never was. But she was, and she was my daughter."

As I left the house, I bit my lip to hold back tears for a life wasted and the grieving mother left behind.

Chapter Twenty-five

The township trustees' meeting at Willow Moon's tea shop, the Dutchman's Tea Shop, had been scheduled to begin at eight. I ran into the shop in a cloud of wind and snow twenty minutes late.

When I burst through the door, Wanda's customers stared at me. I gave them my best winning smile.

One of Willow's waitresses, a teenaged Amish girl, swerved around me with a steaming teapot in one hand and a tray of teacups in the other. She was light on her feet and avoided the collision.

Willow waved at me from a corner table. The other members of the board were already there. Tablets, both electronic and traditional paper, covered the table's service amidst teapots, cups, and small plates of cucumber sandwiches. The sight of the cucumber sandwiches made my stomach rumble.

Farley Jung, former head trustee, pulled out the empty chair next to him and patted the seat. Why did I think he had kept that seat empty on purpose?

I grimaced but sat. "I'm so sorry I'm late."

"What held you up?" Willow asked. She was the only one who smiled at me.

I cleared my throat. "I had stopped at the hotel to check on play practice. I thought you all would appreciate a report on that, and I gave Junie, one of the maids, a last-minute ride home."

Willow clapped her hands. "That was so good of you, Angie. This weather is far too harsh for a young girl to be walking in it."

I ducked my head. "Thank you, Willow." I sat in one of the white mismatched dining chairs around the circular table.

Willow picked up the teapot in the middle of the table and poured tea into my cup. I peered into the teacup. "What's this?" The mixture smelled suspect, and I had been burned, literally, so many times before by Wanda's strange tea recipes that I was wary of them.

"Peppermint tea," Willow said.

It smelled like more than peppermint to me.

Jason widened his eyes in warning over his cucumber sandwich.

Willow beamed. "I'm so glad that you are all here. You can taste my new tea."

A collective "No" went up from the other trustees. I think it was the one and only time that we were all in agreement.

Willow wrinkled her nose. "Oh, you. I made a few missteps in the past. That's no reason for alarm."

"Missteps?" Farley asked. "I think your last recipes burned off fifty percent of my taste buds."

"Oh, pooh," Willow said. "You're exaggerating."

Head Trustee Cramer sniffed. "Now that Angela is finally here, we can start the meeting." Then she pursed her lips. "Find another group to be your tea testers, Willow. We have very important business this evening." She tapped her gavel on the table.

Jason made a grab at his teacup, which threatened to topple over.

"You don't really need to use the gavel, Caroline," Willow said. "That is only for public meetings."

Caroline glowered at her. She pushed the gavel to the center of the table and folded her hands in front of her. "I would like to hear what you learned at the play practice, Angie. Please give a report. I would also like to hear exactly what happened when Eve fell. Willow has already given her account. What is yours?"

"A report?" I asked with a cucumber sandwich halfway to my mouth.

"You were there for the quilt show, were you not?" Caroline arched her brow. "And you were at the progressive dinner itself, so you should know what is going on."

Willow sipped her Christmas surprise tea and hid a grimace. "I suppose it could use a little more peppermint extract or sugar. Maybe the cranberry was a bad idea." She raised her cup to me. "I'm sure Angie knows much more than the two things that you mentioned. She's been sleuthing. Haven't you?"

I felt four pairs of eyes on my face. I wanted to jump across the table and cover Willow's mouth.

I cleared my throat. "Willow and I were both at the

play when the swing broke, killing Eve. I met Eve briefly at the dinner before the play. I thought she was a lovely girl. It's a tragedy for Amish and English in the community."

"It's a publicity nightmare," Farley said. "That's what it is."

I wasn't surprised by Farley's comment. I glared at him. He merely smiled back. My ick factor with Farley went up another two notches.

"Is the sheriff close to solving the case?" Jason asked. Again the question was directed at me.

"Why are you asking me that? You should ask the sheriff."

Jason rolled his eyes. "Come on, Angie, everyone knows that you two are a couple. He had to have said something to you."

"He told me to stay out of the investigation."

"At least that's sound advice," Caroline said. "So you went to play practice tonight. Did they appear to be on track?"

I peered into my cup of not-just-peppermint tea to hide a grimace. I didn't think the stage manager and director getting into a fistfight constituted going well. "Eve had an understudy, Lena Luca. She's already re-hearsing for the part. They mean to continue. I believe they plan to have rehearsals late into the night tonight and more on Christmas Eve and Christmas Day."

Willow clicked her tongue. "That's awful. They should take the holiday off."

Caroline patted the back of her pristine French roll. "No, that is good. They need to have as many practices as they can to make sure this performance goes off without a hitch."

Was she calling Eve's death a mere hitch?

"Let's get back to the task at hand and focus on damage control. Hopefully, with the township practically shut down over Christmas, the Rolling Brook rumor mill will settle down and give us an opportunity to launch the next progressive dinner with much less notoriety."

"You plan to continue the dinners?" Willow asked.

"The show must go on," Caroline said. "We can't afford the refunds. The money is already spent."

"How can the money already be spent?" I asked. "It was earmarked for a new playground. There's like two feet of snow outside. Kids aren't playing outside now."

"Production hasn't started, but we have already signed the contract with the contractor. We are bound to go through with it now."

I bit my lip.

"The contractor gave us a discount to sign early," Caroline said.

"You paid before the work was even started?" Jason groaned.

Farley shook his head. "It is not how I would do it."

Caroline's jaw twitched. "You are no longer the head trustee, Farley. I wish you would remember that. In any case, play practice seems to be on track, so I see no reason to cancel the dinner."

As long as the actors and director can settle their differences first, I thought. I didn't share that concern with the trustees.

She pointed her gavel at me. "Since you're at the hotel for your quilt show, Angie, I want you to keep an eye on the play. Let me know if they look like they are having any complications."

Complications? The play was having more than a few of those.

Willow dumped a full tablespoon of raw sugar into her teacup. That didn't speak well for the flavor of the tea. "I think Angie should find out who the killer is. That will make sure everything goes smoothly. Having a murderer on the loose is a tad unnerving."

I stirred my tea. The acrid scent filled my nose. There was no way I was drinking that.

Caroline frowned. "What if it's one of the actors? Then the play will have to be canceled." She shook her head. "It would be best if the crime was solved after the performances are over."

Willow dropped her spoon. "You can't really mean that."

Jason drummed his fingers on the table.

"Jason, is something wrong?" Caroline asked. "You've barely said two words this entire meeting."

"Are you worried about Amber?" I asked.

Jason's head snapped in my direction.

"What does Jason's daughter have to do with anything?" Caroline asked.

"She and Eve were best friends," I said.

I felt Farley watching me. "My, Angie. You are good at finding out everyone's past, aren't you?"

I ignored him.

Jason pursed his lips. "Amber will be fine."

Willow reached across the table and patted Jason's hand. "I'm so sorry to hear that. I didn't know."

The trustee nearly toppled his full teacup. "My daughter will be fine."

Willow clapped her hands. "Does Amber know anything about what happened? Did Eve say anything to her about being afraid?"

Jason scowled. "My daughter is not involved in this in any way, and I don't appreciate your implying otherwise."

I thought of the threatening letters that Eve had received. Amber knew a lot more than Jason thought or wished to think. Now would not be a good time to tell him that I had already spoken to her. I hoped that she wouldn't tell her father I'd stopped by the library.

"If she was your daughter's best friend," Willow said, "then you must have known her fairly well."

Jason picked up another cucumber sandwich. "I've known Eve since she was a little girl and feel awful about what happened. Her family is devastated."

"Oh, I can imagine," Willow said. She pressed a folded napkin to the corner of her eye. "It's just too terrible for words. And she had a voice like an angel. It's all just such a terrible shame."

Farley cleared his throat. "What I think is that we should draw the killer out, and that will resolve everything."

"But the play," Caroline said.

Farley pursed his lips. "I believe that finding the killer is more important than the play." He turned to me. "Wouldn't you agree, Angie?"

"I do," I said. It wasn't often I agreed with Farley Jung.

"How do we do it?" Willow asked.

"At the progressive dinner, we will make a big show over how wonderful Eve was. We will rub salt in the wound and see if they will confess because of guilt." Farley sipped from a glass of water. Just like every other trustee, he didn't touch his tea.

"And if the killer doesn't feel bad about it?" Caroline asked.

"Then we are dealing with a dark person, indeed."

I shivered. I had faced my share of killers in the last few months, but I didn't want to come face-to-face with anyone like Farley described.

"Who is going to do this?"

"I think Angie should make the speech. She can represent the trustees at the next dinner. You are very clever, Angie. You will know what to say."

Willow nodded. "I suppose it is worth a try if it will bring peace back to our community."

I held up my hands. "Wait a minute. I didn't agree to do this. This is a bad idea. If the killer loses it, it could put the diners in danger."

"No one will do anything with that many witnesses at the table," Farley said coolly. "Angie, you are the best person for the job. Everyone at the play and hotel knows you by now. If another one of us does it, it won't hold as much meaning."

I was always the best person for the job in the trustees' opinions. I don't know if it was because I was most gullible or because I was the lowest person on the totem pole. In either case, I was stuck. At the same time, a tiny part of me thought Farley might be right.

"Will you do it, Angie?" Jason asked.

"If I have a chance." I looked them each in the eye. "I'm promising you nothing."

Farley grinned as if I had said yes with one hundred percent certainty.

Chapter Twenty-six

The next morning, as I drove to the hotel to pick up Ryan for the excursion to Nahum's shack, I kept hoping that he had forgotten about it so Jonah and I could go on our own. No such luck. Ryan waited for me on the hotel's front porch.

He climbed into the car, holding two travel mugs of coffee. He handed one to me. "Extra cream and sugar, just as you like it."

I accepted the mug. "Since when have you encouraged my sugar habit?"

He buckled his seat belt. "Since I've been trying to win you back," he said matter-of-factly. "Watching your high sugar consumption would be a tiny price to pay to be with you."

I sipped the coffee and didn't reply. He had made it just how I liked it. Drat.

Ryan glanced in the backseat. "No Oliver?"

"I thought it would be best to leave him at home with Dodger and my parents. I don't know what to expect at Nahum's and neither should you. The guy is a loose cannon."

Ryan straightened in his seat. "All the more reason I should go along to protect you."

I rolled my eyes.

The woods near Nahum's house weren't discoverable by GPS, and I had to follow the directions that Jonah had given me the day before in the library parking lot. I turned down a one-lane road that I suspected was dirt or gravel under the thick layer of snow. I gunned the engine of my car and pushed through the terrible conditions. In snow this high, even my SUV could get stuck, and the last thing I wanted was to be stuck in the winter on a country road alone with Ryan Dickinson.

"Is it wrong that I have the theme music of *Deliverance* playing over and over in my head?" Ryan asked.

I groaned. "You are such a city boy."

I saw sunlight reflecting off the orange "slow moving vehicle" triangle on the back of Jonah's buggy before I saw the buggy itself. I started to relax. Jonah would provide a buffer between Ryan and me.

I parked behind him. "We're here," I said.

Ryan glanced around. "Where is here?"

I unbuckled my seat belt. "I don't know, but this is where Jonah asked me to meet him, so it must be close to Nahum's home." I opened the door. "Come on, City Boy."

Ryan grinned.

Okay, the teasing was a bad idea. It was only encouraging him.

Jonah raised his eyebrows at me when we stepped out of the car.

"Ryan's coming along with us. I hope that's okay." I pulled my purple stocking cap down over my ears, thinking that I should have doubled up on the long underwear. It was freezing.

"Oh-kay," my best childhood friend said in a voice that implied you had better tell me why later.

I buried my gloved hands into my pockets and tried to make myself as small as possible. The smaller I was, the warmer I would be. "So where's Nahum's cabin? Just beyond those trees?"

Jonah nodded. "*Ya*, but it is a ways yet. This is the closest we can get by buggy. From here, we walk."

"Walk?" Ryan asked, peering into the dense forest. "Are you serious?"

Jonah smiled. "Of course. If you want, you can wait here for Angie and me until we come back. I hope you both have your snow boots on."

I was dressed for the North Pole. Ryan wore a hat, scarf, and leather gloves with his expensive long winter coat. Jonah made a face. "We might have to go through some brambles."

"Fine with me," Ryan said. "I can always buy another coat. Angie is the only irreplaceable thing here."

Jonah's eyebrows disappeared under the long bangs of his bowl haircut. "All right. Follow me." Jonah stepped through the tree line.

I followed him, but Ryan hesitated. I looked back. "You coming? You can stay here like Jonah said."

Ryan frowned. "Of course I'm coming," he said as if he never had any second thoughts.

Once we broke through the tree line into the forest

proper, the snow wasn't as deep and the walking became easier.

"The dense tree coverage holds back some of the snow," Jonah said. "But don't be fooled. There are some very deep drifts back here. Watch where you are walking."

I concentrated on my footing and tried not to think about how angry Mitchell would be if he knew where I was at the moment. Or how much angrier he would be if he knew that Ryan was with me. I sighed. The sooner Ryan went back to Dallas, the sooner my life became less complicated. I glanced over my shoulder. Ryan stared at his feet as he walked. His wool coat was dragging in the snow. An unexpected smile formed on my lips as I watched him. Ryan was a long way from the courtrooms and posh dinner parties of Dallas. So was I.

Ryan looked up and caught me smiling at him.

Shoot. I spun around, but not before a hopeful look lit in his eyes. Bringing Ryan on this excursion had been a very, very bad idea.

I picked up my pace and caught up to Jonah, who moved through the forest with the confidence of a lumberjack. I hopped over a fallen log to catch him.

"Don't get too fancy with your steps," Jonah said. "You don't know what is under the snow. There could be a log or rock that will make you fall."

He had a point. I took my steps much more carefully after that.

Snow crunched under my ugly boots as we crept through the forest.

"I can't believe I let you talk me into this," Jonah grumbled under his breath.

"Come on, you used to always be up for an adventure." I jumped over a fallen log.

"That was before. I have a family to worry about now." He took the edge off his words with a grin. "You know I got in a lot less trouble with *Daed* and *Mamm* when you moved away."

I snorted. "That's not how Anna tells it."

He stepped closer to me. "What's he doing here?"

I sighed. "Ryan figured out where I was going and insisted that he come along or he would tell the sheriff what I was up to."

"We can't have that," Jonah said.

"No, we can't. Mitchell would—"

He put a finger to his lips.

"Do you hear something?" I whispered, listening. All I could hear was the steady crunch of Ryan's footsteps in the snow as he caught up with us.

"I thought I did. It might have just been a squirrel. The woods will play tricks on you if you're not careful."

I stumbled on a rock buried in the snow; then I bounced off a sapling, which dumped its snow down the back collar of my coat. "Yeow!" I cried.

Ryan ran to me. "Angie, are you okay?"

"Could you make any more noise?" Jonah asked.

Ryan helped me up.

"I'm sorry. It caught me by surprise. That's all." I brushed what snow I could off me.

Ryan still gripped my elbow.

"Ryan, I'm fine. You can let go of me now," I said.

He dropped his hand.

"Shh!" Jonah held a finger to his mouth. "I thought I heard something again."

The three of us stood frozen and listened to the woods. In my mind, I heard the theme music of *Deliverance* too. I had Ryan to thank for putting that idea in my head.

A flock of hardy starlings twittered above us.

"Was it the birds?" I whispered.

"I hope so," Jonah whispered back. "Nahum would not like it if he thought we were sneaking up on his cabin."

I shivered.

"Let's keep moving," Jonah said, holding a branch until Ryan and I passed it.

He let go of the branch and it whipped back, releasing a cloud of snow in its wake. "You don't think your *mamm* will bring up the time I broke her favorite lamp when we were kids at Christmas Eve dinner, right?"

I laughed. "What made you think about that?"

"It's been on my mind. I don't think she's ever forgiven me. Maybe she won't. She said nothing to me on the progressive-dinner wagon ride."

"She's biding her time," I teased. "But I predict before they head back to Texas, you will hear about the incident at least twice."

Jonah sighed. "I have a feeling my boys will grow up with some stories like that."

"Ethan and Ezra already have more stories than they could ever possibly share when it comes to mischief making."

Jonah laughed.

Ryan was silent during our conversation, but I knew he was listening to every word.

We heard a snap like a limb breaking in the forest and then the whoosh as it tumbled through the trees to the forest floor.

"Is it safe here?" I asked.

"Sometimes tree branches will crack under the weight of snow and ice."

Great.

"That makes me feel safe," Ryan muttered.

Jonah shrugged. "Just be on the lookout for any falling branches."

Duly noted.

We walked in silence for a few more minutes. I listened for more falling branches.

"I know Amish live off the grid, but aren't they supposed to be close to their district?" Ryan asked.

Jonah glanced over his shoulder. "Most live closer together, but there are loners even in the Amish world. Not many. Amish who want to live outside of the community are looked down upon."

"I'm guessing Nahum doesn't much care what his district says," I said.

"Nahum doesn't care what anyone says about him. He is still Amish in how he dresses and what technology he uses, but he doesn't answer to any district. From what I hear, his old bishop doesn't know what to do with him and would like him just to stay away."

"Then why was he upset about Eve Shelter being in that play?" I asked.

"From what I gather, he still believes in the Amish religion. He just interprets it as he sees fit. I guess Eve's acting didn't follow whatever it is he believes about the Amish." Jonah stepped over a rock peeking out of the snow. "You will be able to ask him yourself soon enough. We are almost to his cabin."

The trees parted into a clearing. In the middle of it was the small building. The word "shack" was a perfect description for it. It had four walls and a roof, but they looked like they were held together by a little glue and prayers. Nahum stood on the roof with a shovel, pushing large piles of snow over the side.

"What is he doing?" Ryan asked.

"He's shoveling his roof. Just like heavy snow can break branches, it can also cave in a roof," Jonah whispered.

"Sheesh, should I be worried about my house?" I asked.

Jonah shook my head. "*Nee*. Nahum's roof is flat. Yours has a peak. It should be fine as long as we don't get five feet of snow."

My mouth fell open. "Does that happen?"

"Rarely."

That didn't make me feel better either.

Nahum's head snapped up. "Who's there?" he bellowed from the roof.

I winced. We had been found out.

Chapter Twenty-seven

"I said, 'Who's there?'" Nahum bellowed again. "Show
yourself." He held the shovel like a javelin as if he
would throw it at us as soon as we appeared out of
the trees.

"Okay," Jonah whispered. "Here's your chance to talk
to him. But when I say it's time to go, it's time to go.
Understand?"

"All right," I said.

Jonah looked to Ryan. "What about you?"

"Fine with me." Ryan folded his arms. "The sooner
we get out of here the better. The man looks deranged."

Jonah nodded and started toward the clearing. Was
he agreeing with Ryan that Nahum was deranged?

Jonah glanced over his shoulder when Ryan and I
didn't follow him. "Are you two coming? You were the
ones who wanted to talk to him."

"He does look a little crazy," I said.

"That's because he is crazy," Jonah whispered before
stepping out of the trees.

Oh well, that made me feel so much better. I followed Jonah into the clearing. Ryan was a few steps behind me.

Nahum pushed a large pile of snow off his roof, and it cascaded over the side like a snowy waterfall. He then climbed down the ladder. "Jonah Graber, what are you doing on my land, and what are you doing bringing *Englischers* here?"

Jonah greeted Nahum in Pennsylvania Dutch. "Stay here," Jonah whispered to us, and cautiously approached the other Amish man.

The two men spoke in their own language, and Nahum repeatedly jabbed his shovel into the snow as if to make a point.

"I'm thinking this was a very bad idea," Ryan whispered into my ear.

I would never let him know it, but I silently agreed. It would have been better for me to speak to Nahum on neutral ground, and preferably somewhere he didn't have access to a shovel.

Jonah waved us over. Ryan and I shuffled within ten feet of them. I hoped that was out of range of the swinging shovel.

"We wanted to talk to you about your niece," Jonah said in English.

"You and everyone else." Nahum leaned on his shovel. "The sheriff and one of his deputies were here just after first light. Doesn't anyone understand that I have work to do? My homestead is not going to take care of itself."

I suspected that he used the word "homestead"

loosely. Broken bits of furniture and farm equipment poked out of the snow in the yard. With the snow as deep as it was, it was hard to tell from where exactly all the pieces of metal and wood originated. We would have to watch our steps. I tried to remember when I last had a tetanus shot.

"What did the sheriff want?" Jonah asked.

Nahum glowered. "Same as you wanted, to talk to me about the girl."

"You mean your niece," I said.

"Anyone who would fall under the world's spell like that is no relation of mine." He spat.

Ryan wrinkled his nose. Nahum certainly wasn't the kind of guy he usually hung out with. The corporate crooks Ryan represented in court were much more refined.

"What did you tell them?" I asked.

"That I didn't have anything to do with her falling. It was *Gotte*'s justice being served. She had it coming for falling away."

I took a step back from his venom.

Nahum glared at Ryan. "Who are you? You look like you're from the city. Are you a fed?"

Ryan cleared his throat. "I am from the city. I'm not a federal agent. I am here as Angie's friend to protect her."

"Protect her from what?" He snorted. "From me? You have no need to worry on that account. I don't have any interest in hurting anyone."

"But Eve—," I started.

"I told you I had nothing to do with that," he

snapped. "Since I am still here as you can see, the policeman believed me." Nahum abandoned his shovel and walked toward his front door. "You can come in if you want. I have *kaffe*."

I raised my eyebrow at Jonah.

"A cup of *kaffe* would be nice," Jonah said, and followed the other Amish man through the door.

Ryan grabbed Jonah's arm. "Do you think this is wise?"

"*Nee*," Jonah said. "But we came all this way for Angie to ask him her questions. It's best to get that over with, and it's too cold to stand out here all day." Jonah followed Nahum into the house.

I waited a couple of beats before I followed.

The door creaked on its hinges when I pushed it in. I definitely would not have gone inside had I been alone. I'm not that dumb. I wasn't even sure if we should be inside the shack with Nahum. Hadn't everyone been telling me for the last two days that he was crazy?

Inside the shack, there was one simple open room. In today's Realtor-speak, they would spin it as an open floor plan. The room was sparse and surprisingly clean. Apparently, Nahum just tossed unwanted items into his littered front yard. A dry sink and small table with four chairs denoted the kitchen area. There were no dishes in the sink, and the counter was bare and dry.

Nahum's sparse wardrobe hung from pegs lining the wall next to his bed.

A black potbellied stove sat in one corner of the single-room cabin. A rocking chair with a worn black leather Bible sat on top of it. Nahum removed one of the cast-iron burner covers with his bare hands. I winced. The metal had to be hot. He filled a blue speckled coffeepot with coffee grounds and scooped snow out of the bucket.

I did my best to hide my grimace. Any of the germs in the snow would boil out. At least that was what I told myself.

"Have a seat." Nahum gestured to the table.

Jonah and I sat. Ryan remained standing near the door. I knew it was for easy escape if need be.

Nahum picked up the coffeepot from the burner on the potbellied stove. "*Kaffe* just needs a warm-up. It won't be long." He looked at me. "It might be a tad bitter for you, but it's how I like it."

Interesting that Nahum would like his coffee bitter. Somehow that seemed the perfect flavor for him.

The Amish man grabbed three empty white mugs from the cupboard and set them on the table. He sat in a third chair. "What can I tell you about Eve? That is what you want to know, right?"

I nodded.

"Eve was the perfect name for her—the first woman to have sinned. Eve Shetler was fallen just like the original Eve." He slammed his fist on the table.

Jonah caught the mugs before they toppled over. Fortunately, they were still empty. Ryan took a step toward the table, but Jonah shook his head. Ryan fell back into his post by the door.

I gritted my teeth. I respected the Amish and their beliefs, but equating Eve's dream of being a star in a play to original sin was a little much for me to swallow. How could this man be Rachel's father? Rachel was the sweetest, kindest person I knew. Maybe it had been for the best that my friend had been raised by her mother's family. I hated the thought that she might have grown up with this man.

"Yes, Eve left the Amish," I said, "but every Amish person has to make that choice. Even you made one. Are you just bitter because she left the Amish for New York?"

"Why should I care where she went when she left the county? I only care that she came back and disgraced our people in such a public way. Don't you realize that those *Englischers* producing the play made everything they could out of the fact that Eve had been raised Amish?" He stood and picked the coffeepot up off the burner. He brought it back to the table and filled the three mugs. The coffee looked as appetizing as one of Willow's signature teas. "They will make just as much out of her now that she's dead. It's all a popularity contest. She did not have to come back here and stir up all this trouble."

I didn't touch my drink; Jonah glanced inside of his mug but made no move to sip from it either. Nahum took a long pull from his coffee, unconcerned that it was blazing hot.

"Maybe she wanted to see her family again. Maybe this was the best way to do that," I said.

Nahum snorted. "My brother won't see her."

"Why did you have such a problem with her being in the play?" I asked.

"Because she mocks the Amish." He smacked his hand on the table this time. Jonah was ready and steadied all the mugs.

"Why do you care?" I blurted out. "You aren't really part of the Amish community."

Jonah looked as if he wished I were in striking distance so that he could elbow me in the ribs.

Nahum peered at me over his coffee mug. "I'm still Amish and can take offense at someone making a mockery of my people."

I opened my mouth, but Jonah jumped in. "Every person must make their decision during *rumspringa* whether to stay within the community or go. Eve made hers."

"Then she should have gone and stayed gone. I went over to that hotel and told her as much. Not that she listened." Nahum's eyes narrowed.

I leaned forward, and the chair beneath me creaked. "When was that?"

"The day she died. A few hours before she went onstage. I went to the hotel to talk to her and found her outside in the snow. She screamed when I walked up to her. I wasn't going to hurt her. I just wanted her to know that she wasn't welcome here."

That must have been right before I nearly hit Nahum with my car in the parking lot. I suspected Eve already knew by that point that many Amish didn't want her in the county, especially those in her own family.

"Why did she scream?" Ryan asked from the doorway.

Nahum turned to him as if he had forgotten Ryan was

there. I knew I almost had because all my energy was intent on Nahum and watching for what he might do.

"Because she was afraid," was Nahum's simple answer.

"Afraid?" Jonah asked.

"She looked it to me. Or maybe she was just skittish. I told her my piece. Whatever good that did, and she claimed she had to stay in the play. She didn't have a choice to back out now, even though she was sorry how the Amish in Rolling Brook felt about it." He gripped his mug. "She had to be lying. She had a choice."

Maybe she didn't.

"Did she tell you why she had to stay in the play?" I asked.

"*Nee*, one of those play people showed up then and told me I had to leave."

"Who was it?" I asked.

"I don't know any of their names. They are all *Englischers*."

"What did he look like?"

"He was a short, wiry man with a mustache. Eve didn't seem to care for him, but she went with him."

Jasper, I thought. "Why do you say that?"

"She said that he couldn't tell her what to do because he wasn't the director. The man turned bright red. If I had not been standing right there, he might have struck her when she said that."

I frowned. If Nahum thought that Jasper wanted to hit Eve, would he have been angry enough to cut the rope of her swing? I swallowed. Poor Eve. What kind of torment had the girl been facing on the day she died?

"She endured a lot to come back and see her family," I said.

Nahum set his mug back on the table. "I already told you that my brother would not have seen her. My brother won't even see me. He believes he is such a righteous man because he follows all the district rules. He is weak to allow the bishop to think for him. I made that mistake once and will never again."

I saw Jonah's jaw twitch.

"What decision was that?" I asked.

He glared at me over his coffee mug. "None of your business."

On a hunch, I said, "Was it about Rachel's mother?"

Jonah's head snapped in my direction. He had not expected that question. I hadn't either.

"What do you know about it?"

"I know Rachel is my dearest friend, and you are her father. I know there has to be a reason that you left your daughter and your district when Rachel was a baby. It was because of her mother, wasn't it?"

Tears gathered in the Amish man's eyes and rolled down his weathered cheeks. "The bishop killed my wife."

Jonah dropped his spoon and said a not-very-nice word in Pennsylvania Dutch.

"What?" I asked.

"He's the reason she is dead. After my daughter was born, my wife was in a bad way. The midwife said that she could not help her. I went to the bishop to ask for guidance." He pounded his fist on the table again. "The bishop told me to take her to the *Englisch* hospital in

Canton. I argued with him, saying it would be better for her here in her home. He told me I was wrong.

"As a *gut* Amish man, I did as the bishop told me. I took her to the *Englisch* hospital, and the doctors hooked her up to all sorts of machines. She died in a most horrible way, surrounded by beeping and whirling. I will never get those sounds out of my head. It was the bishop's fault. And my fault too for not trusting *Gott* that she would get better at home. Instead, we put our faith in *Englisch* doctors. No good comes from the *Englisch* ways—that's what I learned. I left my district."

I swallowed. Did Rachel know all of this? I doubted it. "Did you leave your family's business at the same time?"

"*Nee*. I planned to still work there too, until I saw the bishop's influence washed over my *bruders*. I saw what they were doing in following the bishop's worldly ways. They put a telephone inside the office, and the worst yet, they wanted to sell Christmas trees to the *Englisch*. I had to leave. I would have no part of it. If they wanted to join the world, that was their choice, but they were not taking me with them. I knew what would come of it."

"What about Rachel?" I asked quietly.

Nahum wiped a tear away. "Her mother's sister was a *gut*, steady Amish woman. She was the best one to raise the child. She is better off without me in her life."

I didn't think Rachel would agree with that.

Chapter Twenty-eight

At the road beside Nahum's woods, Jonah, Ryan, and I stood. I didn't know what the men were thinking, but my thoughts were preoccupied with Eve and Rachel. There was no hope for Eve to mend her relationship with her family, but Rachel and her father had a chance.

I broke the silence. "It must have been Jasper Clump, the stage manager, who interrupted Eve and Nahum last night. Do you think that was the person she was afraid of?"

Jonah untied Maggie from the tree. "I would wonder more over what she was doing standing outside the barn. If she wanted to get away from the actors and production for a bit, wouldn't she go back to her room at the hotel?" He climbed into his buggy. "I hope you are satisfied and will not want to speak to Nahum again."

"I won't want to talk to him about Eve, no." Mentally, I added that Rachel was another story. "Thank you for taking us there."

Jonah nodded at me and then at Ryan. "I'll see you both at Christmas Eve supper at our farm tomorrow."

"You will," I promised.

He grinned. "It should be exciting with such an interesting group of people coming."

I glared at him. I knew he meant the sheriff. "Bye, Jo-Jo."

He winked and flicked the reins.

Ryan picked a bramble off his sleeve. "You can take me back to the hotel, and I can change my clothes. Maybe the hotel's laundry will have better luck getting all the brambles out of my coat."

"Thanks for coming," I said.

"You're welcome." His chocolate brown eyes looked into mine. "I would go anywhere you need to, Angie. You have to know that."

He didn't mean that, not really. He wouldn't be willing to stay in Holmes County, Ohio, and give up his life in Dallas if that was what I really wanted. I swallowed the lump in my throat, because I did not want him to stay. I did not.

After a quick stop at home to pick up Oliver (my mother was in the throes of decorating the giant Christmas tree), I arrived at Running Stitch just as Mattie unlocked the front door. "Angie, there you are. How did the meeting with Nahum go?"

I gave her a sheepish look. "He was more forthcoming than I expected."

She frowned. "About Eve?"

"Yes." I bit my lip. "And about Rachel's mother too."

Her mouth made a little "o" shape.

Oliver waddled around the shop, snuffling the ground. He always liked to make sure the perimeter was secure each morning when we came in. Being such a scaredy pooch, he wouldn't do anything about it if he found something amiss though.

"This case is so confusing. In my gut, I think it is someone from the play who cut Eve's rope swing. I've spoken with almost everyone who might be involved."

"Who would you like to talk to next?" my assistant asked.

"There is one more person, but I can't remember his name. He was Eve's Amish boyfriend before she left for New York."

"Oh." Mattie hung up her cloak and wouldn't look at me.

I folded my arms. "Is something wrong with that?"

"*Nee*. Just I know who that is. It's Nathan Eby. He and his family own a buggy shop on River Road just a mile south from the covered bridge."

"Eby? Are they related to the Ebys who own the mercantile?"

She nodded, still not looking at me. "It's the same family. The owner of the mercantile is Nathan's brother."

That could be awkward. I hoped that he wouldn't know my part in solving a crime that put his brother in jail last February. "Thanks," I said. "I had better talk to him today if I have any hope of catching him. Tomorrow and Christmas Day all Amish businesses will be closed. He probably knows about Eve's death by now, so at least I won't have to break the news to him."

"He knows." She smoothed her skirt. "I told him."

I frowned. "Was he the reason you ran off yesterday without telling me?"

"I went to school with Eve and with Nathan. He's a nice guy and my friend." She hit the button on the cash register to open the cash drawer and started to count the money.

"Okay, but why didn't you tell me where you went?"

She set a stack of dollar bills on the counter. "Because I knew this would happen. I knew you would want to talk to him, and I wanted you to leave him alone."

I frowned.

"I can't believe that he had anything to do with what happened to Eve. He's married to someone else now with a baby. They seem very happy, but his wife isn't going to like you asking him questions about Eve."

"You act like I'm going to interrogate him," I said.

Her shoulders sagged. "I know you are just trying to help the police, but I don't know how talking to Nathan will help anything."

"It's probably another dead end, but I know I won't be satisfied until I speak with everyone who might have had a close enough connection to Eve to feel strongly about her return to Holmes County." I straightened the Christmas quilt in the large display window. There were some telltale pinpricks on it, a sure sign that Dodger had climbed it. Maybe Mattie was right and the kitten shouldn't come to the shop until he was better behaved. Who knew when that would be?

I saw the Dutchman's Tea Shop and Miller's Amish

Bakery through the window. "Is Rachel in the bakery?" I asked.

Mattie nodded. "She's there alone. My *bruder* is delivering pies to restaurants in Charm for their Christmas sales."

She adjusted her prayer cap. "Angie, can you tell me what Nahum said about Rachel's mother?"

I shook my head. "Rachel might decide to tell you, but that is her decision to make." I paused. "Please don't tell the other ladies in the quilting circle that I learned anything about Rachel's mother."

Mattie nodded. "I won't."

"Do you mind watching the store? I think Oliver and I will pop over to talk to her while she's alone."

"Not at all." She paused. "And I am sorry for not telling you about Nathan earlier. I should have."

I smiled at her as I opened the front door. "It's okay. You thought you were helping out a friend. I understand that. Just don't do it again." I winked at her before I left the quilt shop.

The bell on the bakery door rang. Rachel came out of the back room with an expectant face. When she saw Oliver and me, she smiled. "*Gude mariye,* Angie. It's so nice to see you on this cold morning. Can I get you a cup of coffee?"

"Do you have hot chocolate?"

She laughed. "Of course. I think I will have a cup too. Hot chocolate sounds *wunderbar* on such a cold day."

Before she started making the hot chocolate, she removed the plastic container from under the counter.

Oliver's rump started to wiggle as soon as he saw it.

She removed two homemade dog treats and tossed them over the counter at my Frenchie. His one black and one white ears flicked back and forth in excitement.

"Ugh," I said. "Come January, Oliver and I will be in a foul mood, as we'll be on our diets."

Oliver delicately picked up both treats in his mouth and carried them under one of the café tables to eat in private.

She laughed. "You are the only person I know who would put her dog on a diet."

"That's because most of the people you know are Amish," I said.

"True." She put the container back under the counter and fixed the hot chocolate.

"What have you been up to this morning? Are your parents enjoying their visit?"

"I gave Mom the project of decorating my Christmas tree. It will be a glitz and glamour monstrosity. You'll have to stop over before I take it down after the New Year to see it. You'll never see anything in Holmes County like it."

She grinned. "I will see it tonight. A group from the district is going caroling, and I put your home on the list of those we must visit." She sipped from her mug.

"Thank you. Mom and Dad will love that." I stirred the liquid in my mug and watched the brown powder dissolve into the hot water. "You asked me what I did this morning." I met her gaze. "I went to Nahum's cabin in the woods."

"Alone?"

I shook my head. "With Jonah. I made him take me there." I thought it was best to leave Ryan out of the conversation.

She lowered her mug. "Oh?"

I swallowed the too-hot chocolate. It burned my throat on the way down. "I went there to speak to him about Eve."

"Did you learn anything?" she asked as if trying to sound disinterested.

"About Eve, some," I said. "About your mother, much more."

Rachel stood up. "My *mamm*? You had no right to speak to him about that. Angie, I know you are just trying to help, but please leave it be. I am a Miller now, and that is my family."

"I know, but do you at least want to know what he said?"

She sat back down. "I wish I didn't, but I do."

So I told Rachel what Nahum had revealed inside his cabin.

Chapter Twenty-nine

I followed the directions that Mattie gave me to the Eby Buggy Shop. The covered bridge made only for buggy traffic over a creek bed looked like a postcard photo, with icicles hanging off the bridge's eaves and snow covering its roof. As Oliver and I drove by on the road that ran parallel to the bridge, a fox dashed out of the bridge and down the bank to the creek. Oliver had his nose pressed up against the glass.

I smiled. "You wouldn't see a scene like that back in Dallas."

He glanced over his shoulder at me and cocked his head as if to ask a question.

"Not that I am considering going back." I turned straight ahead. "I don't think so, anyway."

The Eby Buggy Shop was a freestanding building on the side of the road. It had a large parking lot. A third of the lot was filled with buggies. I didn't know if they were on sale, as they would be at a car lot, or were recently repaired and waiting for their owners to return.

They had only remnants of snow on them as if someone cleared them off each morning.

Not surprisingly, there were no automobiles in the
parking lot. Usually, an English person didn't have much
cause to visit a buggy shop.

Oliver sighed as I put on his boots before getting out
of the car. He had given up fighting me on the reindeer
Christmas sweater, but the boots were a different story.
He kicked his front paws in disgust.

"I know. I know, buddy. The sooner we do this, the
sooner we can go back to Running Stitch and you can
take them off."

He pressed his flat nose against the passenger-
side window. He was ready to go.

The buggy shop appeared to be a converted barn.
The bifold barn doors stood half open.

"Hello?" I called as Oliver and I stepped into the
building.

Wagon and buggy wheels hung from the wall along
with leather reins and harnesses for the horses that
would pull the buggies. Five buggies stood in a hori-
zontal line in front of me in differing stages of repair or
disrepair. The floor was concrete and sprinkled with
sawdust. The soles of our boots slipped on the pow-
dery surface. Oliver picked up one of his paws and in-
spected the sawdust clinging to his red bootie. He set it
back onto the ground with a sigh.

"Hello?" I called again.

There was the sound of the whirl of tires on the concrete. An Amish man shot out from under one of the
buggies to my right on a flat board with rollers like a

gearhead that appears out from under a car's undercarriage. He held a screwdriver in his hand and blinked at me. "Can I help you?" he asked as he stood. "Are you lost? Do you need directions?"

The man couldn't be more than twenty but had a short Amish beard. He was the right age to be Nathan.

"I'm looking for Nathan Eby."

"That's me." Nathan noticed my dog for the first time. "He's wearing a sweater." He paused. "And boots." Nathan laughed.

Oliver gave me his best I-am-totally-humiliated-and-it's-your-fault look.

"He does. He's not used to the cold."

"Oh." Nathan's brow folded together. "Are you a tourist?"

I shook my head. "I'm Angie Braddock."

He frowned. "Where have I heard that name before?"

"I'm a township trustee," I said quickly before he could remember that a crime I solved while visiting my aunt in Holmes County last winter got another Eby sent to prison.

His face cleared, and he walked over to a rolling tool cabinet. It was bright red and looked just like the one that my father had in his garage back in Dallas. "That must be it. Is there something the trustees wanted to talk to me about? I hope it's nothing to do with my business. I follow all of the rules."

"It's not the business," I said. "But the trustees did send me," I fibbed, "to talk about something important."

"What's that?"

"Eve Shetler." I let the name hang in the air.

Nathan dropped his screwdriver into the tool cabinet. It clattered against the other tools in that drawer. "Why would they ask you to talk to me about her?"

"You courted her while she was Amish, didn't you?"

He removed a socket wrench from the drawer below. "*Ya*, but that was more than three years ago, a long time ago. I am married now. I haven't even seen Eve since she returned." He rooted in the drawer as if searching for the right tip to the wrench. "I was very sad to hear about Eve. She was a *gut* person, even if she left the Amish way. But this life is not for everyone."

"I sat next to Eve Shetler at the dinner. I liked her very much."

He smiled wistfully at the wrench. "I'm sure she was the hit of the progressive dinner. She always was at the center of attention even when she was Amish." He nodded. "I did court Eve for a short time. When we were young, I knew there wasn't much hope that she would stay Amish. I suppose my boyish wish was she would remain for me, but the *Englisch* life was what she wanted and I couldn't give her that. I am happily married now. For me, it happened just like *Gott* wanted it to. I have no regrets. Other than I am sorry about what happened to Eve. She did not deserve that."

I shifted my stance. "And Junie?"

"What about Junie?" He slid the bit onto the socket wrench.

"When I spoke to Junie, she mentioned you, and I got the feeling that she might have had a crush on you."

"Junie was like a younger sister to me from the time that I was courting Eve. Eve was so self-confident. Junie is afraid of her own shadow, but I always got the feeling she had a crush on me." He frowned. "These seem to be strange questions that the township trustees would like answered."

"Eve's death is not only a tragedy, but it disrupted the progressive dinner and play. We were hoping that if we found out who did this to Eve, we would be able to stop this from happening again."

He shook his head. "I won't be much help to you because I don't know. I haven't seen Eve in three years." He walked back to the buggy he had been working on. "Now if that's all, I need to get back to work. I won't have time to finish the buggy for the King family over the holidays, and they want it by Christmas Day to ride to see relatives in Knox County."

I nodded. "Thanks for your time." I glanced around the shop for Oliver. "Where did my dog get to?"

Nathan came over to me. "He shouldn't be too hard to find in a sweater and boots. At least we won't mistake him for an Amish dog."

"Oliver!" I called.

A whimper came from one of the other buggies.

Nathan and I followed the sound. Oliver was inside one of the buggies with glass windows. All the doors were closed.

Nathan opened the door, and Oliver hopped out. He marched in place, happy to be free again.

"How in the world did he get stuck inside there?" Nathan asked.

"You would be surprised how many tight spots he gets himself into."

Nathan laughed. "Since he's wearing boots, I doubt that there's anything that would surprise me about your dog." Nathan walked Oliver and me to the barn door. He stopped and said, "I always thought that Esther, their mother, loved Eve more than Junie. That was hard on Junie. I think she hoped when Eve left Holmes County, she would earn her mother's love. Instead, Esther went into a deep sadness over Eve's leaving. It was almost like Eve was dead." He nodded. "And now she's dead for certain. It's terribly sad."

I agreed.

What was it like for Junie to live in a home that pined for a girl who chose to leave but ignored the girl who chose to stay? I felt even worse for the hotel maid. "And were you as upset as her family when Eve left?"

"*Ya*, I was angry and disappointed when she left the way. I thought all of my dreams left with her, but my wife, Susan, has shown me that Eve was not the one *Gott* intended for me. If Eve had stayed, we would have been miserable. We were too different, and we wanted too many different things. My life is just as I want it to be. I pray that Eve's life was like that for her."

I was beginning to have my doubts on that. Yes, Eve had been a working actress in New York, but she'd only been in plays well off Broadway. She took the part in the Amish hotel production because she was desperate for her big break. That thought gave me pause. Had Eve tried out for the part because of Wade's historic career prior to whatever derailed it twenty years ago?

Was she like the others and thought she could ride on his comeback? He certainly had high hopes for what she could do for him.

It was driving me crazy not knowing what had caused Wade's career to derail all those years ago.

Nathan pushed the barn door open wider for Oliver and me. "Thank you for coming in. I hope you and your family have a blessed Christmas."

"Thank you. Merry Christmas." I left the workshop, certain at least that Nathan had nothing to do with the murder, and more certain than ever that Eve was never meant to be Amish if she could leave such a kind man behind for the bright lights of New York. Susan was a very lucky woman.

Chapter Thirty

From my car, I called the sheriff.

"Is this a social call?" Mitchell asked in my ear.

"I hope you think every time I call is a social call," I said.

"I know better than to believe that."

I frowned. "Okay, you win. It's half social, half murder."

He sighed.

I reminded him about the Christmas Eve party at the Grabers, and I also told him about the fight that I witnessed between Jasper and Wade last night at the hotel's barn. Maybe I should have told him about it the night before, but I had been so preoccupied with taking Junie home and making it to the trustees' meeting that I'd forgotten.

"I know Jasper and Wade don't like each other. It was obvious from the interviews with them."

"What did they say about each other?" I asked eagerly.

"I got a Christmas surprise for you today," he said.

"Are you trying to change the subject?"

"Yep." He chuckled. "Is it working?"

"Well, yeah. What girl doesn't like a Christmas surprise?"

There was laughter in his voice. "I'll give it to you tomorrow." He hung up.

I got to Running Stitch and stayed with Mattie in the shop until closing. Business was surprisingly brisk as shoppers came in for last-minute Christmas gifts. At four thirty, Mattie flipped the CLOSED sign around on the front door. "Won't it be nice to have a couple of days off, Angie, to spend with your family?"

I nodded as I swept the floor like we always did at the end of the day. "This is the first day since my parents arrived in Ohio that I haven't gotten a dozen calls and texts from my mother. She and Dad are on a mission to decorate the Christmas tree that he bought last night, and, I think, decorate a large portion of my house. My mother always loves a project."

"That's nice." She tied her bonnet ribbon tightly under her chin as she prepared to go out into the cold.

"Wait until you see the tree. You'll get a chance if you go caroling tonight with Rachel."

She grinned. "Great! I bet it's amazing."

I shook my head, far less certain it would be, but the project was getting my mother off my back, which was worth it.

My cell phone rang. I removed it from my pocket. It was a Holmes County number, but I didn't recognize it. "Go ahead and go home, Mattie. You've worked hard. It's time for you to start your holiday."

"*Danki*," she said, and stepped out the door.

"Hello?" I said.

"Where are you?" an irritated voice asked.

"Martha?" I guessed.

"*Ya*, it is me. Where are you? You are supposed to be at the hotel helping me close up the quilt show. Shoppers are here picking up the quilts that they bought, and I have to deal with it all alone. Not that I should have expected anything more when working with you."

I slammed the heel of my hand against my forehead. "I'm so sorry that I forgot. I will get there as soon as possible."

Without saying good-bye, she hung up.

I sighed. I still had a long way to go to mend that broken fence. "Oliver, we have to stop at the hotel before heading home for Christmas."

The Frenchie whimpered.

"I know, but it can't be helped."

Twenty minutes later, Oliver and I stepped into the Swiss Valley Hotel. I was starting to believe that I was a guest living there myself, since I had been there so often in the last few days.

I waved at Bethanne as Oliver and I made a beeline for the sitting room. The place was neat and tidy. Martha had taken all of the quilts off their racks and had labeled them with the name of the person who purchased each quilt. I noticed that at least five were missing. Presumably, the owners of those quilts had already come and claimed their prizes.

Martha was at the far end of the room, accepting a check from one of the shoppers. Two other women were in line.

I unzipped my coat. "Can I help you?" I asked the next customer waiting.

"Oh, yes, thank you. I'm in a hurry. There's so much that needs to be done before the holiday."

I smiled. "Let's find your quilt then and get you out of here."

Oliver settled under one of the armchairs for a nap.

A half hour later all of the shoppers who planned to pick up their quilts before Christmas had come and gone. The remaining quilts would go to my shop, where the shoppers would pick up their purchases after the holiday.

Martha and I folded a queen-sized Double Wedding Ring quilt. It was from Martha's shop and was quite pretty. I wouldn't say it was better than any of my aunt's quilts, but it was very well done.

"Martha," I said as I took the quilt from her hands, "I'm so sorry. The quilt show completely slipped my mind today."

She packed up her basket with quilt notions, needles, and thread. "Maybe you are too preoccupied with others' business to worry about your own."

"What is that supposed to mean?"

"Everyone in the county knows that you are trying to find out how Eve Shetler was killed. I don't understand why. It's none of your concern."

I placed the quilt on the large stack of others that I would take to my car. "I met Eve and I liked her. I like her sister, Junie. If I can help in some way, then I will."

"That is why you are *Englisch*, and I am Amish. I know when it is not my place." She folded a lap quilt. "Everyone knows Eve got into the mess all by herself. The moment she left the Amish way, she made a choice. Her death is one of the consequences."

I gathered the quilted place mats and stuck them in a basket to take to my car. "You don't really mean that."

"How do you know what I mean?" She glared at me.

I sighed. "Can't we get past this feud over my *aenti's* shop? You have your own store now, and it's doing well."

She frowned. "Yes, I do have my own store now, and it will be everything that yours is not. *Authentically* Amish. The moment you inherited Running Stitch, no one could say that about Eleanor's shop anymore."

I sighed and watched her go. Oliver wiggled out from his hiding place and whimpered. I patted his head. "Not everyone is going to like us, buddy. It's best if we learn that now."

He barked.

After I loaded my car with all the quilts and trappings from the quilt shop, I stopped by the desk to say hello to Bethanne and to ask about the play. I was there after all, and the trustees had commissioned me to keep an eye on the theater troupe. "Is play practice going on?"

The young Amish girl shook her head. "All the actors and crew left an hour ago. They told Mimi that they wanted to go somewhere else to eat."

It was just as well. I was exhausted and knew my parents were waiting for me at home.

I pulled into the driveway just as the Amish carolers began a new song. Rachel, Mattie, and Aaron stood with other members of their district on my front lawn, singing "Silent Night." Oliver barked approval.

Mom and Dad stood in the doorway. Dad had his arm around Mom's shoulders. My mother held a large tray of cookies in her hands. I was certain the cookies were from Miller's Amish Bakery. My heart ached because I missed the two of them. Mom was right; I hadn't given them the attention they deserved since they got to Holmes County. I promised that I would spend the next couple of days while the shop was closed to make up for it.

Begrudgingly, I admitted that I owed the same to Ryan too. I wanted us to be friends. He had been a large part of my life for so long. I had gone from talking to and seeing him every day to nothing. It was a shock to the system, and I hadn't realized how much I missed him until that morning searching for Nahum's cabin. We had many good times together. The problem was I had to make him understand that friends were all that we could be.

Funny, just after I arrived in Holmes County, I would have been elated if Ryan had come to Ohio after me. Maybe a small part of me had secretly hoped that he would, but that window of opportunity had come and gone and a certain sheriff with startling blue-green eyes had stepped through the open door. It was too late for Ryan and for me to love him in that way.

The choir finished the song, and my parents thanked them. Rachel walked over to me. "I'm so glad that you got here in time to hear some of the singing. I asked Aaron to stop at your home near the end of our caroling with the hope that you would be here. I thought you might get caught up in something on the way home."

I smiled. "You know me well. I had to stop by the hotel to close up the quilt show. How are you?"

Rachel's brow furrowed beneath her bonnet. "I'm fine. I thought about what you told me about my father."

I waited.

"And I want to talk to him."

"You do?"

"Not now. After Christmas. I need to talk to him." Tears welled up in her eyes. "Will you go with me?"

"Of course." I hugged her.

"*Gut.* I hate to keep things from my husband, but I think it's best we don't mention this to him until I meet with my father. Nothing may come of it, and I don't want Aaron to become upset over nothing."

I bit the inside of my lip. Her relationship with her estranged father wasn't nothing. I wasn't going to argue with her, so I changed the subject. "Did you go inside and see the tree?"

Her eyes brightened. "Oh yes. It's . . ." She paused as if searching for the right word. "Something."

"I bet."

Rachel laughed and hugged me. "Merry Christmas, Angie. We need to go now to the next home, but you must tell me about your day. You look tired."

"I am beat." I yawned. "I packed a lot into one day.

It will be nice to have a couple of days of holiday and to not think of murder."

Aaron called to his wife in Pennsylvania Dutch.

Rachel smiled. "You take too much on yourself. This should not be your burden to bear."

She was right. As my mother would say, I bring these things on myself.

I went inside the house to find a pink and white Christmas tree. It was furry. I might have been wrong, but it looked like my mother had used a pink feather boa as a garland.

Ryan sat on the couch holding a drink. "It's as if a cotton candy factory exploded in your living room."

My mother carried a cup of tea into the room and cuffed Ryan on the back of the head with her free hand. "It does not."

My heart constricted. My parents were so happy and comfortable when they were with Ryan. Would they ever feel that way about the sheriff? I didn't know. They'd known Ryan for nearly a decade. Mitchell they just met.

Mom beamed at me. "Angie, dear, what do you think? Your father and Ryan have been teasing me all afternoon. But I just love it; don't you? I might use it for my color scheme on my own tree next year. Wouldn't it look amazing in the foyer of the house?"

Dad balanced a plate of Rachel's cookies on his belly and held a huge glass of milk in his other hand. "I could be wrong, but I think one of those sweet Amish girls fainted dead away when she saw it."

"Stop." My mother cuffed him on the head this time.

"And you shouldn't be eating those cookies, Kent. What would the doctor say?"

He grunted. "I'm taste-testing them for Santa. It's a public service."

My mother sighed. "Angie, you haven't said anything about the tree yet."

Because I was struck dumb by it.

"It's pink," I squeaked.

Ryan barked a laugh. "Great observation."

Chapter Thirty-one

On Christmas Eve, I smiled as I turned the SUV into the Grabers' long driveway. This was what I had wanted my parents to experience when they came back to Ohio for Christmas, an old-fashioned Amish Christmas. Maybe it would remind them of the Christmases from their childhood, and maybe it would help them understand why I wanted to stay in Ohio for good.

Ryan sat in the backseat of the SUV with my mother and Oliver. Even though he had a rental car, I had stopped at the hotel to pick him up. I didn't trust he would be able to find the Grabers' farm without GPS.

Snow covered the crop fields on either side of the house and covered the roofs of the house, barn, and outbuildings like frosting on a wedding cake. I frowned. Why was wedding cake the first comparison that came to my mind?

"The farm is beautiful," my mother murmured. "It reminds me so much of Eleanor's farm. . . ." She trailed off.

I turned in my seat to look at her. "Mom, are you okay?"

She waved away my concern. "Of course being here brings back memories of my parents, of my sister."

Dad squeezed Mom's hand. "I'm so glad we are here. We can make new memories with Angie and her friends. They all knew Eleanor. Don't you think your sister would like that?"

Mom sniffled. "She would." She reached into her purse for her mirror to check her makeup. She snapped the mirror shut. "I'm ready."

The Frenchie sniffed the air and lowered himself to the ground.

"What's wrong with him?" Dad asked. "I don't see any birds around."

"But he knows they are there. Jonah has a flock of geese. They are in the far barn, so Oliver doesn't like being here. He was chased by them when we first moved here. The poor guy is scarred."

"I'd be scarred too if I was chased by geese," Dad said.

"Kent, can you help me into the house?" Mom asked as she teetered back and forth in the snow. She wore tall boots with a three-inch spike heel under a long corduroy skirt. Dad held on to her arm so that she wouldn't fall over.

"Go on," I said to Ryan. "Jonah can help me bring all this in from the car."

"Welcome," Jonah said, walking toward us. "It is so nice to have you here for Christmas, Mr. and Mrs. Braddock."

"We're happy to be here," Dad said.

Underneath his black wool coat, now free of brambles, Ryan wore a sweater and jeans. I smiled at the outfit. Ryan was more of a suit kind of guy. It was cute that he was trying to fit in. Ryan caught my smile and grinned back at me.

I turned my head away. Great.

The front door of the house opened, and the children—Rachel's three sons and Jonah's twin boys and ten-year-old daughter, Emma—poured out, followed by Mattie. All of them were bundled up to play in the snow. Emma had a book tucked under her arm. I guessed she was going to find a quiet place to read while the boys played.

Ezra and Ethan made a beeline for me. "Angie! Angie! Come play with us. We are going to have a snowball fight."

I pulled the black stocking cap one of the boys wore down over his eyes. "That sounds like fun, but I should go inside to see if the ladies need any help with the meal."

Ezra laughed, or maybe it was Ethan. "They will just kick you out of the kitchen. *Grossmammi* never wants any help. She only lets *Mamm* and Rachel in the kitchen with her."

That I could believe. Anna does everything her way.

Dad grinned over his shoulder. "Go on, Angie Bear. You work too hard. It's time that you had a little fun. If I remember correctly, you had a strong arm when it came to throwing a snowball."

Dad helped Mom toward the house. Jonah and Ryan remained. "Are you guys going in?"

"No way," Jonah said. "I want a rematch of our snowball fight from when we were kids. You are going down, Braddock."

I put my hands on my hips. "Jonah Graber, that is the most un-Amish thing I have ever heard come out of your mouth. What would your mother say?"

Jonah grinned and punched Ryan in the arm. "Be careful. She plays dirty."

"I know that all too well," Ryan said.

They'd be sorry.

When I was ten, I was an expert at making snowballs. I hadn't made one in more than twenty years, but as I gathered snow to make my arsenal, the skill came back to me.

I had the twins and two of Rachel's sons on my side. We were up against Jonah, Ryan, and the remaining boy.

I hunched down with the twins. "What's the strategy?"

Ethan—I think; I could never tell them apart—said, "You stay here and make snowballs, defend our supplies. The rest of us will go on the offensive."

"What are they teaching Amish kids in school nowadays? How do you even know what an offensive is?"

The twins grinned at each other.

I folded my arm. "Are you making me guard the base because I'm a girl?"

"*Nee*, you are the best at making snowballs."

I decided to take that as a compliment.

A snowball flew into our camp and hit Ezra on the head.

"Let's do this," the twin said.

The boys piled snowballs into their arms and ran into battle.

I peeked over the embankment. Snowballs flew in a barrage back and forth between the teams. Yips and laughter were heard everywhere. Oliver hunched down beside me. He had no problem with staying back in the safety zone.

The next time I peeked over, I saw Ryan staying just ten feet away. He didn't know I was there. I let the snowball go, and it hit Ryan square in the stomach. He doubled over. I dropped the other snowballs I made and ran over to him. "I'm so sorry. That looked like it hurt. Are you okay?"

Ryan rubbed his stomach and, without warning, he tackled me and we fell into the snow, laughing. "That's a cheap shot," I cried. "I was helping you."

I was on my back, and Ryan's face was just inches above mine. I caught my breath. Ryan looked into my eyes, and I swallowed hard. He was going to kiss me. I needed to push him off. Why wasn't I pushing him off me?

"Having fun?" a deep voice asked, and it wasn't Jonah.

I blinked and turned my head to find Mitchell standing over us, holding a deli tray. Jessica, looking hurt, stood beside him.

I pushed Ryan off me and jumped to my feet. "Mitchell! Jessica!" I yelped. "I'm so glad that you came."

"Are you?" Mitchell's lips pursed together. I had seen him have the same look when he faced a killer.

The Graber and Miller boys stood around us. Some of them still had snowballs in their hands. It was as if they had stopped their game in midthrow.

Ryan stood and brushed snow off his coat. "Angie and I were just having a bit of fun with the kids. I hope that doesn't bother you."

Mitchell clenched the tray, and the plastic crackled under the pressure. "Why would it bother me?"

Jessica took the tray from Mitchell's hand. "Why don't I take that into the kitchen?"

I took one step after her. "Jess?"

She kept walking and didn't turn around to look at me. I bit the inside of my cheek. I knew she liked Ryan, but did she like him enough to get so upset? She had to know he was headed back to Texas alone after Christmas, didn't she?

Mattie walked past Jessica and the deli tray coming the opposite way. "Anna says it's time for everyone to come inside and get ready for the meal." She looked at me covered in snow. "Angie, you are going to catch a chill if you stay out here much longer anyway. Come brush off the snow before it melts and you are soaked through."

I brushed at my coat, happy for the chance to concentrate on something other than the fact that Ryan and Mitchell were just inches from each other.

"That goes for you too, boys." Mattie put a hand on one of her nephew's arms. "Inside with the lot of you. We will be eating soon. Has anyone seen Emma?"

I dropped my hands from snow removal. "I'll go tell Emma it's time to go inside," I said. "I saw her take a book into the barn." Before anyone could object, I ran across the yard.

Inside the barn, I leaned against the wall and caught my breath. What had I been thinking? I had almost kissed Ryan in front of all of my family and friends, in front of Mitchell. I hadn't been thinking; that was the problem. I banged the back of my head against the barn wall.

"You are going to give yourself a headache if you keep doing that." Emma sat a few feet away from me. She was cross-legged on a bale of hay with two wool blankets wrapped around her shoulders and a book on her lap.

Across from her, Maggie wore her burgundy horse blanket and ate out of a feed bag tethered to her stall. The barn was dim. A flickering lantern hung from a chain dangling from the ceiling.

I pushed off the wall. "What are you reading?"

Emma placed a piece of hay in her book to mark where she left off. Now, that was an Amish bookmark. "*Sherlock Holmes*. I picked it up at first because I thought it had something to do with our county, but it doesn't."

I laughed. "Really? Which story?"

She held up a thick book. "I got this from the library. It has all of the stories. Right now, I'm reading *The Hound of the Baskervilles*. It's very *gut* and a little scary. Maybe I will be a detective like him someday."

"Don't let you mother hear that."

"*Mamm* wouldn't like it," she agreed.

"How could you be an Amish detective?"

Emma pushed her glasses up her nose with her index finger. "I would have to leave the Amish to be a detective. That would be really hard." She frowned.

"You have a long time before you have to make that choice."

"I'm glad."

I sat next to her on the hay bale. "Sherlock Holmes is one of my favorites."

She scooted over. "Why were you banging your head against the wall?"

"Because I almost did something stupid."

"If everyone hit their head against the wall when they *almost* did something stupid, the whole world would have a concussion." She hopped off the hay bale and folded the blankets.

I laughed. "Maybe you are right. Then why do I still feel bad about it?"

"Maybe it is a sin of the heart? Like if you didn't actually do it, your heart did."

I frowned. I didn't like the sound of that.

"But it is most important you stopped yourself, correct?" she asked, wise beyond her years.

"I wasn't the one who stopped me, but I stopped."

She dropped the folded blankets on the bale of hay. "Then it doesn't matter. You can't be in trouble for something that you almost did."

If only that were true.

Chapter Thirty-two

Inside Anna's house, the living room furniture had been moved against the wall or removed from the room entirely, and the dining room table with all the leaves in it sat in the middle of the room, stretching from end to end. Pine boughs, cranberries, and holly made up the low and simple centerpiece. Five white candles, all unlit, ran the length of the table.

A dark navy cloth covered the table. I counted twenty chairs around the table. A smaller table was in the kitchen for the children. I smiled to see that a "kids table" at big holiday meals was also an Amish tradition. Emma and her twin brother sat at that table along with Aaron and Rachel's three boys. Rachel kept the baby with her.

The men were already seated at the main table. I skirted around the table to the kitchen, I felt both Ryan and Mitchell watching me as I made my way.

While the living room–turned–dining room was the pinnacle of serene Amish simplicity, the kitchen was bedlam as the women put the final touches on the meal. Even my mother was in the middle of it, slicing the freshly baked friendship bread.

"What can I do?" I asked Rachel as she whizzed by with a bowl of green beans.

She spun around and handed me the bowl. "You can start taking things to the table. That would be a tremendous help."

I swallowed, So I would have to walk in front of Mitchell and Ryan a dozen times. "There's nothing else I can do?"

Rachel wrinkled her brow. "*Nee*, Angie is something wrong?"

"I'll tell you later. It's complicated." I took the green beans from her hand and headed into the dining room.

"Jessica will help you," Rachel called after me.

Great.

"Angie, those smell heavenly," my father said as I placed the bowl near his place.

I smiled, taking care not to make eye contact with Mitchell or Ryan. "It's just the start. The ladies have made so many wonderful things. I hope you brought your appetite."

He patted his round belly. "I always do."

I laughed and disappeared into the kitchen just long enough to be given a basket of bread and a tray of pickles. There was so much going back and forth, I knew I wouldn't have a chance to grab Jessica and talk to her. I hoped my friend would let me explain when I got the chance.

I placed them on the table. This was ridiculous. I

wasn't a teenager. I looked up and met Mitchell's gaze. He was studying me, but his expression was unreadable. I gave him a small smile.

"Did you cook any of this, Angie?" Ryan asked in a too-loud voice. "I remember how much you loved to cook. Angie made dinner for me countless times."

Mitchell's eyes flicked in Ryan's direction, and there was no interpretation needed to read that expression.

I swallowed. "No, I didn't make anything today. Anna wouldn't hear of it."

"Angie will be making a turkey for us tomorrow at her house," my oblivious father said. "You should come, Sheriff. She is a very good cook, even if it's not Amish cooking."

"I have my son tomorrow," Mitchell said.

Dad twirled the water in his glass. "Bring him too. He can play with Oliver and Dodger."

"Only if Angie wants me to come," the sheriff said.

I glanced from Ryan to Mitchell. "I want you to come. Of course I do. Be sure to bring Tux, or Oliver will be depressed if you and Zander are there without him."

The sheriff's face broke into a smile, and the tension disappeared. "Okay. We may not be able to stay the entire time. I'm taking Zander to see my parents too. But we'll drop in."

"I'll be there the entire time," Ryan said. "Maybe I can even help you with the meal, Angie? I remember we made a good team in the kitchen before."

I felt my face grow hot. Anger returned to the sheriff's face. I took that as my cue to flee.

Finally, all of the food was on the table, and the ladies working in the kitchen joined us. I sat between my mother and Ryan, directly across from Mitchell, who was between Mattie and Jessica. Jessica wouldn't meet my gaze.

"Please, everyone, hold hands, so that we can say grace," Jonah said from the head of the table.

I inwardly groaned. That would mean I had to hold hands with Ryan. Ryan placed his hand palm up into the open space in the table between us. I put my hand in his and he closed his around mine. Across from me, Mitchell held hands with Mattie and Jessica. That was where I should have sat. It was a safe zone.

Jonah said the first prayer in Pennsylvania Dutch and then said another of thanksgiving in English.

Ryan squeezed my hand at the end of the prayer. I dropped my hand to my lap when he let it go.

There was so much food on the table, I was amazed that it didn't buckle under the weight of all the heavy dishes. A roast turkey sat on either end. Jonah carved one and Aaron carved the other. There were also three kinds of potatoes, stuffing, four vegetables, the deli tray from the sheriff, rolls, fruit salad, Amish casserole, and I didn't know what else. Plates were passed to the ends as the men served. Soon chatter and the clack of dishes filled the room. Occasionally an exclamation came from the kitchen where the children ate. Rachel took plates back and forth for the kids. I wondered how quiet Emma was faring with all of those boys. I bet she wished she was back in the barn reading. I kind of wished I were there with her instead of having to juggle Ryan and Mitchell, both of whom seemed to want to talk to me at the exact same time.

"Angie, I was wondering if you and I could go for a walk later today," Ryan whispered so that I was the only one who heard.

I dished yams onto my plate. "I don't think that is a very good idea, Ryan," I whispered.

"Please," he hissed.

"Maybe you should take Jessica for a walk. She came here to spend time with you. You must know that," I whispered.

"She is a nice girl, but we're just friends." He was nonchalant.

I frowned as I handed him the dish. "Ryan, I already gave you my answer."

"But I think you are considering changing your mind. I am ready to marry you now. Would you rather stay here, until the sheriff gets around to it? He has a child. It will be a long time before he will commit to you."

"You don't know that," I hissed back. "And I never said that I was in a rush to get married."

"You were in a rush."

"Oh, really, waiting seven years with no complaints is a rush." My voice jumped an octave.

The table grew quiet.

"Angie, is something wrong?" my father asked.

"No, no, everything's fine." I dropped my gaze to the table.

"Angie," Mitchell asked, "how did the quilt show go for you?"

I looked up. "Well, I think." I grimaced. "Martha is still as prickly as ever. I wish she and I could make up."

"Maybe she feels betrayed," Jessica said.

"She has no reason to," I said pointedly.

My friend's eyes narrowed. "Maybe she doesn't agree."

My mother laughed. "Oh, let's talk about something much more pleasant than that woman. It is Christmas Eve after all."

I couldn't agree more. The sheriff's cell phone rang. I was never so glad to hear a phone ring in my life.

Mitchell examined the screen. "I'm sorry to disturb our meal, Anna, but I'm on call today. I have to take this. It's from one of my deputies."

Anna nodded. "I understand, Sheriff. Surely, it has to do with police business."

The sheriff went out the front door without his coat. In my gut, I knew the call was about Eve's case. I chewed on my lip. I hoped it wasn't bad news.

The sheriff returned less than a minute later. "I'm so sorry, Anna, everyone, but I have to go. There has been an accident, and I need to go to the scene."

Anna stood. "But you haven't even had a chance to finish eating."

He flashed a smile. "I know and it's all been delicious, but I really must go."

"We'll send some leftovers home with Angie. Since you two live near each other, she can drop off the food."

"I'd be happy to do that," I said. It would give me the perfect opportunity to see the sheriff alone and explain that what he saw in the Grabers' yard had meant nothing. Because it hadn't meant anything.

Mitchell nodded and went out the door. I waited half a second and jumped up from my seat. "I'll be right back. I just need to speak to the sheriff for a moment."

I didn't wait to gauge their reactions. I flew out the door.

The screen door slammed closed after me. Mitchell was halfway to his departmental SUV. He fobbed the car unlocked. "Angie, what are you doing out here? You don't even have a coat on. You are going to freeze to death."

I wrapped my arms around myself, trying to conserve as much warmth as I could. "Is the accident related to Eve's case?"

He opened the door. "Angie," Mitchell warned.

"Mitchell, come on. Just tell me if Junie is okay," I pleaded.

"Junie is fine. There was an altercation at the hotel. Wade pushed Jasper down the grand staircase."

"What?" I dropped my arms. "Is Jasper okay?"

"He's battered and bruised. He's lucky, really, but he wants to file charges against Wade. Deputy Anderson was the first on the scene to arrest Wade because of his past."

"What's that?"

"He was arrested twenty years ago for assault against an actress in his play. The charges were dropped and any monetary settlement happened out of court. By the way, I got your phone message yesterday about the fight you witnessed between the two of them. I wish that you would stay out of all this."

I hopped from foot to foot. "Then Wade might be the one who killed Eve."

"It's possible, and at least he's on ice for the time being."

"What does this mean for the play and the dinner the day after Christmas?"

"You will have to talk to Mimi about that," he said.

The trustees would be so upset if the dinner was canceled. They were counting on that money for the new park, but it was better if everyone was safe. And it sounded like everyone was a whole lot safer with Wade behind bars.

"Now, go back inside and enjoy the rest of your Christmas Eve with Ryan." He closed his car door.

"Mitchell—," I started.

He held up a hand. "We can talk about Ryan later."

"Okay," I said, and stepped back from his car as he pulled away.

Okay, so he was mad and, dare I say, jealous. Ugh. Wasn't murder enough of a challenge to deal with around Christmas?

Chapter Thirty-three

It was dusk when my parents, Ryan, and I said good-bye to the Grabers. We bundled up in our winter coats, hats, and gloves. Jessica pulled on her own coat just a few steps from me but wouldn't meet my gaze. "Jessica," I whispered, "can we talk?"

She chewed on her lip. "Okay."

While my parents and Ryan were distracted by all of the food that Anna was trying to make them take home, I led Jessica and Oliver outside. "I don't know what you saw earlier today between Ryan and me or what you thought that you saw, but I want you to know that nothing is going on between us."

Oliver caught a snowflake on his pink tongue.

She nodded. "I know that."

"Then what's wrong?"

She kicked at a pile of snow. "I'm such an idiot. The first time an attractive man smiles at me, I lose my head. I was willing to throw our friendship out the window because of it." Tears gathered in her eyes. "I'm so sorry."

I hugged her. "There's nothing to be sorry for."

"There is. I was envious of you. It's just . . ." She paused, and then continued, "Christmas always reminds me how alone I am. I don't have any siblings, my parents are gone, and I never married."

"Jessica," I began.

She rubbed her arms. "And here you are, with parents willing to cross the country to spend Christmas with you, and you have two men fighting over you." She swallowed. "I'm so embarrassed by how I behaved. I practically threw myself at Ryan. Now I know the only reason he showed any interest in me was to make you jealous."

"Jessica, I—"

She held up her hand. "Don't worry about me. I'm off to my cousin's now for another huge Christmas Eve dinner. I'll be fine."

I gave her another hug. "How about we plan to do something on New Year's Eve, just the two of us? It will be a girls' night out."

"What about the sheriff?" she asked.

"He won't mind."

Her face brightened. "If you're sure . . ."

"Of course I am."

She grinned. "I'll start making a list of possible exciting activities for New Year's Eve in Holmes County." She laughed. "It might not be a long list." She gave me a final hug and hurried to her car.

Anna's front door opened, and my parents and Ryan came outside. As she stepped into the snow, Mom clung to my father's arm, doing her best not to fall over in those ridiculous boots. "Angie, I'm feeling tired. Can you take your father and me back to your house before you take Ryan to the hotel? It will be nice for the two of you to have some alone time to talk."

"You're not very subtle, Mom," I said, but I didn't argue with her. Through the rest of dinner, I had been itching to return to the hotel and find out more about Wade's arrest. This was my chance, even if it meant spending time alone with Ryan. Was Eve's murder solved? Had Wade confessed in prison? What made Wade push Jasper down the stairs?

On the ride back to my house, my parents chattered about the Grabers and the meal. Ryan said nothing.

In my driveway, Dad opened his car door. "Do you want us to take Oliver in?"

I shook my head. "He can ride along with us."

Mom wiggled her fingers at us. "Have a good time. Angie, don't hurry back."

I ground my teeth, and Ryan moved into the front seat.

"I'm surprised that you didn't put up more of a fight to not spend time alone with me. You've been avoiding me all afternoon," Ryan said as he buckled his seat belt.

I backed out the drive. "I want to go to the hotel before going home. The accident that made Mitchell leave dinner happened there. I want to find out what is going on."

"Does it involve Eve?" he asked.

"Maybe. Mitchell wasn't that forthcoming. He's a little mad at me right now."

"Why's that?"

"You know why. Don't pretend that you don't." I narrowed my eyes. "It's not the least bit attractive."

Ryan chuckled. "I guess Mitchell isn't used to competition. He would never make it in the big city."

"Good. I don't want someone who can make it in the big city. I gave that up months ago."

"You still love me. I saw it in your face today. You wanted to kiss me, and you would have done it if the sheriff hadn't barged in."

I gripped the steering wheel. "I don't want to talk about it."

"Why? Because you are afraid of the truth. Am I so awful that you won't even entertain the idea?"

"I don't want to talk about this." If the conversation kept up like this, it would be torture because we still had twenty minutes to go.

"What was the accident that made the sheriff leave?" Ryan asked.

I watched the landscape as we passed a snow-covered Amish farm. "The play director pushed the stage manager down the grand staircase in the hotel. The stage manager is pressing charges."

"Is the manager okay?" Ryan held on to his seat belt. "He could have broken his neck."

"Mitchell said he was banged up, but you're right. It was a dumb move by the director. He was arrested right away and is sitting in the Holmes County jail right now. I'm sure he is regretting it."

Ryan shook his head.

Finally, we came up to the hotel. I parked in the lot and started to take off my seat belt.

"Are you coming in?" His voice was hopeful.

"I want to see if Mitchell is still here, so I can talk to him about Wade—that's the director who pushed the other man down the stairs—and I also want to be sure Junie is okay. I worry about her."

"You always were one for taking care of other people."

I clipped on Oliver's leash, and we went inside the hotel. Instrumental piano music played softly in the lobby. Instead of Bethanne or Junie at the desk, it was Mimi herself.

"Angie, what a nice surprise to see you here," Mimi said.

I smiled. "I heard you had a rough day."

She flushed. "Yes, it's been difficult. This play has been good for business. Reservations for the hotel are up seventy percent compared to this time last year, but I don't know if I'll ever do this again. It's been a disaster from start to finish."

"Did you see Wade push Jasper down the stairs?" I asked.

"I did. I was right here when it happened. I had given Bethanne the day off."

"What happened?" Ryan asked.

"I heard some men shouting from the second floor, so I was walking around the desk. Then next thing I knew, I heard a terrible yell and saw Jasper come rolling down the stairs. I ran right over. I was sure he was seriously hurt because he didn't move right away. Luckily, he was just stunned. He has a terrible bruise on his cheek, but the EMTs said nothing was broken. It was a miracle."

"So you didn't actually see Wade push him?" I asked.

"No, but when I looked up the staircase, there he was, white as a sheet. The sheriff's department arrived here so quickly. One of the guests must have called nine-one-one when he heard the screams."

"What does this mean for the performance tomorrow? Will it still be on?" I asked.

She nodded. "All the actors want to carry on with it. If you ask me, they want to make it worthwhile that they gave up their Christmases with their families." She started to shake.

"Are you all right, Mimi?" I patted her hand that was on the desk.

A tear slid down her cheek. She brushed it away. "It's been a challenging week, and I miss Eve terribly."

I squeezed her hand. "Are the police still here?"

She shook her head. "I was happy to see them go. The sheriff said he and his deputies will be here for the progressive dinner and play on the evening after Christmas."

"I think that is a good idea. Hopefully there will be no need for it, but I think a police presence will be a good thing," Ryan said.

"I hope we don't need it either. Do you think Wade was the one who killed Eve?"

I shrugged. "I'm sure the sheriff is doing everything he can to find out right now." I decided to keep Wade's former assault charge to myself. "Is Junie here?"

She nodded. "She's in the dining room. I told her she could have taken today and tomorrow off if she liked, but she insisted that she wanted to work. I didn't argue with her. I need the help since most of my Amish workers are observing the holiday. Unfortunately, hotels can't close like most businesses for Christmas. You can go in and speak with her if you like. Maybe you can talk her into taking a break. She has been working like a dog since her sister died."

"Maybe it's how she deals with her grief?"

"Maybe," the older woman said.

I handed Ryan Oliver's leash. "Can you stay in the lobby with Oliver? I don't want him begging all of Mimi's guests for food."

Ryan nodded. "We'll be in the sitting room."

The chatter of the dining room was deafening. Laughing families and couples made trip after trip to the abundant buffet of Amish food. My own stomach rumbled, even though I had eaten my weight in Amish food at the Grabers' just an hour before.

Junie switched trays out at the buffet. She blinked when she saw me. "What are you doing here?"

I removed my winter hat. "I wanted to make sure you were okay after what happened between Jasper and Wade."

She swallowed. "I'm fine. I'm happy that Jasper wasn't seriously hurt."

"Take a break. Mimi just told me that you need one."

She slid the vat of potato salad into its spot on the buffet. "I have too much to do."

"The salad bar will be fine for ten minutes."

She wiped her hands on her apron. "You're not going to go away until I talk to you, are you?"

I shook my head.

"Fine. Follow me."

I followed Junie through the kitchen door. Several cooks were frying chicken and dicing vegetables. They were all English, as Mimi had told me, since all of the Amish except for Junie had taken the holiday off.

"I'm taking a break," Junie told a middle-aged woman.

The woman pointed her knife at the young girl. "Finally. I was beginning to think you weren't Amish, but a machine."

Junie frowned, grabbed her cloak off a peg on the wall, and led me through another door on the other side of the kitchen.

We were outside. The back door to the barn was easily in view and closed. Did the actors hold practice today?

She wrapped her cloak tightly around her body. "Do the police think the director killed my sister?"

I was surprised by her directness. "I don't know. I haven't spoken to the sheriff since it happened. Mimi said that you were there."

She nodded. "I was dusting the upstairs hallway. The two men stomped into the upper sitting room. Jasper was the one following Wade. He was accusing him of hitting a girl." She licked her lips. "I—I thought they were talking about Eve, so I slid behind a potted plant to listen. I know that it's the wrong thing to do, but if they were talking about my sister, I wanted to know about it."

"Were they?" I shivered.

"I don't know. Whenever it happened, they said it was in New York, and I know Eve didn't start working with either man until she came to Holmes County. I wish Mimi would cancel the rest of the performances. The sooner these play people are gone, the better it will be. Now, I must go back to work." Junie went back inside the kitchen.

I went back inside the hotel too and found Ryan and Oliver in the sitting room as promised.

Ryan held out Oliver's leash to me, and I took it. "Thanks for watching him. You can come over to the house anytime you are ready tomorrow. Dad will be up with the roosters. He's like a little kid when it comes to Christmas. We don't have any big plans. We will probably just hang out. Dad will watch—"

Without hesitation Ryan took my face in his hands and kissed me, and I found myself kissing him back.

He was the one who pulled away. "Merry Christmas, Angie." He smiled. "I didn't want you to make a choice without doing that. You need to make an informed decision." He walked away.

Oliver scratched at my pant leg, and I swore under my breath.

Chapter Thirty-four

Outside, the frigid air felt cool against my flaming cheeks. What just happened? And how was I going to face Mitchell or Ryan again? I groaned. "Ollie, we have nothing but problems."

The Frenchie cocked his head at me.

I could see lights shining from the barn. I told myself that I should go home, that my parents were waiting for me. Regardless, my feet propelled me to the barn.

As I walked across the ice-crusted snow, I muttered to myself. "If the back door is locked, I will turn around and go home to spend Christmas Eve with my parents."

I turned the doorknob; it turned without hesitation. "It was just meant to be."

I pushed the door inward and slipped inside. Lena sat at the dressing table. Ruben stood a few feet away from her with his arms folded. "Now, with Wade under arrest, our problems are over."

I scooped up Oliver and ducked behind a Chinese screen. "Shh," I whispered to the Frenchie.

He buried his pushed-in face into my shoulder.

Lena touched up her lipstick in the mirror. "You and I both know this could ruin us if it's ever found out."

Were they talking about Eve's death? Were they the ones behind it, not Wade?

"No one is going to find out. Now that Eve is dead, the secret dies with her."

I shivered. I flattened myself against the wall.

"But what about the letters? What if the police found them?" Lena asked.

"Eve told us that she destroyed all of them," Ruben said.

So Eve knew Lena and Ruben were the ones sending the threatening letters.

"I can't believe you admitted to her it was us."

Ruben folded his arms and watched her in the mirror. "It was a stupid prank, and one I did for you. You deserved this role, not some upstart Amish girl."

"She could have lied." Lena chewed on her lower lip. "Maybe she didn't throw them all away."

"If the police found the letters, they would have arrested us by now. If Eve was smart enough to figure out they were from us, then the police would have to know too."

"I just don't understand why she didn't tell anyone. She could have told Wade, and ruined us both if she wanted to. Instead, she said nothing."

"Must have been her Amish 'turn the other cheek' training. Don't second-guess it. Just be thankful we got away with it and weren't tangled up in this horrible murder business."

A tear rolled down Lena cheek. "I do feel bad that she died. If she hadn't stolen my part, I think that I might have even been able to be her friend."

"It's too late for that now."

Lena stood up. "You're right."

Ruben stepped toward the girl, and she leaned away from him. Despite her resistance, he wrapped her in a hug. "It will all be over soon. We only have two more performances here, and we will be on our way to Broadway. Wade, the little weasel, will have no choice but to give us high recommendations, knowing anyone on this production has the power to ruin him." He took her hand. "Let's go back to the hotel. I think we both need some time in the hot tub to relax." He led her toward me.

With Oliver in my arms, I scooted farther behind the screen and prayed that they didn't stop to look behind it.

The door slammed shut behind them. I took a couple of deep breaths. That was close, too close, but my spying had been worth it. I now knew who was behind the threatening letters. I needed to tell the sheriff.

Back in my car, I called Mitchell's cell number. He didn't answer. I chewed on my lip. Should I try 911? The information that I gathered didn't sound like an emergency. Besides, I knew that Lena and Ruben were behind the letters, but I didn't think they were behind the murder. I hoped I was right.

I started the ignition and headed to the sheriff's house. I had the food to deliver from Anna, after all. If the sheriff wasn't there, I was going to leave the food on his front porch with a note. It was certainly cold enough outside to keep it from spoiling.

I rang the doorbell and heard Tux barking inside. Oliver wiggled with anticipation over seeing his friend. The door opened, and Mitchell stood in front of me with an impressive five o'clock shadow.

I smiled brightly. "Since you missed Christmas Eve dinner, I brought it to you." I held out the basket.

He didn't move.

My arm drooped. "Aren't you going to take it? It's really heavy."

He took the basket from me. "Is Ryan with you?"

I rolled my eyes. "No. He's back at the hotel."

"At least that's some good news."

Oliver wove around my legs and headed into the house as if he owned the place. We heard barks of joy from the living room. He'd found Tux.

Perfect snowflakes fell around us. Some gathered on the sheriff's eyelashes and brows. He didn't seem to notice or care. I wanted to brush them away. He wouldn't let me do that.

"Can I come in? I need to talk to you."

He sighed. "Sure. Are you hungry? Zander won't eat this kind of food. If it's not chicken nuggets and mac and cheese, he's not interested. And I can't eat this all myself."

I smiled. "Well, I think I do have a bit of a second wind, as my father would say."

The front door of Mitchell's home opened into the family room. The television was off, and I had to step over a pile of action figures on the way to the small eat-in kitchen.

Mitchell flicked on the overhead light. "Sorry about Spider-Man and the other guys. Z left them there when his mother picked him up yesterday. I haven't had the heart to move them."

I smiled. "I know it must be hard for you not seeing him on Christmas morning."

Mitchell nodded and set the food on the counter.

The breakfast nook in the corner was the perfect size for him and Zander. There wasn't much space available for another person. I tried not to dwell on that. Ryan's words about Mitchell not being ready for marriage rang in my ears. It was only three more days before Ryan would head back to Texas. My parents were staying through New Year's. It would be nice to have a visit with my parents that didn't revolve around Ryan.

He fixed two plates and heated them in the microwave. The timer beeped and he set one plate in front of me. "What do you want to talk about?"

"There are a couple of things actually. I tried to call you not that long ago. Did you get my call?"

"I did." He cut his turkey into pieces.

I stared down at my food. I seemed to have lost my appetite. "Why didn't you pick up?"

He set his knife on the edge of the plate. "I didn't want to talk to you just then."

I pushed a piece of corn across my plate with the back of my fork. "You're talking to me now."

He looked me in the eye. "It is harder to ignore your cute face than your ringtone."

I smiled. "I have a special ringtone on your phone?"

"Yes, you do. I hope it will last." He dropped his gaze to his plate again.

"What do you want to talk about first, the murder or Ryan?"

"Let's start with the easy stuff: murder."

I told him about the conversation I overheard between Lena and Ruben.

"That agrees with the physical evidence."

"You knew and you didn't arrest them?"

"They aren't behind the murder. It was a prank, nothing more." He swallowed a piece of turkey. "I had planned to tell them that we knew to shake them up a little bit. Maybe next time, they will think twice before being so cruel to an innocent girl."

"They're headed to Broadway." I tapped my fork on my plate.

"Well, maybe not, then." He stood up and filled two glasses with water from the tap.

"Do you think Wade killed Eve?"

The sheriff sighed. "I think that he might have, but I can't prove it. He does have a history of violence, especially with young women. He pushed Jasper down the stairs because the stage manager threatened to tell us about Wade's past." He shook his head. "When he did push Jasper down the stairs, and Jasper, for better or worse, was fine, Jasper of course told us everything. That backfired pretty badly on him. Now Wade's spending Christmas Eve in our jail."

"At least he can't hurt anyone there."

"True."

I pushed my plate away. "I'm sorry. I'm just not hungry."

He smiled. "It's all right. Tux will eat your turkey."

"Don't give any to Oliver. He has had enough snacks this week to last him a lifetime. We are both going on a diet after the holidays."

The sheriff shook his head. "I don't know about Oliver, but you don't need to go on a diet. You are beautiful just the way you are."

I loved him for saying that.

He sipped his water. "Are we ready for the second topic?"

My stomach turned. It was a good thing that I hadn't eaten anything more. "I didn't mean to hurt you."

He shrugged. The cop face was firmly back in place. Would he always be able to use that when he wanted to hide his emotions from me? Why couldn't I do the same? My every thought played across my face like a four-piece orchestra.

"Ryan kissed me," I blurted out.

"I thought that he might." He shook his head. "I have to hand it to him. They guy is determined. He has a good reason, of course, but I would have thought he would have given up and flown back to Texas by now." He sighed. "You are worth sticking around for. I know that and so does he." He paused. "Did you kiss him back?" His voice was husky, revealing the emotion, which he was able to hide behind his eyes.

"I got carried away. I'm sorry. It didn't mean anything." Kissing Ryan had seemed normal. He was my first love, and a part of me would always love him, but I wasn't in love with him. How did I say that to Mitchell without sounding like a bad movie script?

"It sounds to me like it meant quite a lot since you feel the need to confess it like I am a priest or something and not your boyfriend."

"I made a stupid mistake. I'm sorry. I plan to apologize to Ryan too when I see him tomorrow."

"When you see him?"

I looked up from my folded hands. "You can't expect me not to have him to my house for Christmas when he doesn't know anyone else here."

Mitchell sighed. "Why would you apologize to him?"

"Because I don't want him to get the wrong idea. I don't want to lead him on."

Mitchell said nothing.

"It's like you and Hillary," I said. "There will always be something there because you loved each other, but it doesn't mean you want to be with her."

He gripped his fork. "Don't bring Hillary into this."

"I have to mention her to prove a point. She is still in love with you. Ryan is still in love with me." I rested my chin in my hand. "It's just so complicated."

Mitchell barked a laugh. "You're the only woman I've ever met who found matters of the heart more complicated than murder."

I looked up as he fished something out of his pocket. "Murder is complicated?" I asked.

He rolled his eyes. "I have your Christmas surprise."

I swallowed hard. "Okay."

He yanked a piece of greenery from his pocket.

I eyed the sad artificial piece of mistletoe. "It's plastic."

"It'll do," he said. Holding it over my head, he kissed me.

Chapter Thirty-five

"Merry Christmas!" my dad shouted from my bedroom doorway. "Get up! It's time for presents."

I covered my face with a pillow. I was still recovering from the events of Christmas Eve. I felt sick to my stomach every time I thought of it. Mitchell seemed okay by the time I left his house, but I had to talk some sense into Ryan. I couldn't go on like this, even if it was only for three more days. I would lose my mind.

Ryan joined us midmorning, and we were sipping coffee and opening presents around my pink Christmas tree. I don't know how it was possible, but the ornaments appeared even pinker in the daylight. However, I kept my internal commentary to myself because my mother seemed so pleased with her creation. What I was going to do with all the pink decorations after they all went back to Texas, I didn't know.

After we opened presents, I stood up. "Ryan, do you want to go for a walk?"

My mother gripped my father's hand and squeezed. I pretended not to see it.

Ryan put his coffee mug down. "Um, sure." He smiled his killer smile. "Seems kind of strange to hear you ask it since I have been asking you that all week, but all right."

I clipped on Oliver's leash and headed out the door. I waited for Ryan on the sidewalk. "We can walk over to the courthouse. Oliver loves the open green there." I laughed. "Though I guess, right now, it would be an open white."

"I have been interested in seeing the courthouse closer up. It's a nice old building."

Mom pressed a hand to her face. "Go as long as you want. I'll keep an eye on the turkey in the oven, and your father and I will be just fine here." She sounded so hopeful, I hated to think how she would react when she found out what Ryan and I were really going to speak about.

Ryan, Oliver, and I reached the courthouse, and I unclipped Oliver's leash. The Frenchie ran around the grounds in glee, enjoying his newfound freedom. The only thing that would make him happier was if Tux was there, but I wasn't going to say that. It would remind Ryan of Mitchell, and this was hard enough without bringing up the sheriff.

I folded my arms. Snow began to fall. The Holmes County Courthouse looked like a postcard scene. Oliver sniffed a bush and knocked the snow from the branches onto this head.

"Maybe that's the beginning of the big storm we are

supposed to get," I said. "I saw a winter-storm warning in the forecast for the coming week. I hope you will be able to make your flight back home okay." It was easier to talk about the weather instead of what I had to say.

Ryan took my hand and knelt on the ground.

No, no, no, no. "What are you doing?" I yelped.

"Just look at me. Please." He took a ring box out of his pocket. "Angela Braddock, I love you. I never stopped loving you. I made a mistake. Please forgive me and be my wife." He opened the box in a practiced manner because this was not the first time that he had opened it.

I stared at the ring—my ring—in the same box he had given me more than two years ago. As the jilted bride, I had kept the ring, but I didn't want to bring it with me to Ohio. I gave it to my mother and asked her to sell it and give the money to charity. Apparently, she hadn't done that. "How did you get that?" Even as I asked the question, I knew the answer. My mother struck again.

"You are supposed to answer, not ask a question."

Out of the corner of my eye, I saw a handful of diners step out of the Double Dime Diner to watch, including Linda the waitress.

"Ryan, people are watching us." I grabbed him by the shoulders, trying to pull him off the cold ground. "Stand up."

"Not until you give me your answer."

I lowered my voice. "You won't want to hear my answer in such a public place."

"Will you?" He looked up at me with so much hope.

I felt terrible, but my pity for him didn't change my answer. "No, no, I won't."

He blinked.

"Please, Ryan, get up."

He stumbled to his feet. There was a collective gasp from the spectators.

"We need to have a conversation. I need you to know why. I need the closure."

"That's just the problem, Angie. I don't want it to be closure. I want it to be a new start."

I stared into his eyes. They were so sincere; he was so sincere. "I can't, Ryan. I want to stay here in Holmes County. My shop, friends, and life are all here now. I fit here. I care about you, but our time together has come and gone." I curled his fingers over the ring box, and as I did, it snapped closed. "Go home, back to Texas. Find one of my mother's beauty queens to marry. She will be much more suited for the job as a society wife than I ever had any hope to be."

Tears gathered in Ryan's eyes. "I don't want a society wife. I want you."

I started walking across the square. I couldn't stand there with the diner patrons staring at me any longer. This conversation was a dead end. "Oliver, come!"

The Frenchie galloped toward me with a silly grin on his face. Even though he was born in the city, he liked Holmes County better than Dallas too. I snapped on his leash.

Ryan jogged after me and grabbed my arm. "It's because of the sheriff, isn't it? That's the real reason."

I nodded. "Yes, part of it has to do with Mitchell, but

the larger part is me and this place. This is my home now. This is where I want to be. I feel connected to Rolling Brook and to the shop. I feel closer to my aunt here."

His jaw twitched as he stepped away from me. "My life is in Dallas."

"And it should be. You would never find the life you want here, just like I would never find the life I want there."

"So it comes down to geography."

I opened my mouth. "It's more than that, but if you want to blame it on geography, you can."

Ryan dropped his hand from my arm. "The sheriff's such a nice guy; it's hard for me to hate him."

"That's nice of you to say."

"When I kissed you yesterday, you felt something." Ryan said. "Don't lie to me and tell me that you didn't."

"Of course I felt something, Ryan. You were the first man I ever loved, and I will always love you, but I'm not in love with you. I would have been if we had gotten married, but you made a different choice."

He tried to hand me the ring. "You are supposed to keep it since I left you before the wedding."

I shook my head. "No. It's yours now."

Ryan swallowed and replaced the box in his pocket. "I'll walk you home."

"You don't have to."

"Please, Angie. This time I want to say good-bye to you in the right way. No running away."

"Okay, you can walk me home."

We were silent during the short walk. Ryan and I

stood on the doorstep to my house. How many times when we were in college had we ended the night just like that? Maybe it was those sweet memories that made me do what I did next, or maybe it was just anxiety from trying to solve Eve's murder. In any case, I leaned forward and kissed him. As I pulled away, I said, "Stay in touch."

His lip tweaked up in a smile. "I'm sure your mother will make sure that I do. Tell your parents I will see them back in Dallas. I'll fly back tomorrow." He swallowed. "I think I just want to head back to the hotel."

"I understand. I'll tell them."

He kissed my cheek and jogged to his rental car. I waited until his taillights were gone before I went inside the house.

"Where's Ryan?" my mother asked. Her face was expectant and hopeful.

I removed Oliver's boots. Dodger sat a few inches away from us. I could have just been a trick of the light coming off the pink tree, but I think the kitten was chuckling at Oliver's boots.

The Frenchie grunted at his young charge. He must have thought the same.

"He went back to the hotel," I said.

Mom's mouth fell open. "What? But why? What about having Christmas dinner together as a family?"

"Our family is all right here." I stood up. "Ryan's flying home tomorrow."

My mother jumped out of her seat. "What did you do?"

"Mom, please."

"He asked you to marry him, didn't he?" she asked.

I nodded.

"And you said no, didn't you?"

I nodded again.

"How could you do that?" she cried.

"Daphne." My father reached for his wife, but she was already in my face.

I stiffened. "That was nice of you to give the old ring to him. You could have warned me. You could have warned him that I would say no."

"I would have, had I known that you already had a new boyfriend. How fickle you are."

Her words came like a slap across the face. Tears sprang to my eyes.

"Daphne," my father said.

My mother's face crumbled. "Angie dear, I'm sorry. I should not have said that. I just want what's best for you." Tears streamed down her face. "That's what any mother wants for her child."

"I know that, Mom, but Ryan is not what's best for me. Please just let it go."

She frowned. "If my sister were here, she would know what to say to you. Eleanor was always so good at making the other person feel better."

"Aunt Eleanor would know that I shouldn't marry Ryan. Part of me thinks she knew it even when I was here in February, but I wouldn't listen."

Mom sat back down on the couch. "Eleanor was wise. I miss her wisdom." She laughed. "She would be able to make us both feel better by the end of the conversation."

Tears pricked my eyes. "She would."

Mom sighed. "I have to admit, I was sometimes envious of my sister. Everyone loved her, and she always did the right thing. I didn't know coming back here would bring back so many of those feelings."

Dad leaned forward in his chair. "You have nothing to be sorry for, Daphne. Eleanor loved you."

"I know, but I'm sorry about how I felt, even though Eleanor didn't know it." She gave Dad a small smile. "To be honest, I was happy when she met Jacob and joined the Amish Church. I thought I wouldn't have to compete with her anymore. Angie, you wouldn't understand since you never had a sister to compete with."

"Mom—," I started.

"But I do," she said quietly. "Even now that she is gone. I still compete with her because my daughter would rather be here in Ohio with her aunt's memory than with her living mother in Texas."

I knelt by my mother's chair. "Mom, my not wanting to marry Ryan is not a rejection of you or Dad or even the entire state of Texas. It just means I don't love Ryan and want to live here. I love you and Dad; you're my parents."

Tears marred her makeup. "You do?"

I hugged her. "Of course I do."

She wiped at her eyes. "I know I am overbearing and overprotective, but you are my only child."

"I know."

"This means only one thing." She looked to my father. He nodded.

I glanced from one to the other. "What? What does it mean?"

"We were going to tell you at dinner, but your father has been offered early retirement from his company."

"Golden parachute, here I come," Dad crowed.

"That's great. The two of you deserve it."

Mom nodded. "And since you won't move back to Texas, we have decided that we are moving back to Holmes County to live closer to you."

"Isn't that great, Angie Bear?" Dad asked.

I stood up. "You're what?"

"We'll still keep our home in Dallas," Dad said. "Or perhaps even downsize there. Your mother and I have agreed to spend the winters in Dallas and the rest of the year here in Ohio with you. Isn't that wonderful?"

"Really?" I jumped up and gave my father a hug. "That is a wonderful Christmas present."

He grinned. "I thought you might like it." He lowered his voice. "We just have to find the perfect house for your mother. You know she is picky."

"I heard that, Kent," Mom said with laughter in her voice.

"Those drives that you have been going on?" I asked. "Were you going to look at houses?"

Dad nodded. "Guilty."

"Wow! This is really great."

Mom stood from her chair. "If you would excuse me, I'm going to go touch up my makeup."

I sat in her chair in front of the pink tree, smiling. Sure, my mother drove me crazy, but to have her and Dad in Holmes County most of the year was a dream come true.

Something my mom said when she was speaking

about Aunt Eleanor crossed my mind: "Angie, you wouldn't understand since you never had a sister to compete with." She was right. I didn't know what it was like to compete with a more popular beloved sister, but Junie Shelter did. I sat straight up in the chair. Junie? Could I be right? Or could I ever be more wrong? I had to know. I jumped out of the chair, turned to my parents, and said, "I have to go."

Dad blinked at me. "Where are you going?"

"To the hotel." I pulled on my winter coat that I had just removed. "And it's not to see Ryan. I want to talk to one of the maids."

Mom reentered the room just then. "What are we supposed to tell the sheriff when he arrives?"

"I'll call him on the way."

Oliver followed me to the door with one of his boots in his mouth.

"Ollie, don't you want to stay here with Grandma and Grandpa?" I asked.

He went and picked up a second boot with his teeth and dropped it on the floor at my feet. I took that as a no.

Chapter Thirty-six

I parked in the closest spot I could find to the hotel and carried Oliver through the swirling snow to the hotel. The front edge of the promised winter storm was already hitting the county. A large black minivan was parked right in front of the hotel's main doors. Blake stepped out of the hotel with a large crate filled with wires. Blake smiled at me as he loaded it into the back of the van with even more gear from the play.

"Are you packing up to leave?" I asked.

"Yep. I have to say I'm ready to go. The play can't very well continue without a director or the leads."

"Leads? What happened to the leads?" I asked.

"They took off. This morning Lena and Ruben were gone. The sheriff came by last night to ask them some more questions, and this morning they were gone."

Mitchell had come back to ask about the letters; I just knew it. The trustees wouldn't be happy about it when they heard the news. Head Trustee Cramer had better think of another way to raise money for that playground, because the progressive dinner and play idea was a bust.

"Have you seen Junie?" Blake asked. "I wanted to say good-bye to her."

"You're friends with Junie?"

"Yeah. She's a cool girl. We've had a couple of good talks. Junie and I get each other. Neither of us wants to be in the spotlight, but we do want respect."

Respect. That was a funny concept for an Amish person to fixate on.

"Did you have these talks at the hotel?"

"Sometimes, but most of the time, she came to see me when I was alone in the barn, working on the set. Jasper is not a hands-on stage manager. He had me do all the grunt work. She brought me snacks while I worked. I am going to miss the food. The food here is killer."

I shivered when he said "killer" in reference to Junie. The wheels were spinning in my head faster and faster. "What did you talk about? I mean other than your mutual need for respect."

"She was really interested in my job. I showed her around backstage."

My brow creased. "You showed Junie around backstage? Why? It just seems like an odd thing for an Amish girl to be interested in."

Blake blushed. "Yeah, well, she showed an interest in how everything worked backstage. She really saw how our job was even more important than the actors'."

"When was that?"

He thought a moment. "I don't know, maybe the day before the first show."

My pulse quickened. My suspicions couldn't possibly be right, could they? Another shiver ran down my spine.

Blake started back toward the hotel. I hurried and followed him.

"She's a really nice girl. It's a shame she is Amish. She gave me the idea that she might leave the Amish and wanted to get to know me better. Another signal from a girl I completely misread. I don't understand women at all."

I grabbed his arm. "Blake, listen to me. Did you show Junie the swing?"

"The swing that Eve used?"

I dropped my hand. "Yes, the one that she fell from."

"Sure, it was the most important part of the stage until the sheriff took it away. It's a really great prop and took me weeks to make. I made it myself. I can't tell you how upset I was when the police took it. Do you think they will give it back to me? I mean, I could really use it for a future production. I'm not going to be Jasper's assistant forever. I've got bigger dreams than that."

"That's great. If you see the sheriff come in, tell him I am wherever Junie is." I cut him off and ran into the hotel.

"Where's that?"

"I don't know yet. That's what I'm going to find out." I pulled my phone out of my pocket and dialed the sheriff.

"Mitchell."

"Hey, it's me."

"I was just about to leave for your house."

"I'm not at the house. I'm at the hotel. I think—I think Junie cut the rope."

"What?"

"Junie. She did it because she was jealous of her sister, her sister whom everyone loved more than her."

"What are you doing at the hotel?" he asked.

"I came here to ask her."

"You are just going to walk up to her and ask if she murdered her own sister," Mitchell yelled into my ear.

"Uh, yeah. Got a better idea?"

"Yes, stay there and do nothing. I'm on my way."

"But—"

"I said I am on my way." He hung up.

I spun around in the center of the lobby toward the registration desk and was relieved to find Bethanne there.

"Yes, sir," she said into the phone. "Your reservation is confirmed. We will see you on January ten. Thank you for making a reservation."

"Bethanne, hang up the phone," I ordered.

She gave me an alarmed look. "That's right, sir. We look forward to seeing you."

"Hang up the phone now." I made an "end it" signal.

She yanked it away from me. "Good-bye." She glared at me. "Angie, what has gotten into you?"

"Where's Junie? I need to talk to her. It's urgent."

She blinked at me. "She's home by now. Her shift ended more than an hour ago."

"Did you see her leave? Are you sure she left?"

She twisted the tie from her prayer cap around her

finger. "Yes, I saw her walk toward the back of the hotel. That's where the employees' exit is. She can't just go waltzing out of the front door like she is a guest of the hotel."

"How did she seem?" I asked.

"I don't know. Why do you have so many questions about her?"

I couldn't share my fears because there was still a chance that I could be wrong. It was one thing to tell the sheriff, but I couldn't tell Junie's coworker. "Can Oliver stay here with you while I check the dining room and kitchen for her?"

She smiled. "Of course. But I really do think she left. Why would she want to stay around here on Christmas?"

"Thanks," I said, and dashed into the dining room. It was deserted. I went through the employee door to the kitchen, which Junie had taken me through just the day before. I found the English women in the kitchen again, baking and cooking Christmas dinner for the hotel guests.

"Can I help you?" one of the women asked.

"I was looking for Junie," I said. "Have you seen her?"

"Junie? Junie's shift ended well over an hour ago. I bet she's at home now. You can find her there."

I thanked the women and went back into the dining room. Maybe I should heed the sheriff's advice for once and wait until he showed up to keep searching for Junie. I went back through the dining room to the main lobby.

Bethanne stood behind the registration desk.

"I'll take Oliver," I said. "We will go wait for the sheriff in the sitting room."

"He's not here," she said.

"What do you mean, 'He's not here'?" I demanded.

She blinked at me. "Junie stopped by the desk—I guess she was somewhere in the hotel after all—and I told her that you were looking for her. She said that she would take Oliver with her and go find you."

"What?" I snapped.

She pulled back. "Did I do something wrong?"

Give my Frenchie to a possible murderer? Yes, that was wrong. Very wrong. I couldn't tell Bethanne that.

"Where did she go?"

"I—I think I saw her walking toward the barn," the girl stammered.

"Call the police. Tell them where I am, and that Junie is the one who killed Eve Shetler."

"Junie?" she asked in disbelief.

"Yes, now call them!" I ordered as I fled the lobby.

Chapter Thirty-seven

The stage's back door slammed against the wall as I barreled through it. "Oliver!" I cried.

There was a bark in return, and it was from above. I craned my neck and looked up. Oliver and Junie stood on the platform. Junie was precariously close to the edge.

My heart pounded against my sternum. "Junie, what are you doing? You and Oliver need to come down from there right away. You could get hurt."

She looked down at me. A single tear fell from her cheek and landed on the stage like a fat raindrop. "I can't come down. I have to make amends for what I did. I have to face my lot in eternity."

I didn't like the sound of that. I didn't like it at all. And I hated the thought of my beloved pooch up there with a crazy person.

I put my foot on the first rung of the ladder.

"Don't take another step. I will kick him off, I will." She lifted her foot as if to demonstrate.

I froze. "Okay, okay, don't hurt him." I stepped down from the ladder and took two giant steps backward.

High above, Oliver whimpered. He lay as flat as he could on his belly.

Holding up my hands, I moved around the ladder, so that she could see me better. "What are you going to do?"

"The only thing I can do." She turned her back to the open air and crossed her arms over her chest. In her Amish clothes she looked like a pilgrim at the gallows. The back of her heels hung over the edge of the landing. A light breeze would topple her backward.

"Wait!" I cried. "Think about what you are doing."

"I have thought about it. I have thought about it from the moment Eve hit the stage. I knew there was no going back then, and I won't."

Oliver had the good sense to belly crawl farther away from her.

"Why, Junie? Why did you do it?" My neck began to hurt from looking up, but I would not take my eyes off her. How was I going to get her down? Where was Mitchell?

"It went just like I knew it would be when Eve returned. She showed up here and, all over again, it was like I didn't exist. Everyone fawned over her, even my mother, even when she shouldn't because Eve had abandoned our ways." She hit one of the wooden support beams with her hand. The entire platform shook.

Oliver yelped.

Junie didn't seem to notice. "I thought when she

went to New York, I was finally rid of her, but she came back and I was nothing again." She started to cry. "I told her over and over that she should leave, that our parents and our community didn't want to see her. But she refused. I had to make her go, so I cut the rope.

"I thought she might be hurt. I thought she might break her arm. Maybe if she got hurt, it would show everyone that Eve was human, just like me. I wanted her to leave again. I never thought she would die."

"Oh, Junie," I said.

"I know I didn't think it through." More fat tears hit the stage. "I was so angry."

I had my eye on the backstage door. "What do you mean to do now, Junie?"

"I have to do this. It's almost worse now that she's dead. She's all I hear about. *Mamm* cries all night long over her. So does Mimi. So does everyone. I can't stand it."

I waved at her. "Let's go to the sheriff and explain what happened. That her death was an accident gone wrong."

"I can't go to prison. I can't. I'm scared of what may happen to me there."

For good reason. I shivered to think how an Amish girl would fare in prison. Maybe she could claim insanity by jealousy and avoid it that way.

Oliver whimpered. I prayed Oliver would be quiet and not draw attention to himself.

Across the stage, I could see someone moving in the wings, but I couldn't see who it was. I hoped it was Mitchell. Maybe he would be able to negotiate with her.

Why wasn't he coming to help? Should I call out to him? Would seeing the sheriff make Junie jump that much faster?

My mouth was dry. I desperately needed water. "Junie, please don't do this. Please. You made a mistake. Don't take your own life. Please." I knew I was begging, but I didn't care.

"I try to be a *gut* Amish girl, but Eve was always better. Even when she left the Amish, she was better to my mother, to Nathan, to Mimi, to everyone. She was a star and needed all the attention."

I skirted the platform from below. She needed to look at me. When I wheeled around to where I could see her face, I saw her eyes were shut. "Junie, listen to me. Please. This is not how to deal with this. Talk to the sheriff. He can help you." My eyes flitted across the stage. The person I thought I saw there earlier was gone. Had I imagined it?

"Why would he help me? He doesn't even notice me. No one does. He cares about Eve like everyone else. He's trying so hard to find out what happened to her, isn't he?"

"He cares about Eve because he is investigating her case. He has to."

"Would he try as hard if it were me?"

"Of course he would," I said. "I am certain of that. The sheriff is a good man and treats all of the citizens of Holmes County equally."

She shook her head like a kindergartner refusing peas at dinner. "*Nee*, he would not. I'm not as worthy as everyone else. I'm not as important as Eve. Even after I am dead, I won't be as important. She will be the one who is remembered and missed."

Covertly, I slipped my hand into my pocket for my cell phone. I dialed 911 and stuck it back into my pocket, hoping the operator would at least hear some of our conversation.

Junie spoke in Pennsylvania Dutch. The only word I caught was *Gott*. Was she praying? Was that a good sign or a bad sign?

"Junie, listen to me. God would not want you to do this."

"*Nee*, he would not," she said, and with that she leaned all the way back and fell.

Oliver jumped up and grabbed onto the front of her apron with his teeth, but she was too heavy and her momentum was too great. He couldn't hold her, and her dress tore from his mouth. Her skirt floated around her like a cap, and her legs kicked in the air. I screamed as she fell, running as fast as I could to the place where she'd hit the stage. I didn't know if I could break her fall, but I had to try.

But someone else was faster. Thud, thud, thud, the sound of running feet thundered across the stage. Blake sprinted toward Junie's falling body. He made it there just in time.

"Oomph!" Blake cried when Junie fell on top of him.

Junie cried out in pain.

Oliver came away with a long piece of black cotton in his mouth. He looked over the edge of the landing with mournful eyes. I didn't follow his line of sight. I had to get him out of danger first. I climbed the ladder in record time and scooped up Oliver. The Frenchie licked me up one side of the face and down the other.

"Okay, okay, you are okay." I kissed his head before I peered over the side of the landing.

Below, Blake held Junie as she cried on his shoulder. "I noticed you," he said, barely loud enough for me to hear.

Epilogue

Amber Rustle stared out the front window of my car in the parking lot of the Mennonite meetinghouse. Just yards away, the Mennonite minister and Esther Shetler stood on either side of a fresh grave. Mimi Ford was close to the fence, as if she were afraid to get too close.

I watched Amber. "Are you ready?"

"I still can't believe it was Junie." She shivered in her seat, even though I had the heater going full blast. "It's all anyone who has come into the library, both Amish and English, has spoken about. Junie would have been the last person I suspected."

Me too, I thought. Until it was almost too late.

"Why did she do it?" Amber asked. "You promised you would tell me when you found out, but you haven't yet."

"And that's what you really want to know?"

She nodded. "Yes. It won't bring Eve back, but for some reason, I think it will make me feel better."

I wasn't so sure of that.

"There had to be a reason. There is always a reason, isn't there?"

"She was jealous because Eve was so beloved."

"She was jealous? That's her only reason?"

"Not that it excuses her in any way." I ran my gloved hand back and forth over the steering wheel. "But I guess Junie had trouble living in Eve's shadow all her life. She thought that when Eve left the Amish, she would finally stand out in her family and in her community. But as soon as Eve returned to take the part in the play, everything crumbled for her." I paused. "I don't know if it will help, but Junie didn't mean to kill her sister. She just wanted to hurt her and scare Eve enough so that Eve would leave again."

Amber wiped away a tear with the back of her mittened hand. "Do you know what the saddest part was?"

I shook my head.

"Eve loved Junie. She always said Junie was the closest person to her in her entire family. She loved her." She scrubbed her mittens back and forth over her face as if to push her tears back into her eyes, but it wasn't working.

Oliver hung his head over the seat from the back and nudged her arm with his head.

I placed a hand on her arm. "If you don't want to get out of the car, we don't have to. I can take you back home. Whatever you choose to do is fine."

As suddenly as she began, she stopped rubbing her face and dropped her hands. Her face was flush. "No. I'm ready now."

"All right." I patted Oliver's head and told him to stay in the car. As if he understood, he curled up in the backseat.

Amber and I went through the cemetery gate together. I stopped by Mimi, and Amber went on to stand next to Eve's mother.

Mimi touched a tissue to the corner of her eye and smiled at me. "I thought I would give her mother some space."

"Any sign of Nahum around the hotel?" I asked.

She shook her head. "Not since the theater troupe left. A few of them left earlier than the others."

"You mean Lena and Rupert."

It was her turn to nod. "I guess they are finding themselves on Broadway or trying to. They have Wade's recommendation to help them."

"Why would Wade write them a recommendation?" I asked.

"From what I hear, Wade has to write a recommendation for everyone in the troupe because all of them found out about his indiscretion with that young woman all those year ago, thanks to Jasper."

"What will happen to Wade?"

She shrugged. "I know he's out on bail, because he came back to the hotel for his things and checked out. Jasper will sue him for all he's worth for pushing him down the stairs."

I winced.

"I'm glad they're gone." Her head drooped. "The playhouse was a bad idea."

I touched her arm. "No, it wasn't. It was a great idea.

So was the progressive dinner. But maybe next time you should just vet the acting troupe a little bit more."

She gave me a tiny smile and started toward the three people around Eve's grave.

Another car crunched through the snow into the parking lot. It was one I knew well—the sheriff's department SUV.

I met Mitchell at the gate. "You came." I smiled at him.

"You asked me to, and I have." He nodded. "I was able to get away. I put Anderson in charge of any emergencies."

I chuckled softly. "Do you think that was a good idea?"

"Probably not." He smiled. His eyes fell on the tiny group around the grave. "What a sad showing for a girl who was so loved."

I nodded.

"Did your parents get off on their flight okay?"

My parents had left for the airport early that morning to catch a flight back to Dallas. I nodded. "Oh, I forgot to tell you. They are moving back to Holmes County, so you had better start thinking of ways to impress Daphne Braddock."

Mitchell's mouth fell open. I folded my hand into his and led him to Eve's gravesite.

Amish Quilted Snowman, the Perfect Holiday Gift

by Angela Braddock, Owner of Running Stitch

The holidays are right around the corner, and if you're like me, you want to give a homemade gift to those you love. At Running Stitch, we are here to help you find all the sewing and quilting supplies that you need to make the perfect gift for your friends and family. However, you may be stumped on what to make, and time is running out to decide. Why not make a quilted snowman? It's a quick and easy project that is guaranteed to charm your loved ones and bring smiles to their faces.

Supplies

  fabric
  scissors

thread
needle
polyester stuffing
variety of buttons

Step One

Choose a quilting pattern and create three quilted squares of varying size: one twelve-by-twelve inches, one ten-by-ten inches, and one eight-by-eight inches. The twelve-by-twelve-inch block may seem large for the project, but it's better to begin with too much fabric and cut off the excess than to run out. I suggest that you use white or cream fabric.

Step Two

Take polyester stuffing and form a ball to place inside the completed quilt block. Wrap the block around the ball and stitch closed. Repeat this for each block.

Step Three

Now you should have three quilted balls of descending size. Cut off any excess fabric. Stack them so that the stitches holding the balls together are hidden. Stitch the balls together in the form of a snowman, taking care to bury your stitches deep inside the body of the snowman so they don't show.

Step Four

On the face of the snowman, use buttons to add eyes, a nose, and a mouth—or, if you prefer to have you project in the Amish style, don't add a face.

Step Five

If desired, add accessories such as a top hat. You're done!

Read on for a peek at Isabella Alan's next
Amish Quilt Shop Mystery,

MURDER, PLAINLY READ

Available from Obsidian in October 2015

"Whoa!" Rachel Miller called to her buggy's horse. The buggy shuddered to a stop behind a yellow school bus, which three Amish children climbed into. The youngest boy's Spider-Man backpack bounced as he disappeared through the door. I smiled. Clearly he was a member of one of the more liberal Amish districts in Holmes County. A year ago, who knew that I would be able to know the difference? When I first moved to Millersburg, I, like so many outsiders, had thought that all Amish were the same.

Next to me on the buggy's bench seat, Rachel's bonnet cast a shadow over her delicate features. "It shouldn't be too long now," Rachel said. "Austina telephoned the bakery to tell me the bookmobile would be parked in front of Hock Trail School."

Austina, a county librarian, had commissioned a quilt for her ailing mother from my quilting circle. The ladies had finished the quilt during our meeting the previous night. It was breathtaking, with a purple, rose, and periwinkle blue Ohio Star. The colors weren't traditionally Amish, but Austina had chosen them because they were her mother's favorites. The quilt was so lovely I almost wished I could keep it in the shop for display, but I thought that about every quilt my circle created. Each one seemed to be more beautiful than the last.

I scratched my faithful French bulldog, Oliver, between his ears. He leaned into my caress like a cat. I sighed. "I hate for the ride to end. This reminds me of leisurely buggy rides I would take with my aunt and uncle on Sunday afternoons. It's nice to take a breath every so often and think about that time." My throat tightened as I thought about my Amish aunt. She had been gone for more than a year now, but every so often the pain of losing her was like a baseball bat to the chest.

The crease in Rachel's brow smoothed. "Angie, you need to move at a slower pace. You are so busy with Running Stitch and being a township trustee. You need to take a breath. When was the last time you had a quiet evening with the sheriff?"

I found myself blushing like a sixteen-year-old girl. "It's been a while. He has Zander, who needs his attention. I don't begrudge Z that at all. He's a great kid. And now that my parents have moved to town, they're taking up a lot of my time."

After my father's retirement, my parents had moved to Holmes County from Dallas to be closer to me, and my mother was in the middle of colossal house renovation, the likes of which my Amish friends had never seen.

I zipped up my jacket against the cool autumn wind whipping in through the buggy's open windows. "The latest debacle has been over throw pillows for their living room couch. Please don't ever ask me to help you choose a throw pillow. According to my mother, I'm not up to the task."

Rachel chuckled. "Jonah told me your mother put two chandeliers in the house."

I rolled my eyes. "Jo-Jo exaggerated. There's only one."

Rachel's horse turned the next corner. A half mile down the road, I saw the silver-and-green library bookmobile parked in front of a one-room schoolhouse. A small swing set, slide, and metal teeter-totter were next to the bookmobile, but there weren't any children on the playground. In fact, I didn't see any children at all. I frowned. It was autumn and school was in session. I was about to ask Rachel about it when my friend whispered, "Oh, dear."

"What—" I started to ask, but soon my question was answered. Austina Shaker stood in front of her bookmobile with her arms folded across her chest. Her right foot jutted out, and she leaned back as if waiting for the perfect moment to throw a punch. Despite her bright pink cardigan and the eyeglasses perched on the end of her nose, she looked more like a street fighter ready to go ten rounds than a rural county librarian. The Amish man standing across from her appeared just as fierce, but I would categorize his look more like an angry Pilgrim than a street fighter. It was as if the crossing on the *Mayflower* hadn't agreed with him.

Rachel's horse came to a stop, and I hopped out. Oliver joined me, although he checked the area for incoming birds first. Oliver hated birds.

Behind me, Rachel said, "Angie, I don't think you should . . ."

I glanced over my shoulder. "I won't get involved. Don't worry."

My best friend sighed. She knew I was lying to her and to myself if I thought that was true.

From the doorway to the schoolhouse, children stared openmouthed at the arguing pair. Their wide-eyed teacher, a young redheaded girl who didn't look a day more than sixteen, watched with them.

The Amish man pointed a bony finger at Austina. "You have no right to be here. I strictly forbade you from coming. You have to leave the school yard immediately."

Austina snorted. "You can't tell me what to do. I'm not a member of your church."

Rachel joined Oliver and me. We stood at the edge of the playground about four yards from where Austina and the Amish man argued. Austina was facing us, and I could see every expression that crossed her face. I saw only the back of the man's head. He stood erect, like there was a board hidden under his navy coat, and his black felt hat sat perfectly straight on his head.

"Do you know who the man is?" I whispered to Rachel.

My friend nodded. "That's Bartholomew Belier. He's the bishop of the strictest Old Order district in the county."

I frowned. "Do I know anyone in that district?"

"Joseph Walker was a member." She watched me out of the corner of her eye.

I grimaced. Joseph Walker was an Old Order, extremely conservative Amish man I'd met when I'd first moved to Holmes County and who I later found dead in the stockroom of my quilt shop. I didn't have a lot of good memories where Joseph Walker was concerned.

The bishop glowered at Austina. "You're interfering with the members of my church, and you have no right to do it. I, with *Gotte*'s guidance, am the one who should be telling them how to live, not the books you insist on giving them."

"You act like I'm peddling vacuums door to door. Your church members come to me. *They* ask for them. All I'm doing to providing books to patrons to read. It's my job."

"It's disrespectful to our culture."

The librarian arched her left eyebrow. "I will not censor. Now, I think it's time for you to leave."

The bishop shook with anger. His hands balled into fists. He wouldn't hit her. It was not the Amish way. At least, I hoped that he wouldn't.

Austina stuck out her chin as if inviting a blow from Bartholomew.

Slowly he relaxed his hands and his arms fell loosely at his sides. His voice was low. "You will be sorry you ever drove that *monster*"—he pointed at the bookmobile— "into my district. You think you have the *Englisch* law on your side, but I have *Gott* on mine. We will see who has the last word when this comes to an end." He stamped away, straight toward Rachel and me.

We jumped to the side, and Oliver dove under the teeter-totter. Bartholomew didn't even acknowledge us. His pockmarked face was molten red. I suspected he saw red too. The young schoolteacher and the children in the doorway filed back into the schoolhouse.

Austina looked as if his threat meant nothing to her, and she had single-handedly run him out of the school yard herself. After a moment, she noticed Rachel and me hovering nearby. Her round face broke into a smile. If I hadn't witnessed it myself, I would never have known she'd been yelling at someone just a moment before. "Angie, Rachel, I'm so glad you are here. Did you bring the quilt?"

"Of course, the quilt." Rachel slapped her head. "I left it in the buggy. I will go collect it now."

"That looked intense," I said after Rachel left.

Austina waved away my concern. "If you're referring to Bartholomew Beiler, he is nothing to worry about."

He sure looked like something to worry about to me. You wouldn't see me going toe-to-toe with an enraged Pilgrim, especially this close to Thanksgiving.

The librarian started back toward the bookmobile. "Don't wrinkle that cute little nose of yours at me, Angie. Bartholomew is a blowhard. He isn't the first Amish bishop I've argued with about my books, and I doubt he will be the last."

Rachel returned with the quilt, and she and I unfolded it, holding it up for Austina's inspection. Tears sprang to the librarian's dark eyes. "Oh, it's more gorgeous than I imagined it would be. Mother will love it." She ran her fingers over a rose triangle in the design.

"I'm glad," I said as Rachel and I refolded the quilt.

Rachel took the quilt from my hands. "Where would you like me to put it?"

"Put it on my desk inside the bookmobile, please, " Austina said.

Rachel disappeared inside the mammoth vehicle.

I cocked my head. "So, what was the bishop so upset about?"

"I didn't think you would let me drop the subject that quickly," Austina said. "He's mad about the books I provide and believes I'm corrupting his followers with new and scandalous ideas. Small men always fear new ideas."

Rachel tripped down the bookmobile steps. Her lips were set in a thin line. She was open-minded, but she was still Amish and believed in that way of life.

"He wants to take away your books?" I asked.

Austina shook her head. "He wants to keep them out of his district. I guess he caught some of the teenage girls reading romances and flipped out." She snorted. "They weren't exactly steamy. I mean, maybe the characters shared a smooch at the end of the book. Nothing more."

"What are you going to do?"

Oliver wriggled out from under the teeter-totter and was now inspecting the bookmobile's tires.

"I don't censor for anyone. If a teenager from his district comes to me looking for a novel, I will give it to her. It's not my position to tell people what to read. In my business, any reading is good."

Rachel looked as if she wanted to argue, but my Amish friend was far too polite to do it. Instead she said, "I think we should be on our way, Angie. Aaron will be wondering what's taking me so long."

"Before you leave," Austina said, "I have another job for you, Angie."

That sounded ominous. "Oh?" I squeaked. By her tone, I doubted it was another quilt.

"Yes. Stella Parsons, the chair of our Friends of the Library board, had the nerve to break her hip and now she can't manage our library book sale this month."

"She broke her hip?!" Rachel exclaimed. "Is she all right?"

"She'll be fine," Austina said. "As soon as she gets out of traction." Her dark eyes zeroed in on me. "Angie, I want you to take over for her."

I pointed at myself. "Me? Why?"

"Because you are the best person for the job according to the head township trustee, Caroline Cramer," she said matter-of-factly. "When I spoke to her about needing someone to take on the job, she suggested you right away."

I bet she had.

"Isn't there someone else in the Friends who can take this on?" I asked. "I've never ran an event like this before. Your Friends are the ones with experience."

She shook her head. "Most of them are pushing eighty, and the ones that aren't I wouldn't trust with a kid's lemonade stand, let alone a library book sale."

"B-But—," I stammered.

She jabbed her fists into her sides and looked as fierce as she did when she was staring down the irate bishop. "Don't tell me you won't do it. You'd be letting the entire county down."

I rolled my eyes. "That seems like a gross exaggeration."

She picked a piece of lint off of her cardigan. "It could be great publicity for your quilt shop."

She had me. I was always trying to grow my business. "When and where will it be?" I asked in a whimper.

Austina's lips curled into a small smile. She knew she was the victor. She'd had the same triumphant expression on her face when she had shooed away the bishop. I wondered how long that smile would remain.